The Desert Will Sing

Dr Howard Fortescue

Contents

Chapter 1

Sand stretched in every direction for miles under the merciless Arabian sun. In the distance there were some rocky outcrops; difficult to judge their size. The most distant ones were lighter from the haze in the air, that lightness was there for the closer ones too but not so pronounced. It gave a depth to the scene, like a Japanese painting of ranges of mountains fading into the distance. This was distance that Mike and his team would have to travel to get back to their base.

The British Army Land Rover was running well, it wasn't particularly new but it had all the enhancements needed in the desert and, being right hand drive, gave the driver a good view of the nearside of the road; useful if the road was wide enough to have a nearside. It was called the Syrian Desert, although they were actually in Northern Iraq, and they were travelling west on a minor road, more like a track, towards Jordan.

The mission had been accomplished and once they were back Mike would only need to report to his Commanding Officer. He knew everything he would put in the report, and it would be typed up for his superiors. It would be read by a select few and then redacted in such a way that it might as well say, 'a squad of soldiers went on a mission somewhere.'

Mike Collins was leading this mission as usual, and if he was honest, he was enjoying it and his military career generally. He had seen a lot of faraway places and he had made many solid friendships. He now had a well trained and organised team and he was good at his job.

Although these thoughts were in the back of his mind, Mike knew better than to let them interfere with his concentration on the here-and-now.

He was scanning the landscape near and far and occasionally referring to the map, compass or GPS; he believed in having a backup for everything where possible. His driver was concentrating on the road and nearby ground and his squad in the back were scanning to the sides and rear.

Mike was sitting in the front seat next to Jock his driver. Jack, Harry and Bob in the back, made up the rest of the team. It was to be their last mission in that arena and should have been straightforward. The area they were in had previously been controlled by insurgents but there had been no reports of them or any action for a year.

There should have been no hazards on that road, so if there was anything there it would be a left-over from previous activity. What they drove over had been dormant since the insurgents had gone and had lain unnoticed and further concealed by windblown sand. The explosion rocked the Land Rover. A piece of shrapnel from the IED came up through the floor and pierced Mike's left boot cutting flesh and bone. His driver was unlucky too and was hit in his right thigh; his leg went rigid and jammed the throttle down.

Mike slammed his right boot down on the clutch as he pushed the wheel over to keep the truck on the track, simultaneously he pulled up the handbrake hard. They came to a halt in a cloud of dust and Mike shouted, "Get a pad strapped on that," and then he pulled his left boot lace as tight as he could and tied it. Harry jumped out from behind the driver, pulled the door open, strapped the driver's leg and lifted him out onto the ground. Bob and

Jack had automatically deployed outside the truck, scanning for hostiles.

Mike made a quick assessment as he slid over into the driver's seat and said, "The engine is still running, so let's get going before it gives out, there must be damage." They lifted the driver onto the back and set off.

The IED almost certainly wasn't meant for them and the hostiles who had planted it were long gone. Mike guessed that the Land Rover had some serious damage and that he would have to make new travel plans; the priority was just to get back. He started moving with the engine ticking over and his right foot gently slipping the clutch, then he drove without the clutch until he found a safe spot where a helicopter could land and he parked the truck amongst some rocks.

"Jack, signal for air extraction."

Bob noticed and reported a small pool of oil under the engine, then he added, "Oh, the dripping has stopped, we wouldn't have got much further."

"Keep a sharp lookout in case anyone heard the explosion and comes looking," said Mike, "Muwaffaq Salti Air Base in Jordan is the closest and it's three hundred kilometres west so if we get a lift in an hour we'll be lucky."

Three quarters of an hour later Harry reported, "I just got a message, there's a Wildcat about fifteen minutes out."

"Mike, do you want me to rig charges to dispose of the truck?" Bob asked.

Before he could answer Harry had another message. "There's a Chinook coming too to take the truck," he reported, "our friends over there must be having a quiet day."

They were lucky that day, the helicopters arrived only an hour after Harry's first call. The Wildcat hovered to provide cover as the Chinook pilot positioned over the Land Rover and dropped cables. Bob and Jack secured cables to the Land Rover while Mike and Harry helped the injured Jock to a flat location where the Wildcat could land. The Chinook lifted off to safe distance with its load, the Wildcat landed and the team embarked. The helicopter was full with its crew and a medic plus Mikes team.

Jock was attended to first and laid out comfortably, the medic made Mike lay down too. He saw the hole in the sole of the boot where a pad had been bandaged in to stem the bleeding. He decided not to disturb it for the present. Mike felt a prick in his arm and shortly relaxed into an anaesthetised sleep.

He woke up feeling groggy and felt that he was still laying down but on a softer surface. Mike kept his eyes closed and listened. When he heard voices speaking English with British accents he lifted his eyelids just enough to assess his surroundings. It was OK. He opened his eyes and spoke to the nurse nearby.

"How is my driver?"

"He lost a lot of blood but he's going to be fine."

Mike relaxed, then, "How about my foot?"

"The doctor will be here shortly, he'll explain."

That didn't sound so good, "Where are we?" Mike asked.

"Sovereign Base Area, Cyprus, you were flown here from Muwaffaq Salti Air Base in Jordan."

"Thanks," said Mike just as the doctor arrived.

"We've managed to save most of your foot, it was a real mess. Whoever tightened your bootlace, kept it all together and reduced the bleeding probably saved it. That must have hurt." The doctor assumed a medic had tightened the lace.

"Yes," Mike murmured.

4

"Anyway, the good news is your big toe is still OK, the bad news is the others are gone along with a good part of the foot. We have to get you back to the UK for more surgery, a prosthesis and physiotherapy."

"Thanks Doc," said Mike, not really internalising that this could be the end of his military career as he knew it.

Chapter 2

It was autumn. Tony was embarking on the biggest adventure of his life so far. His big brother, Mike, had already left the nest and this would be Tony's first extended stay away from his family home.

"Are you sure you don't want us to take you Tony?" his mother asked.

"It's a long drive from Dorset to Edinburgh. You'd have to take time off work, at least a couple of days, maybe more."

"Mum and I are happy to do it," chipped in his dad.

"It would be great if you could take me to Bristol. Easy jet flights from there are cheap and it would be much quicker," he proposed. Tony had researched the possibilities already. He was close to his family but his parents realised that university would be a big new chapter in his life. It was time for him to spread his wings and they readily agreed to his plan.

They arrived at Bristol Airport in good time. Tony checked in his bag. They said goodbye at the bottom of the escalator to security and departures. He knew airport procedures well enough from the family ski trips but it was his first solo venture. It was exciting but he still felt a few butterflies.

The biggest surprise, when he arrived, was the October temperature in Edinburgh compared to Dorset. The clothes he had left home and travelled in were way too light for autumn in Scotland. On the airport bus he recovered his ski jacket from his suitcase and felt a good deal more comfortable.

Around Corstorphine another young man on the bus near Tony appeared to have noticed the same temperature problem and was rummaging in his bag, unfortunately half the contents spilled out on the floor. Tony helped him pick up the stuff and held the bag while it was all stuffed back.

"Thanks for that," the young man said diffidently.

"No problem, I might have had the same problem."

"It's my first time in Scotland and it's really cold."

"It is a bit chilly; nothing a good coat won't fix though. I'm Tony."

"Oh, my name is Freddie. Are you a student?"

"Yes, I'm just starting, heading to my hall."

"So am I, Pollock hall, but I've no Idea how to get there."

"That's lucky," said Tony, "that's where I'm staying too and I think I can find the way."

"But you're new too, how do you know?"

"Google Earth and bus maps on the internet. If we get off at the Waverley station its a short walk to the Bridges and there are four or five buses that go down to near the Halls"

"What if we miss the Waverley station stop?"

"Don't worry Freddie, the bus route finishes at St Andrew's Square and that's not far from the Bridges either."

Freddie's face was growing clear with relief at this help and visibly started to relax.

They got off at the terminus, walked down to the Bridges and got the first bus that was going down Newington Road.

Freddie was somewhat in awe of Tony's knowledge of Edinburgh and his confidence, compared to his own nervousness.

They got off and headed down East Preston Street towards the Halls as planned.

The check-in and finding their rooms went smoothly and they agreed to meet later for a pint and some food.

When they met, Tony said, "I saw a few pubs from the bus just before we got off. Shall we walk over there?"

"Sure I'd like to explore a bit," answered Freddie sounding a little concerned.

They walked back the way they had come from the bus. They chatted all the way along East Preston Street right up South Clerk Street. They soon found a very comfortable pub that did food.

"That's a ski jacket isn't it?" Freddie asked.

"It is. We go skiing every winter in the Alps if we can," answered Tony.

"I've been twice with school but I'm not that good. Do your Mum and Dad ski as well?"

"Absolutely! They are really good and they started taking Mike and me when we were tiny."

Freddie looked surprised, "My Mum and Dad aren't that outgoing. It's great that you have a brother to do stuff with," said Freddie, who was an only child.

"You are right there Freddie. He's great. He left home a couple of years ago to join the Army and I haven't seen him much since then."

"I suppose you miss him Tony."

"Yes, but we did have a great ski holiday in *Méribel* last winter."

They had a couple more pints and chatted about the courses they were starting.

"I'm really looking forward to starting the physics course. What are you doing?" Tony asked.

"I was never good enough at maths to do real science. I'm doing history."

"Maybe I'll see you at some freshers' event," said Freddie as they walked back to their rooms.

Fresher's week was hectic with meeting other students, staff and all the clubs wanting new members.

Tony settled into the hall and the academic and social life and found he liked it a lot.

The lecturers varied a bit, all were helpful but some better than others at keeping the students' attention and getting their subject over. Generally though the academic side was fascinating and he had to do a lot of work, enough to get by anyway.

The social life was good, he met with a lot of students from different disciplines and backgrounds. He got on well with practically everyone and found that there were fascinating and boring people in all the different courses. He found students from some courses more interesting, but maybe that was because of the higher numbers of girls in them.

Tony hardly saw Freddie in the first term but in January he came across him with some lively company in a pub he hadn't visited before.

"Hi Tony, how are things going? Come and join us."

Tony was surprised and pleased to see the change from shy schoolboy like fresher to a confident student. "Thanks Freddie, that would be great." He hadn't planned anything that evening.

He'd heard that some on his course liked this pub, so he was just looking for a quiet drink and maybe some food with some of his course mates, but this looked a lot better.

There were some introductions but too many to remember.

"Megan! Tell Tony about the Ski Club, he's a big skier." Freddie shouted to one of the girls.

"We all ski," said Megan.

"Oh, I do like to ski, I've been with my family since I was little," replied Tony.

"I haven't seen you at the Ski Club before," she said.

"I'm not in it and I don't have any kit up with me."

"You don't have to worry about that," said Freddie. "The Club has everything and you have got that nice ski jacket."

"So what about it?" Megan asked. She had long auburn hair and an open smile, perhaps that influenced him.

"Well, maybe I'll give it a go. What's involved in joining?"

"You mean, how much will it cost you?" she replied in a lilting Western Isles accent.

Freddie chipped in then and explained the club subscription and the other costs involved in going on ski trips. When the weather was right they went to the Glenshee or Cairngorm areas.

A week later at five o'clock on Wednesday morning it was really icy cold.

"I'm glad you decided to join," said Freddie, his warm breath condensing into a cold bright mist in the streetlights as they carried their kit to Megan's car. "It's not actually called the Ski Club you know. It's called snow-sports or something like that and it's huge. We're just a little bit of it but we love it."

Tony was amazed how Freddie's confidence had grown since their first meeting on the bus and it gave him a good feeling.

The four of them had managed to free up the morning and they all had the afternoon for sport anyway. The snow forecast looked fantastic and they had a chance to get there early if they set off before dawn.

Megan was scraping the windows in a cloud of her own breath. They strapped all the skis on the roof-rack and piled in.

10

"I hope nobody is going to need a pee, we need to hammer it if we want to get on the snow early." Megan would get petrol money back through the club for using her own car on a trip.

"I'll drive there but on the way back someone else is going to have to help with the driving because I'm going to be knackered."

"You know I'll help as long as you let me sleep now," answered Freddie as he snuggled as best he could into the seat and promptly went to sleep.

"Now that's a skill I'd like to acquire," said Tony watching Freddie in amazement.

"He's good at that," said Jo who was the other passenger. "He's been practising."

Tony actually nodded off too, just after the bridge and woke around Perth. It was still dark but the roads were quiet.

Megan got them through Aviemore before eight thirty and they were in the carpark at the Cairngorm Ski Centre well before nine when the funicular would start.

They piled out and surveyed the snow appreciatively; it looked great.

"Lets get boots on and get to the train. Has everyone got all they need," asked Freddie.

They collected all their kit, locked the car and hobbled ski boot style to the train. While they were waiting to get on they put on their gloves, helmets and goggles.

The top was awesome.

"This looks as good as alpine snow," said Tony.

"This is exceptional," smiled Megan, "sometimes there's great snow here and we can't get to it for blocked roads."

"Let's head down White Lady before it gets crowded," said Freddie. They all nodded and Freddie set off followed by Jo, Megan and Tony. They roughly followed each other's tracks which were almost the only ones on the slope. By the time they were halfway down they had passed all the other skiers and were on virgin piste.

"That was a great run," said Tony as they waited to get back on the funicular at the Mid Station. When they reached the Top Station, Jo and Megan wanted to do the White Lady again and they agreed to meet with Tony and Freddie at Base Station.

"OK, where now?" asked Tony.

"If you are up for it we can try the East Wall of the White Lady. It's off piste but I've never heard of it looking this good," said Freddie.

"I'm up for it," said Tony, "I'm told you have to lean back on powder, at least tip the skis up to get through."

The first hundred metres they didn't get going very well; they both piled into a drift and came up laughing.

"I couldn't see much and wasn't too sure of direction," said Freddie, "it looks like mist is coming in."

"We'd better get down," said Tony, "and keep each other in sight".

The slope seemed to be steeper now and it felt like their speed had increased in the lower visibility. It got fairly hairy and the adrenaline was pumping through both of them. They whooped as they slipped into clear air. Pumped up as they were, they shot down the slope in plumes of powder all the way to Base station.

They arrived sweating, exhilarated and feeling on top of the world.

"I was getting worried when the mist came down," said Freddie.

"Yea, but it was great when we got going and out of it," replied Tony.

They took their skis off and carried them back to the car chatting about the runs.

After a while Jo and Megan arrived. They dug out the flasks of hot chocolate and the sandwiches they had brought, sat in the car and discussed the morning's skiing.

"We came down White lady and then when we saw the mist coming down we carried on down Home Road. How did you get here before us?"

Freddie and Tony told them about their off piste adventure and Megan jumped in, "You must have hammered the last part then."

"I suppose so," said Tony.

"Damn right we did!" burst in Freddie.

"The mist is going up already," said Jo.

They skied until the light started to drop on the slopes and then piled into the car and headed home tired but very satisfied with the day.

Freddie drove home as promised. Jo was in the front passenger seat. Megan jumped in the back and was almost instantly asleep. Tony was beside her and was soon asleep too.

Tony opened his eyes around Perth and only Freddie was awake. Megan was sprawled across the back of the car with her head on his chest and her arm wrapped round him. He smiled and closed his eyes.

Shortly after that trip, Tony and Megan became an item which worked out very nicely in a lot of ways, not least for future ski trips.

Chapter 3

When the ski season was over, Tony turned to a sport that was new to him because he wanted to learn to sail. The university club had sailing dinghies but he had to get his own wetsuit for the cold weather. He became proficient and also enjoyed handling the safety boat; a RIB with a hundred horsepower outboard motor.

University wasn't all fun sports and pubs there was a lot of academic work too. The physics was his passion; he especially enjoyed the practical sessions. Optics was a favourite but he found everything in the course fascinating.

All the lecturers knew their subjects thoroughly; although the presentation styles and skills varied, he took it all in.

Final year involved a lot of work and when it came to the results he got an upper second class degree and he was happy with that. During his Viva he realised that if he'd worked a bit harder during the course he might have been able to achieve a first.

Megan and Tony were still together at the end of their final year but unfortunately after graduation they ended up living far apart. They tried to keep in touch but neither had any idea how busy they would be in their new working roles. Their planned visits rarely materialised but they agreed to stay friends.

Tony hadn't been sure what he wanted to do next but his department proposed the possibility of going on to do a Doctorate. He had been so interested in the undergraduate course that he chose a research PhD in Condensed Matter. This study mainly involved understanding the interactions between the constituent particles of solids and liquids.

The basic physical principles were described in terms of quantum mechanics, electromagnetism and statistical mechanics. He understood these to some extent from his undergraduate physics studies, but had to delve much more deeply into them.

Although the institute covered a wide range of fields, he was particularly taken by Extreme Conditions Physics, so that's what he enrolled in.

The university had a world renowned centre dedicated to research into extreme conditions. The Centre for Science at Extreme Conditions (CSEC) involved collaboration between several science schools, and one of them, Physics and Astronomy, was where he had been based as an undergraduate.

His research involved investigations with novel materials and their properties when subjected to extremes of pressure and temperature. They used very high power lasers to attain the high temperatures needed for some work and collaborated with institutions in the US and elsewhere.

He was trying to rapidly heat a significant mass of a novel material and he couldn't easily get enough energy in with the laser, so he reverted to a more natural energy source, the Sun.

He traveled to the solar furnace in the French Pyrenees at Odeillo which has an array of mirrors on a hillside, heliostats, all reflecting sunlight onto a huge parabolic mirror which then reflected the energy onto the furnace itself.

His research was very successful and he stayed on at the university after he received his PhD.

His Post Doctoral work started with control systems for heliostats which he carried out in the physics and astronomy school. During this time his interest in alternative energy sources was stimulated.

He published a paper titled, "A Comparison of Solar Power Generation Systems." This work gave him a good background in the costs and performance of the various projects going on around the world. Most were very expensive and he often thought about the possibilities of making more affordable systems.

Chapter 4

Tony sat in the meeting feeling a little nervous. He was in the same meeting nearly every month with the same group of people, but this month was a little different because he was giving the presentation.

Each month one of the department's staff members gave a presentation about a new technology or a project they were working on. Tony was a little nervous because what he was presenting was in no way new but just a different slant on existing technology.

The last participant arrived and the chairman started the meeting giving a few practical notices and departmental news. Then he called on Tony to give his presentation.

Tony walked to the end of the room next to the screen and addressed the group.

"Good morning ladies and gentlemen. What I'm going to talk about today is not a brand new technology, it's about a particular use of that technology. No doubt you've all heard of a Solar furnace."

"Like the one in Odeillo in the south of France?" Laura interjected.

These meetings were always quite informal and questions were expected throughout the presentations.

"Yes, that's right."

Tony switched on a slide which showed a schematic of the solar furnace and went on to fill in some details.

"This system reflects sunlight from sixty-three heliostats onto a parabola which in turn focuses the light onto the furnace. The heliostats move to keep the direction of the reflected sunlight static. It is capable of raising the temperature of a sample faster than any other type of furnace. It reaches temperatures in excess of three thousand five hundred degrees Celsius within a few seconds which has been very useful for some of my earlier research.

"The version of the furnace which I'm proposing does not need to be such a high-tech device. What I am interested in doing is utilising the sun's energy in countries which have an abundance of sun.

"The vision I have is for a poor nation to be able to use this technology independently and sustainably.

"The first stage of the project is to set up one solar furnace which can melt scrap aluminium. This will be used to make further mirrors to set up more Solar furnaces, and so on.

"Later project stages will be to use the high temperatures to generate electricity by conventional means or to provide energy for many other industrial processes."

The presentation and questions went on for some time until Laura asked,

"How would you make these mirrors without spending a fortune, especially the parabolic one?"

"In our case we don't need so much power as Odeillo so our parabola can be smaller. The mirrors need to be reflective so the polishing has to be good but imperfections in the form are not so significant. That's because we're not trying to produce an image, we're only trying to collect the energy onto a relatively small area."

Andy the senior technician asked; "So will the mirrors on the hillside, the heliostats, all need control systems to cope with the relative movement of the sun?"

"That's exactly right Andy, we'll need control, and servo motors on each mirror."

The chairman commented, "I believe something like this is being used in the US and Spain to generate electricity?"

"Indeed, it is used to generate electricity, they are called Solar Power Towers and there are about a dozen around the world. Some have heat storage features which enable power generation when the sun has gone down. However these are mostly sophisticated and capital intensive systems. My proposal is more basic, lower power and it is aimed at being self sustaining. The first plant will generate raw materials for the second and so on.

"I favour the Namibian Desert and this slide shows some of the advantages to that area."

He put up the slide and went through some of the advantages:

"There's a lot of sunshine there, it may even be the best location in the world for sunlight.

"Namibia is stable politically, it isn't heavily influenced by any of the great powers.

"There isn't too much time difference between UK and Namibia so communications would be relatively easy."

Time was flying by so Tony summarised.

"The concept is to set up a furnace which can melt aluminium scrap. This aluminium can be used to make more mirrors and eventually more solar furnaces. Not only does it provide a good recycling solution for drink cans and similar materials, but the whole process is self-supporting.

"It will bring economic and environmental benefits and it doesn't require costly external resources, just the knowledge. Also we can collaborate with the Namibia University of Science and Technology, N. U. S. T. in Windhoek."

The chairman asked, "Are there any more questions?"

There were one or two queries and a lot of positive feedback.

Tony's presentation was well received probably because it relied on physics and technology which all those present understood, and they could all see the benefits to a developing country because of the project's simplicity.

Chapter 5

Jim Jones, known as JJ, was in his fortieth floor office high over London. The massive floor-to-ceiling windows gave panoramic views over the city and the small people below. He was going through a list of potential projects with his researchers. JJ was the New Projects Director for Renshaw & Collier and, as such, had to make appropriate proposals to the board.

Renshaw & Collier financed environmentally friendly projects in the energy field. So far they had received a lot of great publicity but hadn't made much of an impact commercially. That was okay for the bottom line though, because their main investments were in Oil and Gas and they could easily afford this sideline. However it was very important for image.

"What's this last one on your list George?" JJ asked.

"It's a Solar Power idea from Edinburgh University. It uses mirrors to concentrate the Sun's energy and generate heat which can then be used for small industrial processes and possibly power generation," replied George, one of his researchers.

"That's a bit old-hat isn't it," said JJ.

"It's certainly not new but the science is sound Apparently we could power the whole world from the sun, everything, even if we only used a tiny fraction of its power," replied George.

JJ thought about Renshaw & Collier's oil and gas business in this context and a small shudder went down his back.

"The other thing this project has going for it is that, because it is old technology, it won't require a big R&D budget," added George.

"So why do they need our support?"

"Well, they don't really, I think it will go ahead anyway with other support. I just thought it might be interesting."

'It would go ahead anyway would it,' thought JJ, 'but without our involvement, that didn't sound comfortable.'

"OK, we will get involved in this one," said JJ.

The researchers all knew that the decision was made. Nobody questioned JJ, whatever they thought.

George was sent away to make the financial arrangements and 'Make them jump through a few hoops but not too many' as JJ had put it.

After the researchers were dismissed, JJ got on the phone to make some other arrangements.

Chapter 6

Getting a project like this off the ground was a much bigger task than Tony had envisaged. He had thought about the science and technology involved and thoroughly understood that. There were engineering challenges and he had a good handle on those too but a lot of the rest was new.

Managing a project entailed a whole lot of new activities, and he was the project manager.

He was getting help though, there were people in the department's administration with a lot of management experience which they were happy to share. Most of the academic staff were available too but probably the biggest help came from his fellow post-doc worker Laura who allocated a slab of her time to the project.

She always seemed to be nearby and was great for bouncing ideas.

"Hi Tony, have you got that overall plan written down, the one we talked about?"

"Hello Laura, yes, after a fashion. I haven't had time to learn Microsoft Project yet, so I've roughed it out in Excel."

"That should be a good start," said Laura, "I've used Project quite a bit, I could set it up and put the data all in if you like."

"That would be fantastic, you're an angel," he replied.

"No wings yet," said Laura. "You email your Excel file and I'll have a look at it this afternoon."

At half past three in the afternoon Laura guessed where she would find Tony, and she was in need of a cup of tea too. When she came in he was just stirring his. She put her laptop down on his table and made herself some.

"I've put in all the tasks and durations," she said, "now I need to add all the dependencies."

She opened the laptop and the list of activities was already on the screen.

"That's great," said Tony, and they started working together on the project plan.

"OK," said Laura, "so that's all your tasks done and the bars to the right show how long you estimated each one would take but, there are no dependencies and they all start at the same date."

"I get that, we have to say what has to be done before what," said Tony.

"That's right," explained Laure, "but we have to decide which is the first activity and you've got several starting at the same time, and that doesn't work for the planning particularly the critical path network. We have to start the project on one activity."

"But they do all start together," said Tony.

"OK," she replied, "then we have to add one start activity like 'Project Start' or 'Project Authorised' so that we can get the critical path network to work properly."

"All right, I guess that makes sense," said Tony.

They added 'Project Finance Authorisation' as the first task as they knew they weren't supposed to do anything before that was done.

"You know I've started working on some of these things already," said Tony. "How will we incorporate that?"

"We'll just put them where they are supposed to be in the plan and if some work is already done, we'll just reduce the duration of the task when we get to it. It's a bit of a fiddle but it'll work in practice."

They spent the rest of the afternoon and early evening putting in dependencies and updating durations.

By eight in the evening they had a presentable Critical Path network to look at. They had moved back to the lab where there was a big monitor to display it.

Tony looked at his watch, "Look at the time!It's after eight! Time for some food and a drink, I'm buying."

"I've just realised I'm starving too," she replied. "Let's go."

"I needed that, Tony," said Laura as they were finishing their meal.

"Yea, me too. I think my brain is working again now," he replied. "Did you notice that the heliostat control systems featured a lot in The Critical Path on our diagram."

"Yes, I did see that," she replied. "We'll have to look at that, another pint?"

"Thanks Laura, that would be great."

The following morning Tony was talking to the Physics department's technicians over coffee.

"So do you plan to put this project together in the desert?" Andy asked.

"That's right but with a lot of preparation," replied Tony.

"It seems to me that you want to use really basic technology, not high tech, in that environment," said Bill.

"You don't want to rely on something that has a ten week lead time from a big semiconductor manufacturer," added Andy.

Bill chipped in again, "You really want stuff that you could knock up in your garage or shed."

"That would be great but some of it will require technical solutions." Tony answered. "The main thing I'm concerned about is the heliostat steering system. We have planned a central computer with an interface unit which sends control signals by fibre to the unit on each heliostat."

"Fibre will be robust," said Bill.

Tony went on, "Yes, that's the reasoning. Each Heliostat has a bespoke unit which receives the optical signal, decodes it and controls the motors. The encoders on the motors go back to that board too."

"What if something goes wrong with that heliostat unit?" Andy asked.

"We have quotes from the best LSI chip and multilayer board manufacturers and we'll make spare units too."

Andy and Bill would not be swayed from their lower tech ideas, they knew that the LSI chips were just what the acronym said Large Scale Integration. The final result was a cheap unit price once numbers were being made but it was expensive and time consuming in the design and testing stages.

"If it has to have a proper control system," said Andy, "you could have some basic cheap modules that are off the shelf, like the Raspberry Pi micro computer. You can program them with a laptop."

"And," put in Bill, "if you need sensors for the sunlight you'd be better with old fashioned photodiodes, resistors on a board, all discrete components. They can be soldered up by anyone with a bit of training and a low tech soldering iron. And you can repair it when it gets broken. You would need some power components to drive the motors but that shouldn't be too complicated."

Afterwards, when Tony was in his lab with Laura, he was reflecting on the discussions with the technicians.

"I was talking to Bill and Andy over coffee. Those guys are really practical, they approach thing in a completely different way. I've been thinking about complex centralised control systems and fancy actuators for the heliostats but I'm beginning to think there could be big problems in a harsh environment. And, with very little technical back up locally, it could be a struggle to keep things working."

"Well, what can you do about it?"

"We'll continue with the plan at the moment but I'll be doing a lot of thinking and talking to people about it. I think we might need simpler more modular systems like Andy suggested, as a backup."

A week later, Tony was feeling a bit happier about the project direction and went to find Laura to explain his thinking.

"Hi Laura, remember what I said about my discussions with Andy and Bill?" he asked, knowing that she would. She nodded.

"Well, I have an idea about a Plan B," he started, "and I have to thank the technicians for stimulating these ideas and providing practical information. It's at an early stage but here it is.

"I worked out that we could start with a hundred one metre square mirrors. More would be better but a hundred is a good start.

"Until we start making aluminium mirrors on site we can buy bog-standard glass mirrors for about fifty pounds each. They won't last all that long but should get us started and for only five grand.

"We'll need a tilt mechanism and actuating motors. I favour small twelve Volt DC motors with a lot of gearing and encoders for position. They don't need to move the mirrors very fast and are really cheap and replaceable."

"You could control them with off-the-shelf Raspberry Pi micro computers," Laura jumped in excitedly, grasping where Tony was going.

"Exactly!" Tony enthused. "Have you been talking to the techs?" he added.

"Not recently but I know they're mad about those little single board computers."

"And," Tony went on, "if we add the WiFi to the Pi then we won't need control cabling to each one, only power and they could each have a twelve Volt battery which we could recharge with a solar cell."

"You'd have to work out battery and solar cell sizes, " Laura added thoughtfully.

"Right, but the biggest challenge could be building the tilt mechanisms."

"Hm, isn't there a simple way to do that?"

"I'm thinking Meccano," grinned Tony. "We could make it out of basic steel and nuts and bolts. Look, I made some sketches."

Tony leaned across the desk, spreading papers out before them. "See, I estimate about two hundred and fifty pounds each for materials, but it will be labour intensive so there will be a big job to do organising the labour.

"There are some drive electronics between the Pi to the motors but I think that Bill was right about using discrete components where possible so they could be made and repaired locally. The components will be a bit more expensive than a large scale integration but the easy repairs and low setup cost should more than compensate. What do you think?"

"Wow," said Laura with a smile, "I think it's a real Plan B. Do you think it can really work?"

"It's worth a try," Tony grinned back. "I think it will be under a thousand pounds per Heliostat and we forecast a budget of millions based on what the new American one in Nevada costs. If we add this it would just be backup parts, like a contingency."

"Yes, but we don't know yet if we'll get backing."

Tony smiled wryly. "There's something I have to tell you. The Prof. called me to his office first thing to tell me. A venture capital company that sponsors environmental projects has written to him to say they will finance the whole thing."

"You are kidding!" Laura exclaimed.

"No," said Tony. "He showed me the letter. They want a proposal with business plan but they implied they would definitely fund it if we can make a reasonable case."

"That's fantastic news Tony! Why didn't you tell me that first?" she said punching him on the arm.

"Ouch! Well, I guess I'd just spent a week looking at this backup plan and I suppose I thought it might be irrelevant after we got big finance."

She smiled at him. "I don't think it's irrelevant. It sounds like a great backup. You should try and squeeze the costs in as prototyping or spares but don't include all the detail in your budget."

"Why not?"

"Because," she said, "they might just decide to only fund the backup because it's much cheaper."

The penny dropped. "Oh, I guess so."

"You'll need a lot of funding for all the trials you have to do here before you start thinking about going to the desert," she added. "And now we have sponsorship we can place some firm orders. The best company for the LSI Chips and the circuit boards is Rossborough Electronics; they've been around a long time and have a great reputation and their quote is really good."

"I agree, I looked at their quote a couple of days ago and it's definitely the best," confirmed Tony.

Chapter 7

Laura was in her own lab when her mobile vibrated in her pocket. It was about two weeks after that Plan B discussion with Tony, She took it into the corridor and answered it.

"Hi Laura," said Tony. "Are you free, there's something I have to show you."

He sounded so excited she decided to see what he wanted to show her.

A quarter of an hour later she felt as though she was in a sauna. She was in the basement next to Tony and an oven which was mostly used for melting metal samples. There was a steel bowl on a stand with gas torches playing on the underside. It looked about half a metre in diameter. This was one of the things on the technology side that Tony was keen to try."Have you made a paraboloid already?" Laura asked examining the bowl.

"Not quite, it's only roughly parabolic. The techs made it with blow torches and hammers. It's on bearings so we can rotate it and pour in molten aluminium. That's when we should have a decent paraboloid. Watch!"

He handed her safety glasses and moved her away from the bowl as it started slowly rotating.

"How fast does it rotate?" asked Laura.

"Twenty-one RPM." he replied. "That gives a focal length of about a metre. It has to stay very steady though."

"That looks like a lot of molten aluminium," she queried.

"Yes, there's nearly four litres, about ten kilograms. We needed to make it nearly two centimetres thick because of the irregularities in the steel bowl."

"I thought you were going to cast a concrete bowl," she said.

"That was the original idea but it was going to be a lot heavier, even with thinner aluminium so we went with this first." Tony paused, "I think we are ready. OK guys are you ready to pour?"

There were nods from Bill and Andy who were wearing full face shields, gloves, boots and long leather aprons.

Tony projected his voice, "OK everyone we are going to pour. Stand well back incase there's any splash."

Bill and Andy picked up the hot crucible with long double handed tongs and carried it to the bowl. As they tipped it in, it spread across and up the sides of the hot metal bowl. There was an up-stand at the outside edge to prevent spillage.

"That looks good," said Laura

"Fascinating," said Tony. "We all knew what would happen but seeing it is just mesmerising."

There was general agreement. The bowl was still being heated so the aluminium had flowed well.

"I think you can turn the gas off now and let it rotate until tomorrow, I want it to be really cool when we examine it."

Andy added, "I've set up a time lapse camera to watch it so we can see what happens with the contraction."

"That's great," said Tony appreciatively. "You've done a great job guys." He looked around at everyone and they all looked as tired as he felt but also as buzzed as him.

"It's late," he said. "Who wants a pint?"

The two Techs, Laura and Tony headed off together to get some food and a well earned beer.

"We videoed the pour as well," said Bill. "So we should have some nice pictures to show."

"That's brilliant," said Tony. "You guys are stars."

"Pity that with the full face shields the stars of the movie won't be showing off their handsome features," said Andy.

There were groans. "It must be your round Andy," said Bill.

The next morning they were examining the rather dull-looking silver surface of the aluminium.

"We've got some ideas for cleaning that up," said Bill.

"But we'll have to stabilise it in the steel frame first. See there's a three millimetre gap because of the differential expansion, or rather contraction," pointed out Andy. "We'll separate it all round first then pack all the gaps evenly around the circumference."

"Then we'll rotate it and buzz it with this electric sander with finer and finer paper then some polishing compound," said Bill holding up a sander with a head about ten centimetres across.

"If we can rig up something we'll clamp the sander and just let it run, probably under it's own weight."

"That sounds like a good plan," said Tony. "Thanks again guys."

"More beer on the horizon I think," said Bill quietly to Andy but loud enough for Tony to hear.

They all had a laugh and then went about their respective tasks.

Chapter 8

Laura more or less took over logistics and the procurement of the equipment that would be needed. She and Tony sat down at least every week to discuss the timetable. Tony concentrated on proving as much of the technology as he could.

"How did the parabolic mirror turn out Tony?"

"It was pretty good but it needed a lot of polishing," he replied.

"It's feasible though?"

"Yes," he said, "it's a good process and we won't need to do it very often."

"That's great!" said Laura, "I've been getting the suppliers lined up but I need to go through it all with you."

"I have to see the Prof. about the financial support, can we meet at lunchtime and spend the afternoon on it?"

"That'll be good," she said, "I have a couple of items to check up on. Bring your laptop to the pub, I'll bring mine and we can get something to eat too."

Around one o'clock Tony arrived at the selected pub. Laura was already at a table with her laptop open and two untouched pints.

"That looks great, I'm parched after that meeting."

"How did it go?"

"The sponsoring company is Renshaw & Collier and it's footing the bill for everything," answered Tony. "The Prof. and the Uni bosses are delighted because they get all the kudos and it doesn't cost them a penny."

"So is the budget enough?" She asked.

"It's unbelievable, they have added twenty percent contingency onto our proposal but reading between the lines I think it's a drop in the ocean to them."

"We already added some contingency," she said, "even before we set the budget and I am hoping for some cost reductions. That is great. Let's order some food and we can start going through this."

The beer and the food was good, the company and the project was good. In fact they were both very happy, everything today was good.

After the lunchtime crowd disappeared and the bar was quiet, they carried on working there, topping up on coffee periodically until it started to get busy again.

"I think we should move on soon," said Laura.

"Yes, it's going to get a bit noisy."

"It is Friday," she added.

"My stomach is telling me I need more food but we have a load more to go though."

"I don't mind carrying on after food if you are free," said Laura.

"I am definitely free." He said, "What about fish suppers, my place is just round the corner from the chippy; we can eat and work there."

"Suits me," said Laura.

They had their fish and chips on Tony's sofa and carried on working all evening.

Tony eventually nodded off and so did Laura. He looked at the clock near the TV, it said two o'clock. Laura had fallen asleep leaning on him and had slid down nearly horizontal, sleeping soundly.

He must have nodded off again because the clock was saying two forty-five and Laura was stirring, her arm was right across his belly and he could feel her fingers touching his side, it was warm and pleasant. The fingers slid under his tee-shirt and gently pressed his side. They were both very warm and relaxed. Her hand gently moved up inside the shirt as she explored his chest. They were both awake now and it seemed only natural as their lips came together for a long kiss.

"I need to go to bed," said Laura and before Tony could say anything, she added, "Where's the bedroom?"

Tony pointed in the direction of his room and she got up and started heading that way.

"You're coming too, aren't you?" she said over her shoulder.

"Sure, I just need the loo first."

A couple of minutes later he heard her voice outside the bathroom.

"I need the loo too."

She was waiting for him to come out in her bra and pants and smiled as she squeezed past him. Tony went to the bedroom his brain whizzing, Laura was a great looking girl and he liked her a lot but he'd never thought of her in a romantic way, he wondered at himself for that. He had a vague idea that she had a boyfriend or a partner.

"Are you going to bed with your clothes on?" she asked as she came back in and took off her remaining underwear.

He smiled and shook his head.

She came over to him and slipped her hands under his tee-shirt.

"Arms up," she whispered and he obeyed smiling.

She slipped the tee-shirt over his head pressing herself against his chest as she reached up. He unbuckled his jeans and she slipped her hands down his legs pushing off his Calvin Klein's as well.

"Posh underwear," she said as her hair brushed against him.

They slipped under the duvet and came close together.

Tony woke at ten in the morning and he was alone in a very tossed bed.

'She's gone' he thought, 'Maybe last night wasn't such a good idea. It was great though.'

The front door of the flat clicked shut and two clonks sounded on the floor. A couple of minutes later Laura came into the bedroom.

"Don't look so worried, you were sleeping so soundly I just slipped out to the pharmacy."

His worried look persisted, then the penny dropped.

She read his face, "That's right, morning after pill."

"Have you taken it?" he asked.

"Well," she said slowly. "It is morning, but I'm not sure it's after yet." She slipped off her outside coat revealing that she had nothing underneath and slipped in beside him.

Later, Tony went to the kitchen and made some coffee; he took the cups back to his room. As they were sitting in the bed drinking it Laura said, "I've had a great time but I'm exhausted now. I think I'll take that tablet and have a shower."

He heard her moving around in the kitchen and then the shower started.

She came into the bedroom with a towel wrapped round but made no effort to cover herself as she got herself dried.

'This is a fine way to start a weekend,' Tony thought and went to the shower himself.

He felt it a bit odd as they settled on the sofa again in front of their laptops. She sensed his mood, she had been thinking about their work relationship too.

"Are you OK?" she asked.

"Well, I kinda had an idea that you had a boyfriend or partner somewhere."

"Kinda - is right," she replied thoughtfully. "There is a boy, a man now, that I've been close to for a long time but he's in Cambridge and we haven't seen each other for ages." They were silent for a while, "He's studying medicine."

"I hope I'm not putting you in an awkward position," he said.

After some thought she opened up and answered, "No, last night was really good, your company and everything but I'm not in love with you and I'm still passionate about the project. If I ever get together with my doctor again I think he will be the one to settle with for good.

"There, you know more about me than anyone, including him I think."

He had wondered if this weekend would mess up their work relationship but it was going to be OK and he didn't think he was falling in love either.

"Well," he said eventually, "working with you is great and this weekend is fantastic but I don't think I'm falling in love either. In a funny way you are too good a friend for that. Does that make sense?"

"I think it does," she answered.

They started back on the project and continued till early evening when they went to the pub for some food and a drink. They went back to their respective accommodations, each needing an early night.

When Tony was back in his empty flat he felt a bit disappointed to be on his own but he knew he needed some sleep especially as he had arranged to sail with the commodore of the university sailing club the following day.

Monday morning Tony was in the lab with Bill and Andy.

"How was your weekend?" asked Bill.

Tony's heart seemed to bump extra loud for a few seconds before Andy answered.

"After that quick pint with you I met up with a couple of old friends for a few beers, turned into more than a few and I slept most of Saturday. I did a ten-K run on Sunday and watched Netflix to relax."

"Fairly normal then," said Bill. "How about you Tony?"

Tony didn't want to relate his full weekend and as he'd had a bit of time to think he said, "I went sailing on the Forth, one of my club mates asked me to crew for him, we had a fair wind and a great time."

Laura walked in. "You guys chewing over the weekend as usual?" she quipped.

"How was your's?" asked Bill.

"Good, but we've got work to do," she said looking at Tony quite seriously but he thought he detected a sparkle in her eyes.

They settled down to their planning as the techs went off to fix some equipment. "All work and no play that girl," said Andy quietly to Bill.

They spent two weeks refining the project plan and the technology. The Professor made the first contact with Namibia University of Science and Technology (NUST) in Windhoek, and now Tony was talking to some of the staff; they were very keen on the project and Tony felt they would have a lot to offer.

It was about eight o'clock on a Friday evening and Tony was staring at his laptop screen not really taking anything in. A voice broke through his tiredness, "You are really tired, you have to stop."

He looked up, "Yes, you're right Laura."

"And you need some food, let's go and get some, I need it too."

The pub was busy as expected for a Friday night but they did get a couple of seats squashed together in a corner. They had the first beer and the food came just after Laura collected the second drink.

They ate quietly, comfortable in each other's company. When the food was finished they were very relaxed and most of the way down their second pint. Tony was contemplating a third when Laura's hand rested on this thigh. She leaned towards him and said quietly, "Since we're both tired, how about coming to bed at my flat, I could use a nice snuggle." Her hand slid l bit further up his thigh; he was convinced already without that encouragement.

They slept late on the Saturday morning and had just about finished brunch of bacon eggs and tomatoes with some lovely brown toast when Laura's mobile rang.

"Who's phoning on a Saturday?" Laura muttered as she went to get the phone from the table. Tony could only hear her end of the conversation.

"Hello, Laura here," there was a pause while she listened.

"Your name didn't come up on my phone have you changed your number?" A fairly long explanation must have been given then.

"Well, don't tell any of the drug companies your new number. So what's the occasion to call me?"

"You are kidding, that's great! When?"

"Yes of course that'll be fine."

"Call me when you are going to arrive and I'll meet you. Bye."

She turned round with a big smile on her face and saw Tony as though she was surprised to see him. He looked quizzically at her.

"I'll make some more coffee and then explain," she replied.

The phone call had been from James her long time friend, the doctor in Cambridge. He had a new post at the Royal Infirmary of Edinburgh and would be moving up soon. Laura had happily agreed that he could stay with her.

Short and sweet, that was the end of their weekend romps.

Chapter 9

"Will we be seeing more of you when you finish school?" asked one of the regulars, hopefully, as Maria passed him the pint of lager she had just pulled.

"I plan on going to University in October so I might be here in the holidays but that's all," she answered. She went on to serve some other customers.

He was disappointed to hear that but he knew she was smart and the best looking girl for miles around.

"She's out of my league anyway," he muttered to himself.

Maria grew up in a country pub, almost at the seaside in Cornwall. It was called The Smugglers and was in a tiny hamlet with only a handful of houses.

She liked to be outdoors and there were plenty of opportunities. She helped in the pub when needed and at hay making time she helped some of the local farmers.There were always more hands needed to get the bales into the barns. She'd walk miles along the cliff paths and loved to swim in the sea.

Like many eighteen year olds leaving school with A levels, Maria went off to university without a real idea what she wanted to do with her life.

She knew a few things she didn't want to do: sit behind a desk shuffling papers or typing on a PC, Medicine, and definitely not teaching children. She'd experienced how many of them didn't want to learn anything except how to make their mates laugh.

She chose the most interesting degree course she could find, not really thinking of what career might follow. It was electronics and she enrolled in the university in the October.

The Fresher's Fair, where all the clubs and societies tried to get new members, was a fun occasion. Their success appeared to be based on the charisma of the presenters much more than the actual activities. Her academic schedule would only give enough spare time for two or three activities at most. The Engineering Society although it had a boring name appeared to be dedicated to brewery and distillery trips, including sampling in each case. There were too many sports clubs to choose from but the Martial Arts club was actually there with members throwing each other about on mats. The Ski Club was there with a lot of kit but she'd done that with her family and was already competent.

Eventually she plumped for the Engineering Society as a social activity. As a balance she wanted something physical and chose the Hybrid Martial Arts Club (HMA) and Archery. She wasn't to know till much later how important these choices were.

About half way through her first term Brian, the Engineering Society chairman, called across the canteen, "Hey! Maria! Are you coming on the next Eng-Soc trip?"

"The last one was good so I probably will. Is it a Brewery or a Distillery?" Maria asked half joking but knowing that these were favoured attractions.

Brian looked a bit sheepish then. 'Perhaps we should focus on some other industries,' he thought. 'But then everyone liked these trips. There was usually a good complimentary bar at the end of the tour.'

Aloud he answered, "It's a brewery actually."

"That's fine, you usually choose well," she said, much to his relief.

These venues were good but having Maria along added to the attraction, particularly as the majority of members

42

were male. Maria was good fun, and extremely good looking too. She got on with the other girls and her presence would encourage them to come. It turned out to be a great trip.

The HMA was a totally different experience.

She soon found out not to call it Mixed Martial Arts. MMA is what cage fighting is called and was far from what she studied with the HMA club.

Hybrid Martial Arts turned out to be what the name said; a study of a variety of martial arts from Judo and Karate to Kendo. It was great for her fitness and energy.

Her university life wasn't just socialising and sport, there was a lot of work to do as well. She could handle the theory stuff but most of all she enjoyed applying it to the practicals.

The study of transducers and sensors was fascinating. She loved to be able to put something together that had some interaction with the real world however simple.

Also she found that she had a talent for fault finding and mending things. Mostly she worked on electronic circuits but she also found that she could turn the same skills to mechanical things. It was very rewarding and when her final year came she was sad to be moving on but she also felt ready for some new challenges.

Chapter 10

During the final year it was common for big companies to visit universities to try to get the pick of the upcoming graduates. The students had called it the Milk Round for years. Maria's final year was no exception. The main hall in the university was set up like a business exhibition with tables, banners, corporate backdrops and video presentations galore.

Just inside the entrance to the hall the university had a modest table with some members of staff giving information to the students and sometimes the exhibitors.

Some of the staff were familiar and some just had that academic look except for one.

He was an older man with white hair and a beard. He wore a very smart pale cream suit and tie and he wore it well. He appeared to be observing and taking no part in the proceedings.

She walked around the show looking at the presentations and taking the occasional business card. She didn't want a carrier bag full of leaflets and magazines that she'd never read; she could do backgrounds on the internet. Banks, insurance companies, consultancies, civil service, accountants, manufacturing and many more, nothing particularly peaked her interest.

By mid morning she was gasping for a drink and went for a coffee; black no sugar but there seemed to be no free tables. As she looked around, the gentleman from the university table caught her eye and indicated a free stool at the small round table he was occupying.

"Thank you, you aren't expecting anyone else are you?" she asked as she sat down with her coffee.

"No, I'm here alone."

"Oh! Aren't you with the University?"

"Not exactly, although we have some common interests. Have you found any suitable opportunities this morning?"

"There hasn't been anything that has jumped out at me."

"There are a lot of banks and accountants," he mused with a smile. They exchanged pleasantries while they drank their coffee. He didn't look like a banker or accountant, she wasn't sure what to make of him except that he was extremely well presented and quite charming.

"Would you like another coffee? Black, no sugar?" He asked.

"How did you know?"

"The first one was black; the no sugar was a.." He hesitated just the right amount of time. "A lucky guess." He smiled and went to the counter.

She tried to weigh him up as he ordered. He could have said any number of flattering things about the sugar but he didn't, what he did say with that subtle pause was just right. He certainly was charming.

When he returned with the coffees she thanked him and asked him if he was recruiting.

"Well, indirectly. I liaise with a number of organisations which are looking for good people. Perhaps you would like to tell me about yourself and I'll see if any of those organisations might like to talk to you."

She hadn't prepared herself to give a presentation but he was so easy to talk to that she described herself, her background and just talked about her skills and her achievements. ***

At the end of the summer term Maria phoned home, "Hello Mum I just got my results."

"How did you do darling?" her Mum sounded as excited as she was.

"I can't believe it!" she exclaimed, "I got a First."

"Oh well done! A First Class Honours! All that work was worth it."

"It was an interesting course, I chose well," she said to cover her slight embarrassment as she didn't think she had worked all that hard. Certainly not as hard as the other student who received a First.

"What will you do now?"

"I'll stay here for a few days, there's going to be a celebration tonight with all the graduates and lecturers. Then I will let it sink in and have a long think about where I want to be."

"Well, call if you want to talk about it and you know we are always here if you need us."

"Thanks Mum, I'll call on Friday." Maria usually called her mum early on Friday evenings.

It was a great party that night and most people stayed for it. At the start of the evening while most were still holding coherent conversations, she was approached by Sue Davies a senior control theory lecturer and researcher.

"Have you thought about staying on to do a second degree?"

"Thank you for asking. To be honest, I hadn't really thought too much further than the finals. I'll take a few days now to think about my options. I'm staying up here till at least the weekend."

"Well, you know where I am if you would like to discuss it. I'm sure it would be the start of a great academic career."

A PhD sounded interesting but that last phrase put her off, 'academic career'. It sounded so defined and prescribed. She would have to think about it.

46

The next day, Thursday, everyone was either hung over or at least extremely tired, the party had gone on very late. She went for a swim in the afternoon and went for a quiet drink with a couple of friends in the evening.

Friday morning she was having coffee when her mobile rang.

"Congratulations on your First, I expected nothing less."

The voice wasn't familiar and at first she was at a loss how to answer but her hesitation was minuscule and she answered.

"Thank you, that's very kind of you to say so." She wondered how he knew.

"I would like to speak with you about a career opportunity, do you have some free time?"

She'd relaxed, she'd cracked it, she knew who it was. It was the charming gentleman from the Milk Round. He had not actually told her what organisations he was scouting for but he was so interesting that she took the decision immediately to see him.

Chapter 11

Mid August was roasting hot in the UK and it had been five years since Maria had started in this industry. She had now moved to Sellick & Arrowsmith Security - S&A to the insiders - and was based in HR getting to know the admin staff and security personnel from the vantage of head office. Some of the security people were very professional but some were what she thought of as 'the heavies' and she suspected that they were employed for just that reason.

Her boss asked her to interview one of these 'heavies' because there had been a complaint about his behaviour towards one of the girls in the office. A bit of checking had revealed that this wasn't the first time and probably wasn't the most serious. However this was the first girl with the nerve to report it. There appeared to be a culture of something close to fear regarding these 'heavies'. Because this was a first official complaint it would be a verbal warning although most in HR would have preferred a final warning or dismissal.

The meeting was arranged for mid morning and the big open plan office was packed. The interview room was a glass box known as the goldfish bowl, at one side of the open plan area. As Mr Mason swaggered across the office several sets of eyes turned away. When he saw it was not the head of HR and it was just a young girl, he continued his swagger into the goldfish bowl.

Maria indicated the other chair and, preempting his opening salvo asked, "Would you like coffee?"

"That would be good little girl, do you provide any other services?" he laughed crudely. She detected a slight South or West Country accent, not Cornwall or Devon, maybe Dorset.

"Since you are being rude we'll skip the niceties," said Maria pleasantly. "You are here to receive a verbal warning concerning your conduct towards another member of staff. Consider it delivered. Do you have anything to say about it?"

"Who would dare to complain about me?" he growled staring aggressively out into the office.

"Oh!" Maria said deliberately looking surprised. "Am I to take it from that comment that you've abused more than one member of staff?"

He was becoming agitated and demanded, "What's this verbal warning supposed to mean!"

"I make a note of it on your record and if you misbehave again you will be brought in for a written warning then if your behaviour doesn't improve you will end up with a final written warning and eventually dismissal. Does that answer your question?" Maria asked politely.

"I know how to behave little girl," he said more aggressively.

"It appears that you do not Mr Mason," she said firmly.

"You cheeky little slut! You'll not talk to me like that!" he shouted and stood leaning aggressively over the desk.

She ignored his aggressive stance and reached into the desk drawer for a printed form which she began completing.

He was becoming enraged and the whole office stared and held their breath.

"Don't you dare ignore me!"

"I'm not ignoring you Mr Mason. This is for you."

"What the hell do you mean?"

"It's your first written warning …"

49

She didn't finish the sentence because he lost it completely and swung a wide slap at her face.

Maria moved her head and body with the direction of the hit to reduce the impact leaving only some redness and some fingernail scratches which bled a little but it was worth it.

He made a second swipe, this time with a balled fist but it made no contact. He felt a surprisingly strong grip on his wrist then pressure near his elbow and he was flat on his face on the floor with his wrist up between his shoulder blades before he knew what was happening.

There was a knee on his back and the little girl whispered in his ear, "If you move I'll dislocate your shoulder and maybe break your arm."

The wind had been knocked out of him both physically and mentally both with the impact on the floor and the speed with which he had been incapacitated by a little girl.

The next voice in the room was the head of HR.

"Are you all right Miss M?" he knew her name but didn't want to use it in front of this man. Anyway it was a common shortening in the company, usually for security reasons.

"I'll be fine thank you Mr Prior," as she turned her face towards him blood from the scratches dribbled impressively for such minor wounds.

"Mr Mason, you will give me your security badge and leave the premises immediately, " said Mr Prior with some internal relief to be rid of this problematic man.

"You'll be invited back for a final hearing but I consider that your behaviour here constitutes gross misconduct and that your employment will be terminated."

Later that morning Maria sat with the Mr Prior in his office. He began with, "Are you sure you are OK?"

"I'm fine, only a couple of scratches."

"Good, well there is something else we need to talk about."

'Oh Oh, here it comes' she thought, 'I've crossed a line.'

"It's your position in this department."

"I was only defending myself."

"Yes, yes, you aren't in trouble, in fact a new opportunity has come up which might better suit your talents."

"Oh, that sounds interesting."

"I would like you to consider working directly in security, not admin. You can visit the facility this afternoon and we'll discuss it again tomorrow morning, say 10:00 here."

"Thank you Mr Prior, but I believe it's out of town, I walk to work and I don't have a car."

"That's not a problem, someone will pick you up at your desk at 13:00 and drive you there if that's OK."

"That's perfect thank you," she said, thinking that she would have time for a bite to eat.

Chapter 12

At 13:00 a smiling chauffeur arrived to collect her and they drove out of town on the M4, off towards Windsor then turned west and south on smaller roads. In about forty-five minutes they arrived at what looked like a farm with no signs or company identification. It turned out that everyone had called it the farm for so long that The Farm had become its official designation within S&A.

The senior instructor was in the largest building waiting for her.

"We don't get many girls here, would you like to try to throw me on the floor?"

She sensed potential problems but actually it turned out to be good humoured banter.

"The floor looks a bit hard here sir," replied Maria.

"Good answer, and it's just Ian," he laughed.

He showed her around the training facility and explained the nature of the work and the training she would get. Mostly it was protection of important people: visiting foreign politicians, heads of state, business people and sometimes celebrities.

They talked about the benefits and dangers of the role and half joked about the US security culture of taking a bullet for the President.

"Mostly it's keeping the press from trampling the client and when we do have potentially vulnerable VIPs, we have some special cars and we use bullet proof vests like this one, just in case," he explained.

She tried it on and was surprised how snug it was.

"You'll probably need a size larger jacket when you wear one of these."

The HR interview at ten the next morning wasn't really taxing, the job was her's if she wanted it and she did.

This was the opportunity she had been waiting for and she knew she would jump at it.

Maria lived in a flat off Shepherd's Bush Green and it was only a half hour walk to the office near Hammersmith Bridge. If she went for the training she would be living at the Training Centre for the duration but that was fine.

She was given a list of what she would need there and what not to take; she could have figured out most of it herself.

She had the rest of the day off to buy anything she needed and to pack. The smiling chauffeur would pick her up at her flat the following morning.

She arrived at The Farm with all her stuff in one big duffel bag which she dropped off in her room and went immediately to meet whoever was there.

The training was great, especially the martial arts which she loved.

All the other skills were more or less as she had expected including the fitness training. There were no other trainees as such, but the regular operatives were required to refresh their skill regularly and keep their fitness levels high. There was only one other female operative, Alison, who was very fit and competent; the two got on well together and sparred whenever the opportunity arose. They also sparred with the men, all of whom were all much fitter and more astute than Mason and his cronies in London. Even so Maria and Alison held their own well.

Ian was in George Sellick's office at the The Farm. Mr Sellick was a founding director of S&A, and his senior instructor was updating him on Maria's progress.

53

"First the physical stuff, self defence and the like," said Ian. "She looks light, but that doesn't matter because of her speed and skill. She has been doing various martial arts for several years so there is no problem on that side. Also we did a couple of exercises simulating VIP protection, threw in a few random problems and she handled it all well."

"That's all good but when do you think she'll be ready to go on the road?" Mr S asked.

"She's ready now," answered Ian, "I'd only suggest some low profile jobs in the field as a start."

"That's fast."

"She's a fast learner, bright girl."

"OK then, pass her on to Operations."

Operations immediately scheduled her on an airport pickup.

Phil Arrowsmith, the other founding director of S&A, was in charge of Operations. He was giving the briefing on Friday afternoon in the small meeting room at the Farm.

"OK people, this is Miss M's first outing with operations. You will be doing a meet and greet at Heathrow, escorting a Mr Brown to the car which Mr C will be driving. Mr D will be in the Arrivals hall observing."

Maria eyes flicked up at D at that point, a slight movement but Phil Arrowsmith noticed.

"He's not observing you Miss M; he's got your back and is keeping an eye out for threats."

"Everyone clear so far?" There were nods all round.

"Good. Miss M will be holding this card with Mr Brown printed on it. Here is a photograph of him. There's no unusual Tech on Monday. Miss M will be using her company mobile phone with standard wired Headphones as if listening to music, actually you will be. Before you get to the arrivals gate you will call Mr C and you'll keep that call open until Mr Brown is safely in the car. Mr C will have music on in the car so that you know you are still connected.

"When Mr Brown arrives he will approach you. You will remove the left earpiece leaving the one with the microphone in your ear.

"You will say, 'Good morning Mr Brown, how was your trip?'

"He will reply 'Good thank you Miss M.'"

"What happens if he doesn't say that?" Maria asked.

"Good question. If something is wrong he will say, 'A bit bumpy Miss M.'

"This isn't very likely on this job but our protocol is then to ask the client what extra assistance you can provide and try to find out what is wrong while immediately ushering him towards the exit. Mr C will phone Mr D who will scan for threats and move closer to Mr Brown but will not join you straight away. The team would be on alert and Mr C would inform the Farm. You proceed to the car.

"If someone approaches you who does not look like the photograph, remember there may be another Mr Brown coming through Arrivals, you say, 'Good morning Sir. What is your company?'

"This will alert the team. When he gives you another company name just say, 'I'm sorry I'm collecting a different Mr Brown.' Explain where the meeting point is and make sure your sign is still easily visible for our Mr Brown."

"What is Mr Brown's company?" Maria asked.

"You'll get that information on Monday morning."

"Will you cover the impersonation or switch possibility?" Mr D asked.

"Might as well get it out of the way," said Mr Arrowsmith.

"The only other feasible, though very unlikely, possibility is that Mr Brown has been abducted. Perhaps dumped in the toilets and probably his phone, wallet and baggage snatched.

"As before you will you say, 'Good morning Sir. What is your company?'

"If he gives Mr Brown's company name or insists in any other way that he is the correct Mr Brown, then alarm bells ring but show no sign and offer to escort him to the car. Again Mr C will have alerted Mr D and The Farm. The Farm will contact airport security and inform them of the problem. When you arrive at the pickup point the car will be there. Mr D is following and will arrive at the car at the same time. Mr D will get in the back with the imposter, Miss M, you get in the front. Mr C will have engaged the child locks on the back doors, he will then drive to the Farm. During the drive Miss M will turn in her seat and engage the imposter in conversation.

"Is that all clear so far?"

Again there were nods all round. Although this was aimed at Maria, Mr C & Mr D didn't mind a revision of these unlikely scenarios now and again.

"OK. In the event that it is the real Mr Brown, Miss M will escort him to the car, Mr D will join them and Mr C will drive to the designated location."

"Where will that be?" Maria asked.

"Mr C will be given that information when the client is safely in the car. Everyone happy?" asked Mr Arrowsmith.

Nods yet again.

"Oh just one other thing Miss M," said Mr Arrowsmith.

"If at any time an imposter attacks you or attempts to flee, you will overpower and restrain him using appropriate methods."

Maria was a little apprehensive over the weekend but mostly she was excited at the prospect of getting into the field at last. The use of "Miss M" or "M" instead of her name had been a bit odd at first but she found that the company used the first letter of a name for all its operatives when in the field and it had become habit. It seemed a good idea and she was used to it now. The black chauffeur type jacket and trousers with the white blouse which the company had provided were all a good fit and looked fairly smart.

The Mercedes E-Class Saloon was very comfortable on the drive from the Farm to Heathrow. Mr C dropped Maria and Mr D at the terminal and took the car to a spot where he could get back quickly. They went separately to the arrivals hall where the board reported that the flight was on time, so there was no long wait.

The music in the car was light Jazz from a memory device and M could hear it clearly but not too loudly in her earphones.

"The board reports the flight is on time," she reported to Mr C.

"Roger that," he replied. She wondered if C had a military background.

Fifteen minutes after the flight was reported to have landed a passenger who she recognised from the photo approached her. She removed her left earpiece.

"Good morning Mr Brown, how was your trip?"

"Good thank you Miss M."

'Good start,' she thought.

"This way to the car please Mr Brown. Can I help you with anything?"

They headed to the exit.

"It's OK thanks, I only have the briefcase."

"I'll be there in one and a half minutes," said Mr C in her right earpiece so she slowed her pace marginally. She could see the Mercedes pulling up as they went through the exit door. Mr D appeared and opened the back door for Mr Brown then went round and got in beside him.

Maria got in beside C and they set off.

They dropped Mr Brown at an office block in central London then went back to the company headquarters in Hammersmith to wait. Late in the afternoon they picked up Mr Brown and took him back to Heathrow for his return flight. All went smoothly and they returned to the Farm for a debrief.

"Any issues?" Phil Arrowsmith asked.

"Everything went to plan Mr P." said C and the others indicated agreement.

"OK. Good job. You can change now and relax, you have another job tomorrow afternoon. The briefing is here at 09:00. Thank you."

That was it, so they went off to change and get some food.

Maria spent two weeks on basic pickups mostly with the same team but occasionally some other operatives.

On Monday of the third week Maria went for the briefing at 09:00 as requested. Mr P was presenting but there were more operatives there than usual.

"On Thursday we will be escorting a Middle Eastern gentleman from Heathrow to the Dorchester Hotel in Park Lane. On Saturday we will be taking him back to Heathrow. He is the guest of our most important client and he is not without his critics.

"I will be directing this operation. Today the team will be briefed and equipped. Tomorrow will be a dry run and Wednesday we will review and re-brief. Thursday is the operation itself. Except for the dry run, nobody will be allowed to leave the farm or make any phone or email communications with the outside world until after the operation on Saturday. Except, that is, with my specific permission and under my personal supervision. Is that clear?"

"Yes Mr P," echoed around the room.

The briefing went on until lunchtime. As they were leaving to get food Maria approached Mr P. "I normally call my Mum on Friday afternoon or early evening, she'll worry if she doesn't hear from me, will that be possible this week?"

"Yes, ask me on Friday when you are free, I'll find you an appropriate phone."

"Thank you Mr P."

When they returned to the briefing room each chair had a bag beside it. These were roller type cases and each was labelled. Her's just had a capital M on it.

Mr P spoke again, "Please have a look at what is in the bag. Some of you will be familiar with the contents, others not so familiar."

She took out the company black jacket and was surprised to find it was a bit large. Before she could ask about it, Mr D leaned over and smiled, "You'd better put the vest on first."

"Oh," was all she could think of as reply.

It was a kevlar vest but not like something a soldier would wear, this fitted snugly and was hardly noticeable under the jacket which also fitted perfectly now.

Mr P started again. "Please remove the small black plastic box from your bag and open it. Check that there is a small ear bud in it. And put it in your right ear."

Maria slipped her's in her ear and it fitted perfectly. That made her wonder until she remembered the medical examination she had when she arrived at the Farm.

Mr P had left the room but the briefing continued, in her right ear, "Would you please raise your right hand."

Everyone raised their hand.

"Good, put them down."

Then three people stood up and sat down again.

"Speak quietly to Mr D." informed the earpiece.

"Can you hear me D?" she asked. Mr D was at the other side of the room but she heard his reply clearly in her earpiece.

Mr P went on to explain that he controlled the communication and could talk to one, or any number of them simultaneously. He could also patch any operatives to any other.

There were exhaustive cross tests until Mr P was satisfied there was complete understanding and the system was declared flawless.

Then came the sunglasses! Maria thought that this would just be for the good looks but actually there were two purposes. One, it protected the identity of the operatives to some extent. Two, the glasses were highly reflective with the intention of dazzling flash cameras.

There were also clipboards but the intention wasn't to write anything on them, they were a means of carrying more high reflectors. Also, they were extremely resilient and quite heavy. They could certainly deflect a knife and slow a bullet not to mention deliver a hefty blow if required.

Most of them thought that Tuesday's dry run went smoothly enough but on Wednesday Mr P wanted the operation tightened up which was fair enough. In their business, a mistake was not an acceptable option.

Wednesday found everyone going over the smallest details of the dry run and honing their performances.

On the morning of the pickup, the Middle Eastern gentleman was identified by Mr P as a very rich oil Sheik. He came out of the terminal building with his brilliant white robes flowing in the gentle breeze; his entourage was equally conspicuous. This wasn't a surprise but what was surprising was the gaggle of reporters and photographers who arrived in various vehicles just as he was emerging from the building.

"Where the hell did they come from? And how did they know?" raged Mr P. "Secondary car teams get between him and the press. Make a line in front of the cameras. Backs to the press. Primary car team get him in the car."

This was Maria and Mr D, with Mr C in the driving seat. All were connected by their earpieces.

Maria was standing ready to open the back door of the car. It was a black Rolls, polished to a fine shine. The press were being kept back but edged towards the Rolls. To the team's surprise the Sheik stopped to address the reporters and allowed his photograph to be taken.

"They are too close," said Maria quietly.

She watched the reporters very carefully. There was a tall slim smartly dressed man with a long fluffy microphone among them. She noticed that he didn't hold it well enough to pick up the Sheik's voice. Then everything happened very quickly. The man moved round the press towards the Rolls and pointed the microphone down. Maria stepped towards him. The fluffy cover dropped to the floor revealing a long knife. As the knife came up towards the Sheik, Maria's clipboard came down on the man's wrist and her foot swept his legs from under him. He tried to rise but her foot landed hard on the hand that still gripped the knife giving an audible crack. She saw that Mr D was now at her side of the car and ushering the Sheik inside then placing himself on the seat between the Sheik and the open door.

"Go C!" was all that Mr P said in their earpieces.

Mr D pulled the door shut and the Rolls shot away.

The secondary car teams ushered the entourage into the other two vehicles and they drove away too.

Maria had removed the knife from the broken hand and was restraining the tall man face down with his hands behind his back. She kept her face down too, as the flurry of cameras made their digital clicks.

"Keep your head down Miss M," said Mr P through her earpiece. "H and G are coming to assist."

"Stand back please!" Mr G's deep authoritative voice had the appropriate effect on the press.

He put a zip tie around the man's ankles and another around his wrists.

Police from the terminal were arriving to take control of the suspect and corral the press for their statements and pictures.

Mr P arrived in a white transit van and spoke privately and quietly to the policeman in charge who nodded his assent. Then Mr P looked towards the van and inclined his head slightly, the three operatives climbed in followed by Mr P who drove them away.

There was a debriefing at HQ as soon as they were all back there.

Mr P was in the chair as usual.

"For those of you who didn't travel to the Dorchester, you will be happy to know that the delivery went according to plan with no upsets.

"As far as the Airport collection is concerned I would like to commend you all for your performance, especially Miss M."

That was it for a pat on the back but they all knew that it was high praise indeed coming from Mr P. He went on to go over everything that had happened and he explained that, to his great annoyance, the Sheik's PR people has deliberately leaked news of his arrival.

Since the Sheik had not been cut to pieces, and he would now make the front pages, his PR people considered the leak a success and they probably wouldn't be deterred from behaving with similar stupidly in the future.

However Renshaw & Collier, the Sheik's hosts in London, were not so happy because the project that they were backing with the Sheik was vehemently opposed by environmental groups. In fact they were so unhappy, and as a demonstration of their influence, they insisted on a changed schedule.

Mr P stood up at the Friday briefing, "This briefing has been brought forward because the second part of this operation is going ahead today instead of Saturday.

"Our masters are exercising their muscles and all the business of the meeting was rescheduled to last night and this morning, so get saddled up for a Dorchester pickup at midday."

There were a few more details to cover. Maria was put right to the front of the pickup, partly as she had demonstrated her quick thinking and competence but also as a part of the Renshaw & Collier muscle flexing. It wasn't usual for an Arab Sheik to be directed by a woman.

Apart from a few frosty looks from the Sheik, the pick up and drop off went perfectly and everyone was back at the Farm for a debrief in the afternoon well before dinner time.

As everyone was leaving at the end of the session, Mr P asked Maria to wait.

"As you noticed the Sheik was unsettled by having you as the front security operative, your performance was excellent. Because it is most unusual for a Sheik to be guarded or directed by a woman, he will not wish it to happen again. Therefore it will be a big deterrent to his PR people releasing travel details again. Since the operation is over you can use the regular mobile to call your mother. That's all, thank you."

"Understood Mr P. Thank you."

She left to get some food and call her Mum.

Chapter 13

For two weeks the teams worked on regular meet and greet operations. One Thursday morning when Maria was called to a briefing she could tell it was a high profile job as the zoom was packed.

Phil Arrowsmith started with, "We will be meeting a high profile lady politician from Scotland. There has been chatter picked up by Her Majesty's security services that some fanatics, calling themselves The United Britain Group, has taken exception to her stance on Scottish Independence. Therefore we will be providing meet and greet and protection for the duration of her visit. Are there any questions?"

He asked for questions at this point because he knew exactly what they would ask.

"Who picked up the chatter Sir?" Alison asked.

"You can guess of course but it's not for me to say anything specific about our friends in Cheltenham. Any more questions?"

"Why aren't the people along the river at Thames House covering this? And maybe Special Branch?" Mr D asked.

"Those people are involved but their priority is finding the fanatics and there are also some other operations they have to cover. Anything else?"

There wasn't, so he went on with the briefing for the rest of Thursday and all of Friday.

On the Monday, Alison and Maria were on the 13:00 train from London King's Cross to Edinburgh Waverley. They had been sent to assist and prepare the VIP for the trip.

They arrived at about 17:30 and walked to their modest hotel on Waterloo Place.

09:00 the following morning found them in the VIP's office in the Scottish Parliament Building.

"I have been told that you are Miss A and Miss M," their host said looking from one to the other.

"That's correct Ma'am," they replied together.

"Well, now you are here, perhaps you can explain your visit."

Alison presented a sheet of paper, "This should explain Ma'am."

She took the paper, read the first line and looked up in surprise, she then pulled it closer to her on the desk and continued to read the rest.

'DO NOT SPEAK ABOUT THIS NOTE or ALLOW ANYONE TO SEE IT.

Your office may be bugged and possibly have hidden cameras. This may be true for your home as well. Miss A and Miss M have been sent to escort you to and from your meeting in London. Please take all their advice and recommendations very seriously. A good plan would be to have a casual coffee and small talk and take a walk with them in Holyrood Park well away from prying eyes. They can then explain the situation. Please return this note to Miss A

Very best regards,'

There was a signature which few people would recognise but she did.

To her credit she was very calm. "I was going to have coffee brought up but it's such a nice day, by Edinburgh standards, that I think we could get coffees to take out and drink them in the sunshine."

"Thank you Ma'am, that would be very pleasant," said Miss A as she put the note back in her laptop bag.

They were walking away from the building with their coffees. "Have either of you been to Edinburgh before?"

"I was brought up near Haddington so came here quite often when I was at school." Said Alison.

"How about you Miss M?"

"It's my first visit but I'm sure it won't be the last, it's a beautiful city."

They crossed Queen's Drive and turned left along the path.

"This is very pleasant but …," she stopped as Maria put a finger to her lips.

Alison reached into her bag and produced a small scanner which she discretely moved around their host's body.

"I left my mobile in my office if that's what you are looking for."

"That was very wise Ma'am," said Alison. "But this will also detect micro transmitters which can be attached to your clothes. You don't have any so we can talk."

Maria started the explanation, "There have been messages intercepted which reveal that some fanatics called The United Britain Group pose an imminent threat to your life."

"This would be GCHQ I suppose?"

The girls were silent.

"OK I guess you aren't supposed to know anything about that. So what is your plan to protect me?"

"Do your security people check for bugs in the offices and meeting rooms in the Parliament Building?" Alison asked.

"Occasionally, but not often."

"Please can you get them to check your office over now."

"You are serious aren't you. Can I borrow one of your phones? I presume that they are clean."

"Yes Ma'am, on both counts," said Alison and handed hers over.

She dialled a number and said, "Hello Rhona, please put me through to John Sutherland."

"Right away," was the response followed by a male voice.

"John, please check my office very carefully for bugs and hidden cameras."

"I'll get up there with a team immediately. Shall I call this number back when I'm done?"

"That would be perfect, thank you John."

Alison took the phone and quickly put Rhona in the Contact list.

"I'll delete that when the operation is over," said Alison. " When we get back I'd like to scan your mobile with my laptop if that's OK Ma'am."

That was agreed and as they continued their walk they went over the rest of the plan for the trip. "One last thing for now," said Maria, "if it's OK with you we would like to refer to you as Mrs V, just for the duration of the operation."

She smiled at the young women, "Very cloak and dagger, but I guess you have your reasons." Then she added, "Why V?"

"VIP Ma'am," said Alison.

"Thank you, very flattering."

Alison's phone rang, it showed an unrecognised mobile number, it had to be John. She handed it over to their host.

"OK, I'll come back to my office now, I'll be there in ten minutes."

Alison took the phone back and added that number to her Contacts too.

When they arrived in the office, John's people had just finished packing up.

"We've stuck temporary patches over the two holes, each one had a camera and a microphone, I'm having them analysed. I'm also checking who has been in the room since the last sweep," John informed them.

"What's that box on my desk?"

"We put your mobile in a soundproof faraday cage, just to be sure. I can take it away and get it checked if you like," he answered.

"I think that this lady would like to do that," she said indicating Alison.

"OK," said John. "Mind if I stay?"

They all looked at Alison. "It's OK by me," she said.

When the rest of John's team had gone and the door was shut, Alison asked everyone to not speak until she was finished.

She took the phone out of the box and connected it to her laptop with a regular USB cable then ran a mundane looking app called simply Phone. After a few minutes the screen showed a list of apps with the possibility to keep or remove each one. Above the list it said, Microphone Inactive.

Alison asked, "Are these all familiar Ma'am?"

She went through the list with some help from Alison and John who identified some as harmless and some not.

There were one or two which were definitely not wanted and had the capability of allowing the phone to be monitored.

When they had finished the list Alison selected CleanUp and the process completed in another few minutes.

"With your permission, I'd like to install this tracker app on your phone. It operates in the background and is never visible but we can use it to find the phone's location. It could be useful should anything happen."

John was getting agitated, "What's going to happen. Where is all this coming from?"

Mrs V turned to John and explained, "It seems that there are some crazy people who may attempt to harm me. Miss A and Miss M have been sent here to escort me on my trip to London and make sure nothing happens. I have only found out myself this afternoon and basically you know as much as we do now."

"Isn't this MI5's job? Are you MI5?" John asked.

"No John, we work for a private security company but we are cooperating with the security services, passing relevant information both ways. Also the security services are working hard to find out where this threat originates," answered Maria.

"I see. What do you want me to do?" he added turning to his boss.

"Stay in Edinburgh and find out who bugged my office," she answered. "Also check out my home for bugs too but do it all discretely, there may be someone in this building involved. I would prefer that person to be identified rather than scared off."

John added, "I emailed everyone and told them we were starting a routine security check of the whole building before we started on your office. I'll continue with that."

John left and the others went over the procedure for the next day in detail.

When the girls were back in their hotel they started sorting through their suitcases in preparation for the trip.

"I was impressed with that lady," commented Alison. "She wasn't flustered and she was decisive. I think she will be OK in an emergency."

"I agree," said Maria. "And her security man John was on the ball too. It would be good to keep in contact with him."

Maria and Alison were on Platform 8 in Waverley Station well before the 07:30 scheduled departure on Wednesday. They found John and a small technical team checking the First class carriage which had been reserved for Mrs V and her team. It was at the end of the train so there would be no other passengers passing through it. He also had a sniffer dog and its handler checking for explosives.

"Dinnae mind us, we'll be out in five minutes" shouted one of the technicians from the other end of the carriage.

In few minutes the team was off the train. Maria approached John and said, "You aren't taking any chances are you?"

"Too right," he answered. "That lady is very important to us. And, I won't be put out if you run your scans when we're gone. Some of your toys might be a wee bit more sensitive than ours."

They had intended to do just that and said together," Thank you John."

Alison added, "If we need to, how can we I contact you?"

"I think you have my number already," he smiled. "Here's my card anyway, it's got everything on it. Just call anytime."

"I might just do that," replied Alison with a warm smile.

John hadn't found anything and Alison's sweep of the carriage also found nothing so the girls were happy.

"He's quite nice isn't he," grinned Maria. Alison went very slightly pink near her collar, something not many people would notice but Maria was very observant. "Do you think you'll call him?"

"I might just do that when I'm up visiting my parents. Was I that obvious?"

"No, not obvious, but I sensed some chemistry between you two."

While they were talking they noticed that the dog and its handler were coming back along the next carriage from the far end of the train.

He waved to them as he got off and then waited near the end of the platform where all the passengers would have to walk past him.

Mrs V and her four staff members were at one end of the coach and had been working since they first sat down. A burly police constable and a female sergeant sat at the other end of the carriage near the only access from the rest of the train. A few seats away from Mrs V and her team, Maria and Alison sat at a table rummaging in a couple of flight cases.

Just after Berwick on Tweed, Mrs V announced that she would like everyone to make any phone calls they needed to before 09:00 as she wanted to have an uninterrupted briefing about the rest of the trip.

They departed Newcastle about 09:00 and nobody was on the phone so she called everyone together beside Maria and Alison.

Alison started, "Sergeant, please can you turn off your radios, leave them on your seats and join us. Please bring your mobile phones."

Mrs V then asked everyone to put their phones into a flight case which was divided into compartments. There were name or designation tags in each section and they all complied. Then Maria, with a questioning look, pointed to the pocket of an aid.

"But that's my personal phone, it's on silent," he said.

Another look from Mrs V and it was deposited beside the other phone and Alison carefully shut the case.

"Now, please sit down and listen very carefully to what these ladies have to tell you," said Mrs V.

That done Maria started. "We believe that there is a significant threat to the life of Mrs V. We will use the designation, Mrs V, for the duration of this trip."

There were some gasps and very worried looking faces.

Alison continued with the information, "Your phones have been quarantined because there is a possibility that they have been compromised as listening and or tracking devices. With your permission I will scan each one with a special program on my laptop after which they will be given back to you.

"They are currently in a soundproof box which also allows no signals in or out."

The staff asked much the same questions that John had asked, and more.

Then someone piped up, "This is all a bit clandestine isn't it?"

"Yes it is and it is necessary," answered Alison.

"What if I don't want my phone scanned?" asked the same person.

"My guess," said the sergeant, "is that it will remain locked in the box."

"That is correct," said Mrs V. What she didn't add was that the owner would be escorted off the train at York station by Special Branch.

The little rebellion fizzled out; some people were a bit too sensitive about their rights.

Everyone agreed to the scans and so went back to their seats while Alison got on with her work.

The phones of the police officers had slightly preferential treatment as the sergeant and the constable had been subjected to exhaustive background checks by both Special Branch and MI5.

Alison went through the same procedure on each phone as she had on Mrs V's. She had to remove some dodgy Apps and call some of the staff members back occasionally to verify if they needed a particular App. She didn't ask their permission for the tracking App and she definitely didn't tell them about the other little thing that she installed.

At York station a large suitcase was passed into the carriage by an S&A operative. As they left the station Mrs V told her staff to move to the centre of the coach and Alison and Maria set up a curtain to screen off the end of the coach. Behind it they unpacked the rest of the case's contents.

It was made clear that only Misses. A & M and Mrs V were allowed to see what was there.

At 11:45 Maria came into the body of the coach carrying a flight case,

" We will be at Kings Cross in about fifteen minutes. Please collect all your things and here are your phones."

She opened the flight case and they retrieved their mobiles.

"Miss A and I will not be accompanying you. We will clear up here and see you all again on the return journey."

Maria turned and took the screen down and the group could see the back of their boss tapping her keyboard. As always she was working up to the last minute. As they pulled into the station they all bent to get their things and Mrs V walked past them and stepped out of the door which had been opened by the constable.

Mr D was in command of the group of six S&A people on the platform. He introduced himself briefly and asked Mrs V to walk with him. Four others formed the corners of a square around them as they walked down the platform.

The last member of the team ushered the rest of the party after them.

They all walked down the platform and straight towards the exit which was right in front of them. There were some reporters and a couple of cameramen waiting outside.

Mrs V waved her laptop which she still had in her hand and smiled at them although the laptop spoiled the photos. She was still holding the laptop up as they then turned immediately left towards York Way where a black Mercedes had just pulled up. Before she reached the car Mrs V jerked violently back and a second later D heard the faint report of a rifle. He caught her before she hit the pavement and lifted her bodily under her back and knees. The other four operatives closed in tight formation to obscure any other shot. Then she was in the back of the car and speeding away with her escorts.

The press stood bemused not thinking of any hazard to themselves. They had missed everything, interview, photos and they had only a vague idea what had just happened.

"Ow, that hurts," came the groan from the back seat as she tried to sit up.

"Best stay down," said Mr D. "We'll get you straight to A & E." He looked worried as he could clearly see that there was a hole in her jacket, in the centre of her chest.

At the other side of the station Maria and her associate were walking out of the Pancras Road exit where a white van was waiting for them.

They entered the sliding side door into the back of the van which was isolated from the driver. It was very comfortable, carpeted and with comfortable seats, handrails and rails near the ceiling, with room to stand up but no windows. The van set off immediately and turned right into Euston Road. The driver came over the intercom,

"We are straight now for half a mile, I'll warn you when we approach a turn."

"You have about ten minutes to change Ma'am," said Maria.

And Mrs V immediately took off her S&A uniform, the black wig and the ballistic vest as Maria took clothes out of the bag she'd been carrying and hung them on the ceiling rails.

"I heard something when we were walking down the platform," said Mrs V. "Could it have been a gunshot? Is everything OK?"

Maria was in contact via her earpiece and said, "Miss A has been shot in the chest but it's going to be OK. She had a vest on too and is on her way to hospital for a check up."

"Clearly that was intended for me." Mrs V appeared calm but her heart was racing.

"Yes Ma'am."

In well under ten minutes she was dressed and herself again with hair combed.

The van stopped behind a black Mercedes on the double yellows lines just outside an Italian Coffee shop. They transferred to the car and drove on south towards Trafalgar Square. As they approached the entrance to Downing Street, another black Mercedes dropped in behind them. The two cars were waved into the security checkpoint then quickly passed through.

Mr D opened the back door and Mrs V climbed out and went to the door of No 10. It was opened as she approached and kept open until the occupants of the second car entered too. The delegation was inside by 12:15 on schedule.

The S&A cars departed, that was their involvement over until the meetings were finished.

At 13:00 Mr P was in the communications room in Head Office, he reported to his key operatives over their earpieces,

"As I already informed you Miss A has taken a hit in the chest. However, the new augmented ballistic vest took the round squarely and it didn't penetrate. As she is so fit and strong the result is not as bad as it might have been. She has some severe bruising and considerable pain but she will recover completely."

He was with two of the technical staff in front of a stack of communications and computer equipment. The screen he was studying was a 50 inch UHD TV which was mirroring the display of one of the computers. It showed a map of central London with a number of coloured dots on it.

"I'll go and get some tea," he said. "Let me know if anyone moves."

He left the room to stretch his legs and clear his head and walked down to the canteen.

"Please can you send a pot of tea for three up to the communications room. Oh, and some biscuits too please." He strolled about that floor for a few minutes and then went back up the stairs.

In the communications room the two Techs heard the door open and a tray was brought in. When the door was shut again one commented, "I thought that was a bit out of character, fetching tea for us."

The door opened and Mr P came in and commented, "Ah good, it's arrived."

At 15:05 all three in the communications room stirred, there was movement on the screen.

Five dots moved into the garden at No. 10.

"They're having a break," said Mr P.

Shortly afterwards a sixth dot of a different colour entered the front door.

One of the dots in the garden blinked because of the four phones which had Alison's monitoring bug had become active. "It's a text sir. It should be on the screen in a moment."

The number of the mobile phone was displayed and below it the text message appeared:

'Re the project, there was a technical problem and the first trial failed. I think it best to go on with the second trial. Hope that's OK.'

"Have you got the number it was sent to?" Mr P was a bit on edge and impatient.

A second later, another mobile number appeared on the screen.

"Email both those numbers to Thames House right away, they will locate them. I'll phone too to make sure they pick up the message immediately."

At 17:30 a leather clad courier arrived at No.10 on the pillion of a motorcycle. The courier took both panniers to the door and was admitted immediately. The rider made a leisurely turn at the end of the street and came back to the door of No 10. Then waited for several minutes until the door opened and the courier came out again replaced the panniers and they rode away.

The press were there *en masse* on the pavement opposite the door to No 10, they were awaiting the reappearance of the VIP from Scotland. A white truck drove into Downing Street did a three point turn at the end and stopped right in front of the press. There were cries of outrage as the truck completely blocked their view of the No.10 door. Two black police vans had also pulled into the street, they turned and positioned themselves in front of and behind the white truck. The press were corralled behind the heavy galvanised steel barriers and could see nothing. A mobile phone rang and a photographer answered it. A plain clothes policeman grasped his camera by the long lens and pointed it to the sky. Another enfolded him and whisked him bodily into the black van nearest the gates. The other police van moved to the door of No 10 and six people entered it and drove away. The press saw almost nothing of the occupants.

Just before 06:00 a courier and driver parked their motorbike at the Pancras Road entrance of Kings Cross station and, carrying a pannier each, walked into the station and onto Platform 2. They entered the first class carriage still wearing their crash helmets with visors down. Maria took off her helmet and helped Mrs V to remove her's.

"That was quite exhilarating, whizzing through London on a pillion. I haven't been on a bike for years."

"But it was obvious you've spent some time on one," Maria had noticed that Mrs V's balance was good and she wasn't fighting the tilt on the corners.

Three of the four who had come down on the train with Mrs V arrived and took their seats looking a bit concerned.

"Where is your colleague?" asked Mrs V.

"His phone rang, he went away a wee bit to answer it and some black suits took him away. We asked but they said it was a personal matter."

"Maybe he has family here in England somewhere," said Mrs V calmly, although she knew exactly where he would be by now. "I'm sure he'll be in contact when he has sorted out his personal issues."

They returned to Edinburgh with no further problems

Chapter 14

In Thames House, MI5 section head Rob Riddle looked around the polished conference table. His team leader Rose was there with four staff. Without preamble, he started, "What's the status?"

Rose answered, "We already had surveillance around Kings Cross when we received the mobile numbers from Sellick & Arrowsmith. One of the numbers was answered from a café not too far away. We detained a very smartly dressed Eastern European gentleman with a large cello case. Quite retro but a very good case for the sniper rifle. We think he was remaining nearby in case he was called on again."

"Identity?" Rob asked.

"We're working on that," she replied. "He had no positive ID on him, he understands Russian but I don't think he's a native."

"And the rifle?" he queried.

"It's a MK 13 Mod 5 Sniper Rifle, in use since 2001 with a range of about thirteen hundred metres. It's Easily available in America or Europe to a person of his profession. I think he is a hired assassin, definitely not cheap though. He is being interrogated but he probably doesn't know who is footing the bill, just nameless contacts and phone calls."

"Get his bank and phone records and see if there is any trail there," said the chief. "How about the Scottish Parliament staff member?"

"He isn't a professional, I think he is probably being threatened or blackmailed so we are following up all his phone and financial records and looking into his background."

"OK," said Rob "We have a bit of work to do and I need to know who wants this VIP out of the way, and why."

Late that evening Rob and Rose sat together again, she began with, "The assassin's money trail leads eventually to a Cayman Island based company which is controlled by Igor Solovyov. He happens to be the brother of Vladimir Solovyov a Russian multimillionaire living in London. Vladimir used to have very close links with the Kremlin and he is supposed to be out of favour and exiled but I don't believe that.

"The Scottish Parliament guy was being blackmailed but he doesn't know who is behind it. The only useful thing from him is that his instructions came from someone with an accent which we are now pretty sure is Russian. He has a fairly good ear and we have tested him with samples of accented language. However I don't know why the Russians would want to do this."

"Good progress," he commented, "I think I can shed some light on the why.

"The Russians are delighted by Brexit and they would be even more delighted with the split up the UK. It's not just divide and conquer; if Scotland leaves the UK, it puts our nuclear deterrent in jeopardy."

"Of course," she replied. "SNP is anti nuclear, we'd have to relocate the submarine bases, who knows where."

"Exactly," he continued. "The Russians are still working on zero-sum thinking. Anything that harms the West benefits Russia."

"So Scottish independence would be a real win for Russia. But why assassinate a strong proponent of independence?" Rose asked.

"Simply, to make her a martyr." Rob answered. "If this fabricated United Britain Group is blamed, it could trigger another referendum and give the Russians the UK split they want."

"So we need to squash this United Britain Group fiction," said Rose. "And keep a close eye on Vladimir Solovyov. I'll warn the Scottish administration and send a note to Vauxhall Cross." Rose made some notes on her pad.

"And the press?" Rob asked.

Rose smiled, "They have been told that a stone thrown up from a vehicle wheel hit her in the chest and security, correctly, overreacted and whisked her away from any potential threat. Nobody was injured and her meeting went on as planned."

"What about the gunshot?" asked Rob.

"The shooter was a kilometre away and there was a lot of traffic noise and, luckily, some roadworks too so we don't think anyone could definitely have identified the sound of a rifle," answered Rose.

"Good," said Rob. "You have a few calls to make but that about wraps it up for today."

"There's one odd thing about today's events," said Rose. "The security company Sellick & Arrowsmith; they performed really well, I thought we suspected them of some nefarious activities."

Rob brought her up to date on that, "It's a bit more complicated than we thought. We've been investigating and there are a number of layers to unwrap. The head office and the escort and protection services seem to be bona fide."

"As evidenced by today's performance," she interjected.

"Precisely," he said. "But we suspect another layer and so far we haven't been able to penetrate it. We'll keep investigating them but the Solovyovs are the priority."

Chapter 15

A year after part of Mike's foot was blown off,   he had more or less come to terms with the loss and was thinking that it wasn't as bad as it sounded; it was only a bit of his foot and there was the pension.

The torrential rain running over his boots before he had boarded the intercity seemed to be chilling his left foot. The same conditions didn't chill the other foot the same way. There was no body heat in the metal and plastic prosthesis. Perhaps that's why that foot was affected; he'd have to ask Tony when he saw him.

Mike arrived at Edinburgh Waverley station just as the daylight was fading. He was heading towards Leith Walk so didn't go up the Waverley Steps but headed down past Platform 3 to the rear exit. He crossed the little footbridge and turned left along Calton Road. Under the bridge he saw two young men walking towards him on the same side of the street. From the change in their gait and posture when they saw him, he sensed that there was about to be a problem.

Mike guessed that they were both about sixteen. They were quite tall but not heavy.

They both produced knives and demanded money. Mike was expecting something like this and already knew that he wouldn't be giving them anything that they wanted.

"Put the knives away and go," said Mike, "if you know what's good for you."

The first boy lunged while the second one tried to get behind him. They were fairly quick but Mike was quicker. He grasped the lunging wrist and swung his attacker into the other boy. He bent the hand forward and removed the knife which he then dropped to the pavement. Both boys glanced down which they realised was a mistake when Mike gripped their necks and banged their heads together. One went down without making a sound except the sharp clatter of his blade on the road, the other came at him again and received a fist to the jaw which stretched him in the gutter.

At that moment three shadows separated themselves from the arch opposite, they were a little older, perhaps eighteen, and a bit heavier. They charged across the street cursing and brandishing knives. Had they synchronised their onslaught, Mike would have been harder pressed but the leader outdistanced the others. He came on his blade flashing, Mike pivoted on one leg and sent his other heel cracking into the attacker's chest. He crashed heavily into the second youth who fell to the ground and then felt the sole of a shoe on his wrist and his knife being firmly removed from his weakened grip. He was hurling abuse but quietened when a sharp tap on the head from Mike's foot sent him into oblivion. The first youth had fallen awkwardly and was rendered unconscious when his head made contact with the pavement. The third hesitated then turned to flee but his right calf stung suddenly and collapsed under him; his friend's knife, which Mike had thrown, was deeply embedded there. With professional efficiency the attackers were relieved of their weapons, all knives. A nearby lamppost shone down by a telecoms box. Mike deposited the knives behind that, except the one.

"You'd better leave that in till an ambulance comes or you'll bleed out," Mike told the runner.

He quickly relieved them of their mobile phones to prevent any reinforcements, and their shoes, so thy wouldn't wake up and attempt any heroics. He photographed each face and any reliable looking ID on them, just as a precaution.

He worked on the phones for a minute then discarded three with the knives and tied another high on the lamppost with a shoe lace and walked away up the slope towards Leith Walk.

He shouted back, "I'll be over here watching you boys and I've got your knives so don't even think about moving."

Only Runner could hear him and he wasn't moving anywhere.

When out of earshot he called the emergency services number on the last of the boy's phones. In a broad Glaswegian accent he said, "There's five boys on Calton Road, under the bridge by the back of the Waverley Station. They've been fighting and need an ambulance, better send police too, they're right angry."

He was far away when the boys in blue arrived but watched the scene unfold on the borrowed phone.

"Thank goodness for audio/video Apps," he thought.

The police were searching for weapons at the scene when a disembodied voice from the lamppost announced in a broad Glaswegian accent, "Look behind the telecom box."

The runner groaned, Mike continued walking towards his friend's flat in Leith Walk.

Chapter 16

On Monday morning, Maria came in as usual and was asked to go and see Mr Sellick in his office. The office was glass fronted and looked over the training area from a first floor mezzanine. It resembled a traditional manufacturing facility with the managers overseeing the shop floor. Maria went up the steps and knocked.

Mr Sellick looked up from his screen and beckoned her in.

"Please sit down," he indicated the chair on the opposite side of his desk.

"Would you like coffee?"

"Yes please, if it's OK, I'm supposed to be checking my duties for the week."

"That's OK, I've cleared your absence with Operations."

"Thank you, black no sugar."

"How are things going in Protection?"

"Everything is fine thank you, it's a good team and it's well organised."

"I've been following your progress and it appears everything is somewhat better than fine. I think you are capable of more. Therefore I am going to offer you the chance to be involved in something more interesting but I warn you it can be a little more, how shall I say…," he paused, "stressful!"

"Does more stressful equate to more dangerous?" Maria asked.

"Sometimes that is a possibility and often you would be relying on your own skills and initiative. Does it sound interesting to you?"

"It does sound interesting. I'd certainly like to find out more," she answered.

"Good."

For about an hour he explained about the covert activities the company sometimes undertook. Eventually he asked, "Do you want make the transfer to Covert or would you prefer to stay in Protection?"

She had already made up her mind and she was very keen to do it.

"Yes Mr Sellick, I want in."

"Good, then take this away, read it, sign it and bring it back after lunch. 14:00. It's a sort of non disclosure agreement. Do not show it to anyone, OK?"

"Yes. Thank you."

The document that he had given her was similar to her original contract but was considerably tighter on confidentiality and secrecy. If that was what was needed to do the job then she'd sign up.

At 14:00 she handed back the signed document, Mr Sellick looked at it briefly and put it in his desk.

"Please come this way." He indicated a rather nondescript, barely noticeable door in the wall behind his desk. It could have been a storeroom or cupboard.

Through the door was a short narrow corridor and another door. He placed his hand on a glass panel at one side and opened it. Inside was another world, a modern open plan office with a lot of glass and people at computers. He went from desk to desk introducing people.

"This is Mrs Smith. When needed she can provide a covert operator with a cover story, all the appropriate documents and a background.

"This is Mr Jones. He can provide such technology as is required: mobile phone, trackers, that type of thing.

"This is Mr MacDonald. He can provide suitable clothing some of which has additional features, like the vest with which you are familiar.

"And this is Mr O'Malley. He can provide you with information about many important things."

She didn't believe for one moment that those were their real names, far too corny, however they were useful tags.

They sat in an office which let onto the main room and some coffee arrived, she wondered what the bringer of coffee would be called.

"You will spend the rest of this week with Mr O'Malley coming up to speed with what we can do here. The following week will be with the other key members of staff and getting to know fellow operatives with whom you may work. When a suitable operation requires your participation you will be contacted and come to work for me. If we are waiting for an operation you will go back to Operations temporarily. Is all that clear?"

"Yes Mr Sellick, very clear." She had an idea that: 'Yes Mr Sellick' was going to be a well used phrase.

Chapter 17

As it turned out Maria spent three weeks training, then one week back on Protection before she was called back to see Mrs Smith.

"Good morning Miss M, this memory stick contains what the people at MI5 call a legend. It is your new identity. Your name is Maxine Bassett. The USB stick contains your background, job, interests, and all relevant data for role. There is a great deal of detail in this file which you must memorise. Sometimes you may have to improvise, if you do, where possible keep it close to your own real experience." She handed Maria the USB memory stick.

"Now Maxine, please go to see Mr Sellick whom you will refer to as Mr S from now on. He's in the office over there, he's expecting you. Understood?"

"Yes Mrs S and thank you."

"Ah, Good morning Maxine, please take a seat.

"Your assignment is quite different to what you have been doing with us so far. It is extremely non hazardous, relatively straightforward but will require you to exercise the covert skills about which you were made aware during your training in this section.

"Our client is making, or is in the process of making, a significant investment and wants to get some first hand information of the set up and progress to ensure that the investment is good.

"You will not need any very-special technology," he emphasised the phrase very-special with a slight smile and continued.

"You can use all normal personal items, clothes and so on, but see Mr O'Malley on your way out and he will provide you with a laptop and a mobile phone. He will also give you the email address for your reports and the phone number to use if you need to contact S&A. He will give you some other items and information together with the details of your location, contacts and so on.

"I expect this assignment to require only a few weeks. Is everything clear?"

"Yes Mr S." An even more succinct phrase for regular use she thought as she left the room.

Mr O'Malley was ready for her when she arrived at his desk and started without preamble, "Hello Maxine. This is your Laptop, the password is samsunggalaxy, all lower case with no spaces. Here is your phone, the password is macbookpro, all lower case with no spaces. You may change the passwords to more secure ones but please change them back to the original ones just before you return them to me. Is there any data on your regular company phone?"

"Only the pre loaded company things, and I guess the call log."

"Good, let me have that and I'll lock it away till you are back. How about family numbers?"

"I only call my parent's landline number and I can always remember that. They've had it since I was little."

"Good. Now please sit down, start the laptop and log in," he instructed.

"Now open the Contacts, you can see some have already been completed for you, these are S&A contacts and they are listed as your employer in your legend.

"Now open the browser, Safari in this case. Maria did as instructed.

"Yes, you see you have access to Cloud space. If you send us a large data set put it there, it can hold the entire contents of a hard drive. There is plenty of space."

O'Malley turned and handed her a USB stick. "This is your backup drive. It contains hidden software which can download the contents of all the hard drives on a computer it is plugged into. Most standard computers you will access will have up to two TeraBytes of hard disc storage. The downside of this method, although very secure and non traceable, is you need considerable time."

He produced another small USB device.

"This USB stick uses a different method. When it is plugged into a laptop, it quickly loads a special application to the computer and can then be removed. Whenever the laptop is connected to the internet, the application copies hard disc data to our cloud location. It is relatively slow but carries on sending; eventually it will copy the entire hard drive."

"Won't the user notice that activity?" Maria asked.

"Very unlikely," said Mr O'Malley. "If the keyboard or mouse is used or an application is in use the upload speed slows right down. When there is no activity on the computer it increases the upload speed. Is that all OK?"

"It seems fine so far," answered Maria.

"Anyway," he added. "If you know which files you need, and you have time, just use one of the regular USB sticks.

"Now, these files on your laptop contain details of the people you should contact and information about your assignment. Everything clear so far?"

"Yes," she said, "I'll want to try these things before I need them in the field."

"Indeed you will, in fact I'll insist on it. Now the phone."

She switched it on and unlocked it while O'Malley talked her through the special features and Apps.

It was approaching 13:00 when Mr O'Malley called a halt.

"Time for some lunch," he said. "This afternoon that office will be available for you to try out these things." He indicated a door.

In the afternoon, while she was in the office familiarising herself with the laptop and phone, Mr O'Malley came in and gave her a driving licence, some other documents and a passport to match her legend.

"You may need these," he said simply.

"Thank you."

She wondered why the investor didn't just ask for the information she was being sent to discover, a bit strange.

Chapter 18

Tony was in a café in Marchmont Road in Edinburgh waiting for his brother.

"Hello Mike, can I get you something?" Tony asked as his brother walked in.

"Black coffee would be good."

Tony went up to the counter and ordered two large black coffees. Mike sat down at the table and watched his brother go up to the counter.

'Tony the Technologist,' thought Mike.

Sometimes he wished he had taken up something a bit more stable and less stressful than the military. 'Mike the military man,' he thought to himself with a smirk, 'not very military now.'

He picked up the paper that had been left on the table. Flicking through, a headline caught his eye. 'Battered In Possession'. He read on, 'five youths taken to the Royal Infirmary under police escort.' Mike gave a wry smile. They had later been charged with affray and possessing weapons.

Tony came back with the coffees.

Tony sipped his and asked, "So! What have you been doing for the last year?"

Mike thought for a moment. "Doesn't seem much when you put it like that. There was some surgery and a lot of physiotherapy when I got back to the UK. I guess Mum and Dad filled you in on what happened?"

"Yes. After you left the service you stayed with them for a while."

"That's right. Actually they were great, as always. I needed to rest but also to get my body going again after all the time in hospital beds.

"They just got on with their lives and let me get mine started again. I walked and swam and eventually ran. Swimming in the sea was great. Durdle Door, Lulworth Cove, Studland, just like when we were kids."

"How did you get to the beach from the house?" Tony asked.

"Oh yes. I borrowed Dad's bike. So I guess I cycled too."

"Well, what brings you to Edinburgh, other than the train?"

"I was at a bit of a loose end," answered Mike. "So I came up to see what the city is like and what my little brother is up to?" Mike smiled.

"Still at the university. Doing some research into alternative energy sources."

"So what's new in that business?" Mike asked.

"It's not so much what's new as does anyone have the will to use what's available. There's beginning to be an awareness with global warming becoming more public but things need to happen faster and all over the world."

"So what are you working on?"

"Mostly solar energy now."

"Solar panels?"

"No, something even more basic than that." Tony outlined the project enthusiastically, filling Mike in on his plans and the funding that had been promised.

"Anyway you don't want to hear about my boring work what else is happening in your world"

"I'm staying with an old friend, he has a flat near the top of Leith Walk. We have a plan to visit all the best pubs in Edinburgh. Over a period of time you understand." Mike smiled.

"You could write a book about that; Best Pubs in Edinburgh - a users guide."

"Might be an idea but it's probably been done," said Mike.

"Very likely, but let me know how it goes."

Chapter 19

Tony was in the Meadows early on Saturday morning, The weather was beautiful for taking photographs, the sun was about to come up and mist was hanging over the trees like a weightless grey duvet. The leaves were turning to a fantastic range of yellows, orange sand reds. As the grass was still wet he hadn't moved far from the Walk and he had his tripod set up quite near the hard surface. The camera was lined up towards the sunrise but the sky wasn't so bright yet as to wash out everything to a silhouette. A skein of geese was just coming over high in the sky and was making perfect V. It was that time of year when they were flying south to find a warmer place than Edinburgh for the winter. The perfect shot was just coming when a jogger stopped right in front of the camera turned his back to Tony and just snapped the shot with his mobile phone, then stood prodding the screen for a few moments and jogged off, apparently oblivious.

A voice from Tony's right said. "What a prat! I watched him. I think he'd seen you taking a photograph realised you'd done all the composition and just stepped in."

Tony turned and saw a runner bending over, hands on knees and breathing as though she'd been running hard for some way.

"Did you get the geese?" she said.

"No, but I got some OK shots, the trees look fantastic with the mist."

She nodded in agreement.

"The light I wanted is going now," he said as he packed away his camera and strapped the tripod onto his bag.

It hadn't escaped Tony that this was a very good looking girl.

She slipped her rucksack off her back and took out a fleece.

"Don't let me stop you running," he said.

"No, I've had enough," she finished her water, put the bottle back in the rucksack and said, "I'm still thirsty though."

"I usually go for a coffee in a café up on Marchmont Road," said Tony.

"I don't know that one," she said.

"Would you like to join me?" he asked.

"Yes," she said. "That would be very nice."

So they walked off together and he was surprised how comfortable he felt with this girl having only just met her.

They reached the coffee shop. It was a bright oasis amongst the damp darkened walls of the old town houses, mostly flats now.

They ordered black coffees. Tony had a small dash of brown sugar.

They spent a pleasant time savouring the excellent coffee and chatting about the pleasant décor of the café and the indifferent weather.

"Maybe you'll get the shot you want next Saturday and perhaps I will see you, I'm always running through the Meadows at that time in the morning." And with that she pushed her chair back and ventured out into the increasing drizzle.

Tony sat for a few minutes musing over the encounter. The interlude had been pleasant but he doubted he would ever see her again. He hadn't even asked her name, but then she hadn't asked his.

Chapter 20

The following Saturday morning Tony was in the Meadows again but the scene was not so atmospheric as the previous week. He had taken a few shots but he didn't think any of them were particularly stunning and he was thinking of packing up and going for a coffee.

He got the camera in the bag and the tripod collapsed and strapped on the side.

"Hi there," said a familiar voice. "Did you get the shot today?"

"Unfortunately not," said Tony. "The light isn't so good."

"Well, I hope the coffee will be as good as it was last week," she said and they went off happily to the little café again.

This time he remembered to ask her name while they were quietly enjoying the coffee.

"I didn't ask your name when we met last week."

"It's Maxine Bassett," she answered. "What's yours?"

"I'm Tony Collins," he said and proffered his hand.

They shook hands with a bit of a giggle each. Her hand was soft and warm but firm too. Tony felt a buzz as he held it.

"Do you live in Edinburgh?" he asked.

"No, I'm here with work, I'm auditing one of my employer's operations here. It's HR so I can't really talk about it."

"I work at Edinburgh University," said Tony.

"That sounds a lot more interesting than doing an audit. Is your work secret?"

"No, it's not secret. It isn't rocket science more research into a new technology application."

"That still sounds a lot more interesting than what I do. What field is it in? Not that I'll necessarily understand the science if it's beyond school level."

"It's about using solar energy and concentrating it to a small area to make the heat useable," answered Tony who was now becoming practiced in reducing his project to a few words. That would have been enough for most people but Maria was still looking at him expectantly so he went on.

"It's called a solar furnace. The first in the world was built in 1949 at Mont-Louis in the French Pyrenees then they went on to build the more famous one at Odeillo about ten kilometres drive west. The French use them for research but now some systems have been built to generate electrical power; they are mostly Solar Power Towers."

"I think I read something about Odeillo years ago, doesn't the temperature go up to really high temperature in just a few seconds?"

He was surprised enough that she had even heard of it, but even more so that she knew something about it.

"That's right," he said. "There is enormous power available from the sun."

"Is Odeillo anywhere near Andorra?" Maria asked. "My first ski holiday with my family was in Arinsal."

"It's about an hour and a half drive from Arinsal. Do you still ski?"

"I love it but I don't often get the chance these days," she answered.

They talked for a couple of hours over more coffee and some pastries.

"If you are free this weekend I could show you some of Edinburgh," he offered.

"That would be great but I need to go back to the hotel and change out of my running things, it's in Hill Place off Nicholson Street." She had a. street map, which the hotel receptionist had given her, so she showed him where it was.

"No problem I can find that."

"Can we meet in reception, in an hour maybe?" Maria asked.

"That would be great, I'll see you there," answered Tony. He just needed to drop his camera bag and tripod at his flat and walk up there.

They walked for miles over the weekend and Tony showed her all the interesting places he could think of.

On Sunday night he walked her back to her hotel and they agreed to meet at six the following evening for some food and a beer in a pub not too far from his flat.

Chapter 21

Maria met with Tony almost every night that week. On Thursday, she asked him where exactly he worked. From their walks, it was clear that Edinburgh University had buildings scattered all over the city. Tony offered to give her a tour of his own lab at the weekend.

That Saturday, Tony took time to explain his project and Maria seemed genuinely interested. He turned to look at her, "I think you are in the wrong line of work."

Maria stopped, her heart beating a little faster.

"You should be doing something like this," Tony continued, oblivious to her pause, gesturing widely across the lab. "Especially as you don't seem to enjoy your job that much."

Maria relaxed and smiled. "I'd have to think about that!" She laughed.

When they were walking back from the lab she said, "I think you mentioned that you live around here didn't you?"

"Yes, I was planning to drop off my laptop if that's OK."

"Sure."

"I could make us some coffee there, if you like," he offered.

"That would be good," she answered.

Tony put the laptop on the coffee table in his living room and they went into the kitchen to make the coffee.

"Do you have any pictures of that big solar furnace in the Pyrenees?" Maria asked.

"I can show you on my laptop if you like," he said.

They sat at the laptop while the coffee was percolating and he pulled up some pictures that he had taken.

While she was looking through them he went back to the kitchen to pour the coffee. It was just long enough for her to put a USB stick in a socket to do its work and then remove it.

"These are great pictures, you were there?" Maria asked.

"Yes, I spent some time there during my PhD, it's even more impressive in real life."

They finished their coffee then went out and strolled around happily for the rest of the afternoon. They ended up near her hotel.

"I want to go and have a shower and change," said Maria. "Can we meet up later at that pub near your place?"

"That would be great," he answered.

"Is eight o'clock OK?" Maria asked.

"Sure. See you there."

Up in her room she got her laptop out and logged in to the appropriate server. 'That worked,' she thought. Data was uploading rapidly, files, folder structure, the lot.

Tony's phone rang at seven thirty.

"I'm really sorry Tony, I've just had a call from my boss in London. There are a lot of problems in one of our European offices and he wants me there on Monday morning. I have to get the train back to London tonight and fly out of Heathrow tomorrow. I'm really sorry about our drink."

"Will you be back to finish your audit?" Tony asked.

"I don't know, it might be me or they might send someone else. I'll call you."

"OK. I hope your trip goes well."

"Thanks Tony. Bye," Maria hung up and finished packing.

After the call, Tony realised that he was quite disappointed as he was really enjoying Maxine's company. He decided to call her and wish her a safe journey.

Tony checked his mobile phone log for Maxine's number. The call that evening had been from the hotel's landline so he looked back further. After a lot of searching he realised that every call she had made had been from the hotel phone so he decided to call the hotel to speak to her and get her number.

The hotel receptionist answered and asked how he could help Tony.

"I'd like to speak to one of your guests please, Maxine Basset."

"I'm sorry sir, she has left. She checked out a little while ago," answered the receptionist.

"I don't suppose you have her number do you?" Tony asked.

"I don't think we do sir and I wouldn't be allowed to give it out anyway, sorry."

"OK, thanks," said Tony.

Maria was going back to London but she had made the decision herself and had told her boss she was finished in Edinburgh. There was no European panic.

She was well aware that stealing data was industrial espionage. It was unethical, dishonest and almost certainly illegal but that was her job. This was what she had signed up for and she'd enjoyed it.

Chapter 22

The atmosphere was exactly as one would expect in an exclusive private members club in Berkeley Square, London. Two men in expensive suits sat drinking excellent coffee in comfortable chairs by the window. The view was of trees, well into their autumn colours, and grass still green but scattered with leaves golden from the season. They looked down on the people below going about their business.

The two men had a similar appearance, dark hair solid jaws and very smart. It wasn't surprising that they looked alike, they were brothers.

They had ordered their coffee in good, if slightly accented, English but now they reverted to Russian for a more private discussion.

"This is a very nice club, very private and discreet," commented Igor.

"Yes," agreed Vladimir. "Very private and not overlooked. That's why I'm a member. It also has a very pleasant outlook, quite a perfect location. Unfortunately," he added his tone hardening. "Not everything is perfect in our world. That shambles at Kings Cross with the Scottish woman a few weeks ago, that was shit!"

Igor was just slightly relieved as a large pigeon dropping hit the window distracting them both.

"Kings Cross and this window. Both Shit!" said Vladimir with feeling.

"Yes, that was very unfortunate."

"Do you actually know what happened?" Vladimir asked.

"The press story is of course all lies," he answered. "It appears that two women on the S&A protection detail were much more resourceful than could have been anticipated."

"So they were good," interjected Vladimir. "But that doesn't fully explain the problem."

Igor continued, "GCHQ intercepted some traffic about the threat, it may have originated because of the United Britain Group ruse, we'll have to control that better in future. That intelligence gave them the heads up to put a strong security resource on it. They switched our target with a slightly thinner look alike operative with a very high specification tactical vest. They also bugged all the party's phones and thereby found our plant, tracked his mobile calls and found the shooter. MI5 took over from there. We don't have information from inside MI5 at present."

"OK," said Vladimir, the older brother. "No real harm done as long as they can't trace the shooter to us. We'll reduce any direct action on the Independence issue for now. What progress do we have in the energy sector?"

"JJ has arranged sponsorship of the solar type project in Namibia so that we can effectively control the outcome," answered Igor. "And as a backup we have obtained all the personal files of the project leader. I believe that he is key to the project, it's his baby."

"That's good," said Vladimir. "We're gaining influence again in Africa but so far, not in Namibia."

"Why has that country proved so difficult to influence?" Igor asked.

"The authoritarian regimes are always easier to manipulate," Vladimir explained. "The leaders are always open to improving the balances of their Swiss bank accounts."

"I guess Namibia doesn't fit the profile then," said Igor.

106

"That's right," his brother answered. "But they are vulnerable over energy. They import nearly sixty percent of their electricity from countries where Russia does have a voice."

"So we don't want them to become energy independent," said Igor putting it simply.

"Correct," said Vladimir. He then asked, "Other than observing the project, what else do you plan?"

"We have a few tricks up our sleeve," answered Igor with a sly smile. "And if necessary, we have the resources available in Africa to take direct action."

"Good," concluded Vladimir, "I think it's time for dinner."

Chapter 23

Sunday lunchtime Mike and Tony were on their second excellent pint of Export; they were chatting happily in the Blue Blazer.

"How's the users guide going?" Tony asked.

"Beg pardon," said Mike.

"Best Pubs in Edinburgh," laughed Tony.

"Oh. The research is going well, hard work at times, you have to be dedicated. This one will be in it."

He smiled sipping his pint, "To be honest it's getting a bit repetitive and I'm afraid that my mate may get hooked if we carry on with the same intensity much longer. I'm thinking of moving out and maybe getting my own place. But how about you, is the project moving along OK?"

"Oh yes," said Tony, "I'm making some great connections with the Namibian University."

"That's in Windhoek isn't it?" queried Mike.

"That's right," answered Tony.

"You'll be spending some time in the desert won't you?"

"Eventually yes," answered Tony, "but to begin with, I'll be in Windhoek. Have you ever been there?"

Tony had a vague idea that Mike had served in various parts of Africa.

"I was in Namibia for a while a few years back. It was relatively stable part of Africa back then. I don't know of any recent problems." Mike made a mental note to check that with some old friends.

He knew Africa and he knew people, but talking with his brother about things scientific was a new experience.

"So let me see if I understand this. You put some mirrors on a hillside, reflect sunlight on to another mirror, a concave one, and it focuses the light onto a crucible. And that heats up enough to melt aluminium?"

"That's exactly right," said Tony.

"And with molten aluminium you can make more mirrors," added Mike.

"That's right but it's a bit tricky. To make the steerable mirrors we need a flat, horizontal surface that we can cast the aluminium into and it needs to withstand the heat of molten aluminium. I'm thinking of making a large flat ceramic plate here and shipping it out. Then we have the problem of levelling it accurately."

"What about a pool of cement? That would be level," said Mike. It seemed a straightforward idea to him.

It hadn't been obvious to Tony which he admitted, "That's a good idea Mike, we could just vibrate it and it will be flat and level, just like making a road. But I wonder if it would take the heat."

"Fire backs and the fixing cement get pretty hot and they survive, I expect you can get special cements anyway."

"You're right Mike, that's actually a brilliant idea."

It was great having Mike around, he was good company and great to bounce ideas off. His thought processes were completely different to all the university people, informed but also very practical.

They chatted about their younger days for a while and then Tony offered, "I have a spare room in my flat, how would you like to move in there?"

"That's very kind, it wouldn't cramp your style would it?"

"There's no girl in my life at the moment," said Tony. "I had been wondering what to do about the flat if I'm away in Africa for a long time. You could stay on and look after it."

"That would be great," said Mike, "I can pay rent."

"You don't need to while I'm still here but it might help when I'm away."

They agreed to go back to the flat and see if anything needed doing before Mike moved in. On the way Mike was thinking that this would be good, he needed a base, at least for a while, to settle down and think about his future. The extended pub crawl had been a distraction, and fun, but he'd had enough of that for a good while. What he needed to do was to think and do some fitness training.

Chapter 24

Tony had been on the phone several times to Dr Clara Bella in Windhoek and she seemed very competent but he wasn't getting an impression of what she was really like as a person, maybe a video call would be better.

"Hi Clara, I was wondering if we could have a video call, maybe Skype, FaceTime, Teams or Zoom?"

"That would be good, I think people here use Zoom mostly now," she replied. "I don't know why we haven't done a video call before, probably because we would have to set a time for the meeting and not just call."

"How many people at your end would join?" Tony asked. "Over here it will be either two or four."

"Probably similar from here," she answered,."I'm on my own at the moment shall we do it now and check for any hitches. If you have a computer handy I'll just start a new meeting and send you an invite."

"Great," Tony answered. "I'll stay on the phone till we are connected."

The invite started bouncing on his laptop screen, he put his phone down and clicked the joining boxes.

They exchanged pleasantries about it being nice to meet and it soon became much more relaxed than a phone call. They talked about their own education and about the energy situation in Namibia. Clara explained that the country relied too much on imported electricity and liquid fuels and needed to improve their energy security. There was already a lot of work going on in the country to utilise the sun's radiation.

"How much of your electricity do you import?" he asked

"It's almost sixty percent. But we want to get that energy from the sun and not make pollution."

She was obviously passionate about this.

"Does the government back these efforts?" Tony asked.

"Definitely, we are leaders in the region. We want to install one and a half million square meters of solar collection in the country by 2030. That's more than half a square meter for everyone in the country. That will be made up of many different methods and applications from domestic solar ovens to heating public buildings and industrial applications. Industries like brewing use heat and it's wasteful to burn fuel or use electricity when the sun's radiation is so abundant here. We have one of the highest levels of solar radiation in the world."

"That's one of the reasons I wanted to bring this project there," said Tony.

Although this was supposed to be just a try out of the video and broadband link, they talked on for several hours. Eventually they brought it to an end and scheduled some times for the other members of the teams to meet by video link.

After they finished Tony thought about his trip to Namibia and realised that he was getting really excited about it. It wasn't going to be long before he left for Africa.

Chapter 25

The Lufthansa flight was long but comfortable. Tony had looked at the route well before he travelled, he liked to know exactly where he was going. Hosea Kutako International airport was almost due south of Frankfurt, a bearing of 171 degrees and about five thousand miles. He knew there would be a few variations from the great circle course but the main thing would be little or no jet-lag, just tiredness from the travel.

He'd said goodbye to Mike at the flat at six o'clock on Saturday morning and walked to the Waverley Station. He had a medium sized roll along bag and a laptop bag so it would only take about half an hour. The train to Birmingham was leaving about ten to seven so he had plenty of time. He arrived at Birmingham International before eleven thirty, 'Near enough on time,' he thought.

It only took a few minutes to get to the terminal on the monorail so he got some food land-side as he was early. He didn't need to be there three hours before departure because he wasn't flying intercontinental from there, but Tony liked to leave time for any delays.

He still had time so he decided to call his parents to let them know he was on his way.

"Hello Tony. You are at the airport. I can hear the tannoy," said his mum as soon as she answered her mobile.

"That's right, Birmingham. I've a bit of time before the Frankfurt flight. Are you on your lunch break?"

"I'm at my desk eating a sandwich as usual," she answered.

"How are the bugs in the lab?" Tony asked. She was a microbiologist and they often joked about the bugs.

"They are fine," she answered laughing.

"I just thought I'd ring before I left. I don't know when I'll next call. Is Dad OK?"

"Fit as a fiddle as usual. And don't worry about calling. We're not expecting calls when you are away, especially from the desert."

"Thanks Mum. One less thing to think about.

"I can't remember if I told you, but Mike's looking after my flat, so that's another thing not to have to think about."

They chatted some more and finished with a fond *au revoir*,

There were a couple of people waiting at the Lufthansa desk when he went to check in. The roll bag was checked in and he headed off to Departures, boarding pass and passport in hand.

The Lufthansa flight to Frankfurt was one hour minutes and he had almost two hours stopover. He'd had time for a beer after he had found his International departure gate.

He slept a little on the flight to Namibia and touched down on time at twenty past six on Sunday morning.

He felt a bit guilty dragging Clara out at that time in the morning but she had insisted and he was grateful that she had.

"Hello Dr Tony!" shouted a boy's voice as he walked through the arrivals gate.

"Hello," smiled Tony. He had been expecting to see Clara.

"My big sister is outside with the truck," said the boy as he reached for the handle of the bag. He was so enthusiastic that Tony let him pull it out through the doors into the Namibian heat. He knew it was going to be hot but was still surprised by the blast of roasting air.

114

Clara was at the driving wheel of a white Toyota pickup. Tony and her brother lifted the bag into the back and they climbed into the cab with her. It was beautifully cool.

"How was your journey?" Clara asked as she pulled away. She drove out of the airport and turned right heading westbound on the B6 towards Windhoek.

"Everything went smoothly, Lufthansa was good."

"When did you leave home?" Clara asked.

"Six yesterday morning."

"You must be tired," she sympathised.

"I am a bit," he replied. "I did get some sleep on the plane but it has been a long journey."

"You don't have much luggage, you'll be here a long time."

"I packed some other things in with the equipment," he explained. "I think I'll have enough stuff. Has the container arrived?"

"It arrived at the university on Thursday so we decided to wait for you to open it," she said.

"That must have taken some self control."

"Yes," she said. "I had to fight off the technicians."

"I can imagine. My techs in Edinburgh would be the same. What's your name?" Tony asked her brother.

"I'm Ben," was the reply.

"And what do you do Ben?"

"I'm at school. I'm doing O Levels now and I plan to do A Levels in Science and go to University."

"He's doing pretty well too," said Clara proudly. "We have booked you into the Hilton for the first few days. It'll give you a chance to acclimatise."

"Thanks that sounds very nice."

"The Prof. has booked a table for dinner," she continued. "It's at the Hilton so we will meet you in the in the lobby lounge at six thirty this evening if that's OK. You can get a drink in there too."

"That will be great," said Tony savouring the idea of a cold beer even though it was still early morning.

After a drive lasting about thirty-five minutes they arrived at the Hilton Windhoek. Tony lifted his bag out of the back of the truck but Ben insisted on pulling it into the reception.

"I'll see you at six thirty," called Tony to Clara as he went inside.

She smiled back. He'd never met anyone who could send such warmth in a simple expression.

Clara and her professor arrived in the lobby as planned and he had brought his wife, Dr Hamutenya. She was also a scientist so the four of them had much in common and there was no lack of interesting conversation. They discussed the work of the university generally and the solar project specifically together with a wide range of other scientific and environmental topics.

After the dinner they went to the Skybar which offered fantastic open views of the city . The conversation was relaxed but still focused on real issues for Namibia.

When Tony eventually reached his room after saying goodnight to his hosts, his body was tired out but his brain was racing.

It seemed that energy security and clean water were major national issues. He was fascinated by the discussion about Solar Stills and was convinced that his mirrors could increase efficiency. He eventually fell asleep thinking about the design of a new type based on higher temperatures supplied by mirrors.

Clara arrived with the pickup in the morning as arranged and they set off on the ten minute drive to the university.

"Did you sleep well, Tony?"

116

"Soundly thanks. I didn't realise how tired I was until my head hit the pillow. It was a great evening, your Professor and his wife are very interesting people."

"Yes, I agree," said Clara. "She is well respected in academia and by the government. She advises on energy and water purification and lots more I think."

"Hence the discussion about Solar Stills I suppose."

"We are all interested in making clean water in Namibia," she replied.

Over the next week the container was unpacked, its contents sorted and extra labels added where needed. An inventory was made and checked against the delivery note and it was all stacked carefully.

"What are these?" Liode asked, he was one of the technicians and was examining the boxes containing the Raspberry Pi and other Plan B things.

"Just log them as spare parts, we may not even need them," said Tony. "Ah! Here's the parabolic mirror we made in Edinburgh." He was sliding a box about a metre square and half a metre high out across the floor.

"That looks big," said Liode.

"The mirror is half a metre diameter, the rest must be packaging," said Tony.

They opened the box and took off the top packaging layers, it was still bright and reflective.

"Wow, that looks amazing," said Liode. "It must have taken some polishing."

"Indeed it did. Andy and Bill did sterling job. It took many hours."

"I guess I'll have to do more than a 'sterling job' when we make bigger ones," said Liode. He was not familiar with the phrase 'sterling job' but he grasped the meaning and enthusiastically added it to his vocabulary.

"I hope you have some help when the time comes," said Tony.

"Speaking of help," said Clara from the doorway. "We need to have a coffee and probably water. You haven't stopped since you got here this morning, and I have something to tell you."

"Can I try this in the sun?" Liode asked.

"It could be quite dangerous," started Tony.

"It'll be fine," said Clara. "Liode is very capable."

As they were drinking their coffee, Clara started to explain the plan she had. "We need to get this equipment safely into the desert and set up to start our trials."

"Yes, but I thought we would do most of the work here first and then ship nearly finished systems to the desert."

"Well," she said slowly. "There are a couple of issues. The first is space, we haven't emptied the container fully yet and the store rooms and labs are already getting full. Secondly, there is a feeling amongst the team here, that we need to prove that we can do things in the desert without the backup of all the university facilities. That will prove that the systems really can work in a hostile environment, and it will be fun," she added with a grin.

He smiled back, he had been getting concerned about the amount of space they were taking up. "But what about manpower, or woman power. We surely can't take all the technicians from the department and if not we'll need a lot of people to help."

"There is a potential solution," Clara said. What she really meant was that she had the solution and Tony guessed that's what she meant.

"What is the potential solution?" he obliged.

118

"We need a lot of hands, not all skilled, as will be the case in the future. As you know Africa is a continent of tribes. And people retain strong bonds with their tribe. My tribe is based north of Windhoek and I'm sure that they would be very happy to be the first tribe involved in this project."

"Do you think you can convince them?" Tony asked.

"With my father's help, I am sure I can."

"Where does your father come into this?" Tony asked.

"Well," she said with a smile. "He happens to be the headman, the Chief."

Chapter 26

At the weekend Tony found himself in the Toyota again, being driven north by Clara to meet her father and some of his tribe. Tony had no idea what to expect of the village or a tribal chief.

The houses were made of block walls with what looked like traditional coarse thatch roofs. Around the village there were fields surrounded by fences made of wood posts, which were just branches stuck into the ground, with wire strung between them. There was something growing in the fields but he couldn't be sure what. One looked like maize about five feet high but some of the others looked fairly bare. There were goats corralled in one area. There was an outside area with logs to sit on and a rough wood palisade around the sides.

Clara had explained on the way that her father was much younger than most headmen and that he was quite forward looking. When he and Clara walked into the palisaded area, Tony guessed that the whole village was there.

"Welcome to our village Dr Collins, I am honoured that you have come to visit us so soon after your arrival in Africa," boomed Chief Daniel Bella.

"Thank you Chief Bella, I am honoured to be made so welcome," replied Tony.

"I think this country is very different to your home," smiled the Chief.

"Yes, very different, and I think it is awesome," said Tony.

"We have some challenges but I believe the government knows this and is attempting to address them. Projects like yours are extremely welcome and we plan to help you to succeed."

This appeared to Tony to be a well thought out presentation which he guessed may have been for the benefit of the other villagers as much as for him. He answered in the manner he thought would suit the whole audience.

"I too will do everything I possibly can to make it successful."

Chief Bella stood up, which appeared to be a known convention in the village. "My guests will now join me in my house."

The rest of the village gradually went back to their homes or tasks and the Chief ushered Clara and Tony away and into his house.

Ben was in the house as they entered, "Welcome Dr Collins, both to Namibia and to our home."

"Thank you Ben, I am truly grateful for the warm welcome."

"Now," said the Chief. "We will sit down, have some food, drink a beer and talk about your project, or may I say, 'our project'? And Dr Collins, please call me Chief Daniel."

"Perhaps you would be more comfortable being called Dr Tony," said Clara.

"And perhaps you should be Dr Clara," said Tony smiling.

They chatted over the beer and some fruit for a few minutes and then the Chief brought the conversation back to the project.

"Clara has explained the basics of the project to me and I am very happy that the ideas are so straightforward that even I, with my rudimentary scientific education, can understand."

"He is too modest," broke in Clara. "He has a university degree in Mechanical Engineering."

"That was some years ago Clara, and I have been an administrator rather than an engineer for ten years. Anyway Clara knows my thoughts on this and she knows the technology so I think it's best if she explains what my people can offer."

As the day went on Tony was more and more impressed with Clara's father and his obvious ability to both lead and understand the technology.

It was late afternoon when they were driving back to Windhoek.

"Your father is great," said Tony.

"I'm glad you like him. I think he's great too. What's your father like?"

"My dad's an engineer. When we were kids Mike and I were into building stuff. Dad would chip in with advice if we asked but he didn't take over. The projects usually worked out OK."

"Mike is your brother? What does he do?" Clare queried.

"That's right, he's a couple of years older than me and he was in the army."

"Not anymore?"

"No, he did nearly ten years. He's very fit and pretty tough."

"My dad can be tough too if he needs to be." Clara added.

Tony didn't doubt that, he also didn't doubt that his respect for Clara was growing and, he hoped, their friendship.

Chapter 27

There were four white Toyota Pick Up trucks outside the University building. Men from Clara's tribe were loading them under the direction of Liode the technician.

"We aren't going to get everything in these trucks," said a worried looking Tony.

"Don't look so worried," said Clara. "We'll just do another trip, or trips as needed."

"Won't that take forever with trucking everyone back and forth and someone will have to stay on site?"

"Don't worry. We'll just unload everything and send the trucks back with only a driver."

"But who's going to load up the next trip? Liode can't do it on his own."

"I'll call my dad, he'll send another team here to help Liode. He already told me he wants more of his people involved."

Tony just smiled and kissed her on the cheek.

"That means thank you," he said. He thought she blushed but he couldn't really tell. "Let's get on with the loading."

Once they had all the project kit loaded Clara asked, "Do you have all your personal stuff loaded Tony?"

"I do, I just have my bag that I brought on the flight and the box I shipped in the container and I haven't even opened that yet."

"Do you have all yours?" Tony asked.

"Yes, I'm all set to go."

Clara drove the first vehicle with Tony beside her. The others following in convoy. The last one was driven by Liode and the middle two by men from Clara's village. Clara had already reconnoitred the site and the university administrators had arranged all the appropriate permissions. They drove south on the B1, turned onto a C road and then cross country on tracks through desert scrub.

It was five in the afternoon when they arrived. All that was there was a marker flag with the University logo and name on it. The area around was more or less devoid of scrub and there was a slope to the south side.

Clara stood by the marker facing north and called to everyone to gather round.

"We only have an hour of light to set up camp," she said. "The village will be over there," she pointed in front of her and to the right. She handed a rope to Tony and Liode, "Please take this rope, one at each end. Both take about a hundred paces, Liode on a compass bearing thirty degrees and Tony ninety degrees." She pointed the directions with her arms. "When the rope goes tight stop and peg the ends down, that will be the front line of the village." They followed her instruction and to some's surprise it worked. She grabbed two small tents and went to a point at the centre of the rope. The rope had tags tied on at intervals. She put the tents down next to the tags marked Clara and Tony.

"There's a tag there for the first six man tent," she said pointing along the rope. "We should get the tents up in daylight and then build a fire and get some food."

It all happened as Clara had planned.

She knew this level of order wouldn't last but at least she could start the way she wanted.

It always surprised Tony how quickly it became dark in Africa, but they had the three tents erected and had started a fire by the time the last rays disappeared.

The men had their big frame tent in order, their bedding sorted and were sitting round the fire with thick jackets on. They wanted to retain the day's heat as night fell and the desert became cold. Clara and Tony had warm jackets on too, they each had a small two man tent. Tony had brought his from home, he liked it and knew he could put it up quickly.

They dined on a stew that they had brought with them heated in a big pot on the fire. They boiled water for tea too and talked for a while but everyone was tired and soon they all went to their tents and were quickly asleep.

The sun came up just as quickly as it went down and they were up early unpacking the pickups.

Tony and Clara had mapped out the site and had the plan on a fold up table they had unpacked. A sixty degree sector of the circle due north of the central marker was simply marked as "Solar". The centre of the arc due north of the marker was marked "Furnace". The living area was to the east of the Solar area and the working area was to the West. Almost everything from the pickups was for the working area but then most of what they would bring would start there. The two of them had roughly divided the many tasks into technical and admin with Clara taking the admin initially because she knew most of the villagers and so to whom she could delegate.

Tony was desperate to start setting up some of the fabrication facilities but starting on a small scale.

He had the half metre parabolic mirror which Liode had already tested back in Windhoek. There was an M10 tapped hole in the centre and it had come with a length of ten millimetre diameter stainless steel bar tapped at one end. What Liode had found was that when he screwed it in and put it in the sun, the bar at the end got very hot even

125

though it was only a guide and was just short of the focus point. He had polished the bar to a mirror finish so it reflected the radiation and did not get so hot.

In theory, in good sunlight, this little mirror could produce one kilowatt at its focus, but not enough to melt aluminium on its own. Tony would need mirrors reflecting sunlight onto the parabola to multiply the power.

"If I used a hundred mirrors I would have a hundred kilowatts," he muttered to himself. "That would be good."

"Are you talking to yourself?" Clara asked as she walked up to him.

"Yes," he said. "I always get sensible answers."

"And what was the question?" Clara asked.

"Not a question really. I was just mulling over multiplying the power of this little parabolic mirror with more mirrors," answered Tony.

"Well, the hundred glass mirrors you shipped from the UK are in those crates," she said indicating four of the nearest ones.

"I calculated that we need one point four kilograms of aluminium to make a half metre square mirror but only two millimetres thick," he said. "That's not much more than a hundred beer cans at about thirteen grams each."

"I'm surprised it's so few," said Clara. "But only two millimetres will bend won't it?"

"Yes, it'll have to be reinforced," he replied. "I made a few calculations and I suggest we try five millimetre square beads of aluminium along the back. We'll position them along all the edges and three across the middle in each direction in a grid. That will be another point three kilograms."

"That sounds feasible," she replied. "They'll only be about twelve centimetres apart. Will you use all one hundred mirrors?"

"I don't think so," said Tony. "Twenty will produce about twenty kilowatts which should heat and melt that amount of aluminium in a few minutes, given some efficiency losses."

"If it loses heat too quickly and doesn't get hot enough we can always unpack some more mirrors," she added.

That agreed, they set about making the flat slab to cast the mirror on. The trucks returned and departed every day and brought more men, and women and a lot more kit.

They had brought the cement with them, "Fire cement" as they called it. There was plenty of sand and Clara instructed some of the men to collect some buckets of the finest grain they could locate.

Liode had ordered a square steel frame to be made in the university workshop for the outside of the mirrors. He also had sixteen steel plates each twelve centimetres square. There were bars welded on one face of the plates which held them in a rigid grid with a five millimetre gap between each edge.

When he showed it to Tony and Clara their reaction was the same, "That's great Liode."

"Where did that come from?" Tony added.

"I got the techs at the uni to knock it up. The mirror will be fifty point five centimetres square when hot, but drop by about three and a half millimetres when it cools."

"Won't the plates get trapped when the aluminium cools and contracts?" Tony asked.

"I hope not," answered Liode. "The plates have sloped edges so I hope they pop up as they get squeezed."

"That's very good," said Tony, giving Liode a big smile.

The camp became a village and everyone had tasks, either delegated or just taken on because someone had to do it.

The Village men had taken on the job of making the flat concrete bed to cast the aluminium. Tony was sceptical at first after a few failures but they persevered and eventually he was impressed with their ingenuity.

The men dug a shallow hole in the sand and poured concrete in to make a level surface. When this concrete base had set they set about making the top even more smooth and flat. They poured a thin layer of fire cement on top and vibrated it flat by pounding the edge of the concrete base. The women were delighted to see the men pounding with the heavy wooden poles, this was a job the women usually had to do with corn.

Tony looked at the surface carefully when it was dry.

"It's quite smooth," he said to Clara, "but there are some small undulations. What do you think?"

Clara ran her hand gently over the surface.

"Yes," she said. "The roughness is pretty good but there are variations in the form. I think they might have happened during the drying and setting."

The men who had made it had also been making an examination and talking among themselves.

One of them turned to Tony and Clara and just said, "It's not flat enough, we'll have to grind it."

"OK," said Tony and turned to Clare to see what she thought.

"Let them have a go," she said.

It was hot in the sun as usual and everyone went to get drinks.

Tony and Clara sat together drinking coffee.

"I think we should let them try out their ideas," said Clara.

128

"I know you're right," said Tony, "but you know I'm always itching to pitch in and add my own thoughts."

"Whatever they come up with will be repeatable by our people and doable in this environment," she added.

"That's why I know we should let them go ahead," he said. "And also they will be more committed and that's what we need."

So they left the men to it and got on with other aspects of the project.

The following day Chief Daniel collected Tony and Clara to show them what his people had done. It was a strange looking thing. The slab of concrete that had been made before was still there but it was now much thicker and had six timbers protruding from the edge at regular intervals. Tony and Clara were a little puzzled.

"They have cast a second slab on top of the first one," explained the Chief. "The top one was cast on top of a sheet of polythene so that they can lift it."

"So that's what the timbers are," said Clara,."Lifting handles."

"Correct," said the Chief.

There was a smooth steel bar sticking vertically through the centre of both discs which formed an axle.

"They chiseled out the bottom stone for the axle," said the Chief. "But they cast the top stone around it."

"I don't think they will lift that," said Tony quietly to Clara as they watched the men gathering round. "It must weigh hundreds of kilos."

"Oh ye of little faith," she replied.

It was just over a metre in diameter and fifteen centimetres thick and, in fact, weighed over three hundred kilograms.

The concrete disc was lifted about fifteen centimetres above the base by twelve men on the six timbers, each lifting nearly thirty kilograms in unison.

More timbers were pushed underneath at three points pushing the polythene towards the centre and it was lowered onto those timbers.

The polythene was slit and pulled out and everyone looked underneath so see the surface, it was quite smooth.

"I was wrong about that, they lifted it quite easily," Tony conceded.

The women threw water underneath and the men lifted again while the chocks were removed and it was lowered. Then they started rotating the top disc grinding the surfaces. Once it was moving one man stepped away from each timber and the other moved to the end to push. It was hard work and they swopped over regularly.

Tony went off to do some other jobs and when he came back half an hour later they were still pushing and turning but one of the women was laying below the line of the timbers holding a sharpened steel bar to the outside of the rotating stone.

"Is she decorating it?" Tony asked Clara.

"We'll see," she answered with a smile.

They went on turning until dark and it was food time.

Tony was woken the following morning by the sound of one of the truck engines revving. After he was dressed and came out of his tent he stood staring at the scene.

The stone was rotating but no-one was pushing it. Then he saw the cable around the stone stretching away over a couple of pulleys to the electric winch on the front of a truck. They had modified the winch so it was using the cable as a drive belt.

What Tony had surmised was a decorative groove on the stone was a cable guide.

"This is great," said Tony as Clara joined him. "Your people are very ingenious," he was getting really excited. "How smooth do you think we can get the surface?"

"You will have to be patient, the longer we grind it the smoother it will be, up to a point," Clara answered.

Tony went on, "The smoother the casting is the less sanding will be needed before polishing it."

They went on grinding all day but lifting and checking the surface every hour. It smoothed down to what looked like two hundred grit sandpaper by mid day and the undulations on the surface were gone. They tried grinding for longer but it didn't get any better.

While they were eating they discussed their next steps.

"I think we could cast aluminium onto that surface," Tony said thoughtfully over their food.

"I think so too," said Clara. "We have every roughness of sandpaper between two hundred and three thousand grit. There will be a lot of rubbing but we'll get the metal smooth enough to polish."

"We could use some PV solar panels to keep the truck batteries charged if we make more millstones the same way," said Tony. 'Millstone' is what the concrete slabs had been christened. "Do we have any spare batteries?" Tony asked.

"We do have more batteries," she answered,."And I have already ordered PV panels from Windhoek, they should be here tomorrow."

"That's great. If we had an inverter we could use regular mains powered electric tools like sanders for the mirrors."

"I'll order those right away sir," she laughed punching him playfully on the arm.

131

Chapter 28

By the first Sunday in the desert there was a substantial population at the site. On Saturday afternoon the returning trucks brought the Minister from the church near Clara's village. He was met by Clara, Tony and her father who had arrived on the Friday.

Tony wasn't sure how to welcome a visiting Minister so he started with, "Welcome to our site, it's very good of you to come all this way for us."

"It is a great pleasure," replied the Minister,."But as most of my congregation is here it seemed sensible. I hope you will be joining our service."

"Of course," said Tony. He had intended to join but it was clear that he was very much expected to be there.

There was no project work done on the Sunday and everyone, even Tony, was grateful for the rest.

The service was a joyful event with lively African Gospel songs.

The sermon was very long but nobody was going anywhere and Tony noticed a few nodding heads.

The afternoon was mostly a rest period and in the evening the whole company sat together for a meal started with the Minister delivering a grace.

Tony and Clara were sitting together with the Chief when the Minister joined them. "Thank you for the warm welcome and allowing me to minister to your people Chief Daniel," he said and to Tony he added. "And thank you for your welcome and respect also Dr Tony."

"You have always served us well Minister," said the Chief.

"Thank you Chief Daniel. I have a favour to ask."

"Please ask," replied the Chief.

"I would like to remain here. I wish to be able to minister to our people."

After a pause he added "I have other skills which might be useful and make my presence worthwhile."

Chief Daniel glanced quickly at Clara and Tony before he replied, "I think that your presence here would be of great benefit. I know that you will look after our spiritual wellbeing and I also know you have medical experience which might be prove to be vital."

"That'll be great," said Clara. Tony agreed.

As the community settled down and people found their roles and niches the Minister also morphed naturally into a health and safety role.

Chief Daniel lent his considerable muscle, when needed, but also kept his controlling role as well as planning and sharing ideas with Tony and Clara.

Over the next week the project went well, the heliostat frames for the one metre square glass mirrors were gas welded together. The mirrors were fixed in their frames so they could be directed down to the place where the parabolic mirror would be. The next two key tasks were to test the control system and then cast some aluminium. Tony was delighted that the Chief had found a skilled foundry man and blacksmith. He was known as Smoke both for his craft and for his curls of grey hair. His skills were invaluable, he advised on the set up of the crucible and he also had contacts in the scrap metal business who were able to provide truckloads of aluminium drink cans. His real contribution was his knowledge of hot metals, one key thing being, he knew when to pour molten metal just by looking at it.

Tony had been working with the Plan A sophisticated actuation system on one of the heliostats, to check out the electronics and the control. He had everything assembled early one morning sending the reflection of the rising sun down onto a target. The circuits were designed to track the movement of the sun and keep the reflection on the target and it was working. He continued checking it for half an hour measuring the accuracy of the energy on the target and it was very precise.

He looked up to see Clara approaching with two mugs of coffee. "Oh! Clara, thank you. You must be psychic!" he said as she handed him one.

"You were gasping for a coffee?" she queried.

"No, well, yes, that too but I wanted to show you this working."

"Great, but drink your coffee first Tony. Have you had any water? It's getting hot."

"I've had some," he said. "There's a bottle in the shade of the toolbox."

As they drank their coffee he explained what he had done and how accurate the steering of the heliostat had been.

"You can see that it's tracking and still right on the target."

He had a piece of white plywood with a matt black square in the centre.

The reflected sunlight was all on the black square and was hardly being reflected.

They moved to the shade of the mirror to finish their coffee, it was getting hot now.

"Have you adjusted something?" asked Clara as they stood up.

"No, why?"

She didn't answer but asked, "Did you touch the mirror?"

"No, why are you asking?" he said.

"Because I can see sunlight shining brightly from the white of your target."

As they watched they could see the bright area grow as the mirror changed its angle slightly. In a few minutes it had moved completely off the black target.

Tony pushed the Home button on the control box and the mirror went to a horizontal position.

"I'm glad we put that Home there," said Tony,."But I don't know what went wrong."

Clara and Tony spent the rest of the day with the heliostat system checking everything. It would work for a short while after resetting but then drift off again. By nightfall they were no closer to finding the problem and agreed to start afresh the following morning.

They were up before dawn, it was cold in the desert at night and they were wrapped up against the chill.

As soon as the sky brightened a little they were at the Heliostat system resetting it again ready for the sun to appear.

They could see that the reflected light was hitting the black of the target as the sun came over the horizon and it stayed on the black.

They monitored it as the sun rose in the sky and it appeared to be functioning perfectly.

"No light on the white," said Clara. "It's behaving well."

"Yes," said Tony. "Let's hope it keeps behaving." He was pleased it was working again but still worried about the performance of the day before.

"Hello doctors," said Liode. "You look so engrossed I thought you might not stop for your coffee." He handed them a mug each and asked how it was going.

"It's fine so far," said Tony. "Can you see the reflected sunlight on the black of the target?"

"Just about," said Liode. As they drank their coffee Liode kept looking at the target. "I see it now the white edge is bright."

Tony looked up. "Bugger," he breathed quietly.

"I guess that wasn't what you wanted to hear," said Liode.

"No," replied Tony "It means it's starting to drift again."

"Is the frame warping in the heat?" asked Liode.

"Not when it moves as much as we saw yesterday but you may well be right about the heat. We'll watch it for a while and if it's bad like yesterday we'll check the circuits."

"Could we cool it?" suggested Clara.

Tony thought about it for a while, "It wouldn't be a real solution but if we cooled separate parts of the system individually we might be able to figure out which one is faulty."

"Or which ones," added Liode.

The heliostat wandered about in the same way as the previous day and they pushed the Home button again.

Tony took the electronics out of its case and examined it, it didn't seem particularly hot.

Liode appeared with a can of freezer spray, "Is this any use?"

Tony looked at Liode in amazement. "That's fantastic! Where did you produce that from?"

"It was in the container from the UK, there was this note on the box."

Tony read it out loud, "'This should keep you cool. Bill and Andy,' They probably did that as a joke but well…."

They started cooling various parts of the circuitry and checking the performance of the heliostat.

Mid afternoon the mirror reflection steadied and centred on the black square.

"I left this one till last hoping it wouldn't be the one," he explained to Liode. "This is the bespoke multilayer board and the culprit is this bespoke LSI chip. This unit takes the optical signal right through to the motor controllers. Also the encoders on the motors go back to that board too."

Clara arrived with some cold drinks in time to hear the bad news.

"Maybe we could rig something to cool the chip," said Liode.

"It might work but it would be a real bodge," said Clara.

"It might even need someone supervising each box," added Liode.

"We might as well have someone steering each mirror," said Tony in exasperation.

"We could do that," said Clara.

"We could," said Liode. "We have enough men and women and I'm sure they would like to do it."

And so Plan C was born.

They set about installing a mirror in each frame on the hillside. In lieu of a Home button they fixed a weight under each one so that the mirror naturally relaxed into a horizontal position.

This all happened in double quick time. When the community found out that they would be steering, everyone got involved and took responsibility for their mirror.

There was a lot of trial and error and honing of the steering skill required. Anything left on the ground in front of the parabola's position was scorched. Luckily nothing valuable was lost.

The Foundry Team, as they had been named, had been making progress too. By the time the mirrors could all be pointed to the same target virtually everything at the parabola site was ready.

In the evening Clara, Tony, Chief Daniel, the Minister and Liode were sitting around a fire together. It was the day that they had confirmed that the LSI controller was the problem.

"Can't you just buy another chip for the controller?" asked the Minister.

"Unfortunately not," said Tony. "This chip was specially made for us. To get new chips the semiconductor factory has to go through the complete design and production process again."

"And that will take weeks," added Clara.

Chief Daniel looked very severe, "That factory has a lot to answer for and should be held to account financially."

"They will have to make good the work they have done," said Tony.

"And they should cover all the consequential costs," Chief Daniel added.

"The bigger problem is really the delay and I'm sure that the contract says that they are not liable for other costs," Tony answered.

"That is standard," said the Chief. "But you can argue that when you contact them and speeding up their response would help restore their reputation."

Tony agreed, he was gradually learning that the Chief had many talents and his respect continued to grow.

"Will you go back to Windhoek to phone and email?" asked the Minister.

"I won't have to," answered Tony and then explained. "For a few weeks before I left Edinburgh my brother was staying with me. When I told him I would be coming to the desert he insisted I had a satellite phone with me. In fact there are two in a case in my tent which he acquired for me."

"Your brother sounds a very sensible and resourceful man," said the Chief.

"Yes he is," reflected Tony. "He was in the army and he has served all over the world. I'll check the batteries tonight and we'll talk with Laura in the morning. She is at Edinburgh University and has the contracts and all the contact details for suppliers."

Chapter 29

Laura was in the lab talking to Andy and Bill when her mobile started ringing but she didn't recognise the number.

"Don't answer it," said Bill. "It'll be someone from Africa offering to make you millions."

At the mention of Africa, Namibia and Tony popped into her mind and she answered it.

"Laura McLeish," she said formally as she didn't really know who it would be, then after a pause, "Hello Tony, how are things going, are you in Windhoek?"

Andy and Bill waited as Tony spoke for several minutes. Laura was making copious notes and eventually replied, "I've got all that Tony and I'll get onto it right away. How are you surviving the heat and the desert conditions?"

There was another long pause while he answered then she said, "Well that's good anyway. Can I reach you on this number?"

"Good. OK. I'll tell them, they are right here."

She hung up and turned to Andy and Bill, "He says a big thank you for Plan B."

She went on to explain the situation generally and specifically with the control electronics. She also told them about Plan C.

"Well," said Andy. "The lower tech the better in that environment."

Laura started making calls.

While Tony had the satellite phone in his hand he thought that maybe he should call his brother to thank him for his forethought.

When Mike's mobile rang he knew instantly who was calling.

"Hi Tony, are you OK?"

"I'm fine, a problem with the tech stuff in the project. Today is the first time I needed the sat-phone. I had to call Laura at the university and I wanted to thank you for getting me these phones."

"Sooner or later you were bound to need one. Is there anything I can do?" Mike asked.

"The problem is with the control system, there's an LSI chip and multilayer board that was made specially for us and it doesn't work in the heat."

"That's a bit bad isn't it? I presume you specified a high working temperature."

"That's the strange thing, it's a reputable company and we specified absolutely everything, especially the temperature, they shouldn't have got it wrong."

"So who is Laura?" Mike asked.

"She's a Post Doc who's been helping with the project, to be honest she's been essential in the planning and admin, and bouncing ideas." And other things thought Tony to himself.

Mike was more cynical about big business than Tony and something didn't seem right to him.

"Is it OK if I call her to see how things are going?" Mike asked.

"Sure, I'll give you her number."

Mike wrote down the number. Tony explained more about the company and the problem and he described the village which had grown up and some of the people. He promised not to leave it so long before getting in contact again.

Mike Googled Rossborough Electronics, the semiconductor company that Tony had mentioned. He found their website and checked them out on the Company

House website too. It all looked bona fide but he was still puzzled.

At the University, Laura checked the specifications of the control system with the purchasing people and got them to contact Rossborough Electronics.

Purchasing called Laura back the same afternoon, "The sales person was very helpful on the face of it but their production schedules are full and the best offer I can get is our money back but that doesn't help you much does it?"

"It would be better than nothing but I don't think Tony will be very pleased. I'll call him and let you know. Thanks for trying."

Laura called Tony straight away after she got the news and she was right, he wasn't well pleased. However, being Tony he told her to buy more beer for Andy and Bill as their Plan B was looking like the project's salvation.

Chapter 30

In the desert village nobody wanted to wait for Plan B, they were ploughing ahead with Plan C.

Smoke, the blacksmith, had a crucible packed with crushed aluminium cans just waiting for heat.

Liode had the steel surround for the mould waiting on the flat millstone, the bar at the centre had been removed and the hole filled with cement. The whole surface looked smooth and flat.

The frame with the squares welded on it had some long carrying handles fitted to it ready to lift it into position after the pour.

The Minister had cordoned off areas near the crucible to keep people from being burned.

Chief Daniel was overseeing and making sure the people stayed where they were supposed to be.

There were twenty mirrors to be used, they were all in their frames and each had two steerers, one as a standby.

Tony, Clara, Chief Daniel and the Minister had two way radios to keep in contact and control the trial.

The Chief and the Minister were on either side of the heating location. Tony and Clara were up the hill above the mirrors to get an overall view.

The correct weight of crushed aluminium cans had been put into the crucible.

The crucible was standing in the middle of the millstone and the parabolic mirror had been fixed on a frame with its focus on the crucible. The plan was that any stray radiant heat would heat the millstone ready for the pour.

When all was ready Chief Daniel called for quiet and gave the order to lower mirrors. The mirror steerers had been given a number and they would bring the mirrors to bear one at a time. They each took about five seconds to get steadily on target. There was considerable tolerance since each flat mirror was one metre square and the parabola was only half a metre across.

It was late morning and the sun was high and bright, the crucible heated rapidly as did the millstone.

Smoke was standing on a ladder well to one side of the crucible so that he could see in. When he judged that the molten aluminium was at the right temperature he nodded to the Chief and scrambled down.

"Mirrors up!" bellowed the Chief.

All the steerers relaxed and set the mirrors horizontal. Smoke scraped the dross from the surface of the molten aluminium and directed his two assistants to pick up the crucible holder, which was already in position, lift the crucible and pour it into the centre of the millstone.

It flowed but didn't quite reach the edge of the mould. The foundry man ordered the welded square frames to be lowered anyway and they could see the aluminium spreading and rising between the plates.

"Breathe!" bellowed the Chief.

There were sighs and a peel of laughter as everyone realised that they had been holding their breath.

"Steerers leave your mirrors and let's get some more crushed cans weighed into that crucible, and don't touch anything that's hot. Well done everyone," called out the Chief.

When the aluminium had cooled and solidified the welded squares and their frame started to be squeezed up and out as planned. It was lifted away but the aluminium had to be allowed to cool a lot more before it could be moved.

To warn people to keep clear the Minister stayed close by.

As it was cooling Clara, Tony and the Chief ate together.

"The heating went well and quickly," said Chief Daniel. "But the cooling is a long process. I think we need more millstones with a frame for the parabola at each one."

Tony and Clara agreed, that way they could keep the process going. And turn out more mirrors, if indeed they had made one.

After lunch and after looking very carefully, Smoke deemed that they could throw some water on the casting.

The casting had come away from the steel frame except on one side where the molten metal had run over a little. Smoke gave it a couple of taps with his small hammer and loosened it enough for the frame and casting to be prised apart.

The surface of the mirror looked rough but Tony said, "That's what I expected it to look like, now it needs sanding and then polishing. The good thing is it looks flat."

The Chief pointed to two of the villagers, "You have the privilege of being stewards of our first mirror."

They stepped forward eagerly and reverently and happily carried the mirror away.

Tony looked surprised, "Where are they off to with that?"

Clara whispered to him, "They will take responsibility for that mirror, they'll sand it, polish it, and steer it. My father has made a priority list and given the people a specific number to put on the mirror so we can keep track of each one."

"Sounds like a good idea. I didn't know, was it a secret?" he looked puzzled.

"No, not a secret but you have been so busy and this sort of organisation is best delegated and Dad is the best one for it. He knows all his people so he can arrange it without offending anyone. And it helps with motivation by introducing an element of competition."

"All good with me, we'll have to get on with making more and I definitely didn't want to have the job of sanding and polishing."

The Chief, the Minister, Clara and Tony had become a sort of ad-hoc management team. They decided to make four more millstones next to the first one, only these would be two metres across. They abandoned the centre pin and top grinding stone as it would take resources and would probably be too heavy. That meant the millstones didn't have to be round although that was an easy shape to make it.

They cut and broke the original top stone into pieces to use for grinding the new millstones.

Liode went back to Windhoek to the university and made new metal jigs for casting the bigger mirrors.

They practiced with the equipment they had and it took many days but eventually they had a good process running. When the extra frames arrived and were used they could make ten one metre square mirrors in a day.

At the end of the month Tony called Laura on the satellite phone and gave her a detailed update. She noted it all down but then Tony added at the end to leave out everything about Plan B & Plan C in case the sponsors decided their money wasn't needed. She wrote up the shortened report and emailed it to their professor in Edinburgh and also to Professor Hamutenya at NUST. Their Professor in Edinburgh sent a summary report to their sponsor Renshaw & Collier.

Chapter 31

Liode and Clara approached Tony when he was alone one afternoon.

"Hello," he said, "this looks suspicious."

"We have an idea and we want you in on it," said Clara.

"This sounds interesting, carry on"

"Well, it's my Father's birthday soon and I want a special present for him."

Liode couldn't contain his enthusiasm, "And we have a great idea."

"Yes," said Clara. "It's both traditional and modern."

"OK," said Tony getting impatient to hear the idea. "Tell me, what is it? It sounds as though you think I'll need some convincing."

"It's just that it will take resource from the project," she answered.

Liode could contain himself no longer, "We want to make a traditional African shield in aluminium. Like a Zulu shield but with a mirror finish."

Tony was surprised but he immediately started to think through some of the implications and after a short pause he answered, "I think it's a great idea."

Clara gave him a big long hug which Tony returned with feeling. Liode wasn't quite sure where to look.

When they separated Tony continued, "With the new bigger millstones we would just need a new steel jig and to do a few calculations on the mass of aluminium."

Liode looked down towards his feet, obviously slightly embarrassed.

Tony knew his Edinburgh technicians and he was sure Liode was from the same mould. "You've made it already haven't you," he laughed. Relief flooded through Liode. Clara too was relieved that Tony was so relaxed about it.

They went to one of the pickup trucks and Liode lifted a canvas cover to reveal the steelwork, it barely fitted in the truck.

"I guess this has to be a surprise," said Tony. "We'll have to cast it when the Chief isn't around."

"He has a meeting with the village elders tomorrow," said Clara. "That will be our best chance and it will give us three days to get it polished before his birthday."

The opportunity presented itself as planned, they told the villagers about the secret shield and word spread like wildfire. Everyone wanted to help with the polishing.

Tony worked out how much aluminium was needed and all was prepared. With the experience that they now had with the process the casting went smoothly and even the small extra metal lugs which were added after the first pour were successful. These were to fit leather handles so that the shield could be carried.

The villagers disappeared with the shield and set about carefully sanding and polishing so Tony didn't see it again until the Chief's birthday.

It was Saturday and no work was planned for the afternoon. There was singing and dancing and plenty of beer.

In the mid afternoon Chief Daniel's special song was sung by the whole village and the Chief sat cross legged with his wife and son who had both travelled there for the occasion. The Minister, Tony and Clara sat with them.

Liode nodded to Clara and she got up and went to him.

She returned with Liode leading a group of villagers and she asked for quiet. Clara projected her voice to the assembled company, "Chief Daniel, we offer our blessings and good wishes to you on this special day and we have a gift for you which has been prepared with the help of all your people."

She was passed the shield from within Liode's group. Tony took a sharp breath, the shield was not a mirror but leopard skin. Had someone broken the mirror shield?

Clara presented it to her Father and as he admired it she pulled a draw string and lifted the leopard skin away revealing the shining shield.

Tony relaxed.

"The whole village has helped to polish this," said Clara. "And your elders acquired the skin as a cover to protect it."

Although the shield weighed over five kilograms, Chief Daniel slipped his arm into the leather straps and easily held it up high flashing sunlight around his people.

He smiled broadly at them and boomed, "You honour me my people. This is a great symbol of our success here. With work such as this you honour yourselves and our whole tribe."

Drinking and celebrating continued into the night with much praise for the Chief and his shield.

The Sunday service was still a happy occasion but was a little more subdued than normal, also the sermon was much shorter than usual as the Minister nursed a rather sore head.

Chapter 32

The members of the management team were sitting together by a fire after finishing their evening meal.

"The shield," said Chief Daniel, "was a wonderful gift. There has never been such a shield."

"It's not too heavy to carry?" asked Clara.

"Not at all," he replied. "It is very sturdy and it's lighter than the one metre square mirrors."

"We have made a hundred of those mirrors," said Tony, "which is enough for this project. We have to work on making a bigger parabolic mirror to make the best of the heliostats and I need to start work on the Plan B control system with the more basic electronics."

"But we don't want to just stop using the system we've developed," added Clara.

"We can make some ingots of aluminium to use in future or even sell," said the Minister.

"I think that my people may find that, how can I put it, uninteresting," said the Chief. "We could spend some time making ingots but I suggest we make more shields."

"That would certainly keep our equipment and process in good condition and improve and refine everyone's skills," said Tony. "Would we give a shield to each of your people?"

"That would be hugely appreciated by my people," answered the Chief.

"Smoke has been training one of the young men in foundry work so it will be a good opportunity for him to practice," added Clara, "So you can get Smoke to do the big parabola."

"I think that Smoke has christened his assistant Spark," said the Minister with a smile. "Although Christening is supposed to be my job."

With guidance from Smoke, Spark and most of the villagers enthusiastically set about casting and polishing the shields. There were three slightly different designs of shield because Liode's colleagues in Windhoek had made another two sets of metalwork with slight variations in case the first one had a problem. Liode had his colleagues make two more of the first type so that all five millstones could be used.

Tony, and a smaller team, made a new concrete base near the others. Liode had ordered a two metre diameter steel plate with an upstanding ring at the outside. It looked as though the university technicians had made a huge shallow baking tin. It had a bearing under the centre with another plate on the bottom to support it.

When it was placed on the centre of the millstone it rotated easily with gentle hand pressure. They had a small electric motor at one side with a band around the baking tin to rotate it.

They checked that it rotated smoothly with the motor and Tony measured the rotation speed to check that it was constant.

With it rotating, they carefully poured cement into the bowl until it gradually flowed into a parabolic surface. The cement was very watery so that it could flow, consequently it required a long time to set and dry out. It had to be continually rotated. Fortunately the temperature was high as the season was approaching its hottest time. It was rotated until the following day and then examined carefully. It seemed to be dry but Smoke wan't happy that all the water was gone so they kept it going another day.

151

This was to be the biggest casting they had ever made both in diameter and mass of aluminium. To give this mirror some physical strength and stability they carved grooves in the surface of the cement to give ridges on the back of the mirror.

The heliostat steerers had just finished a melt on the furthest right millstone. One of the senior villagers who was endowed with a strong voice was acting as the melt controller and called for, "Mirrors up."

The half metre parabolic mirror was transferred to the frame by the rotating baking tin. Smoke asked the melt controller to call for one mirror.

With that light he adjusted the parabola so that it was focused precisely on the crucible. They moved away to a safe distance and the melt controller called, "Mirrors down!" The steerers had to maintain concentration longer than usual as this melt contained so much more metal but after five minutes and Smoke's word, they heard the melt controller call "Mirrors up!". They had one hundred heliostats now and the power was enormous.

Smoke moved in with his assistants and examined the molten aluminium. He took extra care with the crucible and particularly skimming all the dross from the surface, when he was satisfied he called his assistants to pour, constantly giving them instructions to control the way they did it. The concrete was already hot and the molten metal flowed well over the surface creating the hot parabolic mirror.

The motor was kept running for several hours until they were sure the mirror was stable. It had shrunk away from the sides of the mould but balanced in the centre as planned. When it was cool enough a thin slurry of cement was poured into the gap, this was left turning to stabilise until the following day.

Tony was dozing in his tent that night but he could hear the motor driving the big mirror and was restless. He wrapped up warm against the cold desert night and went out to have a look.

As he approached he saw a figure standing next to it.

"You are out late Clara," he whispered.

"I couldn't sleep," she replied.

"Me neither, is anything wrong?" he asked.

"No," she replied. "I think it is just that the sound of the motor is different to the normal desert and camp sounds that we are used to."

"Probably the same for me."

"Let's walk away from the motor noise and listen to the desert," said Clara taking his arm and guiding him away.

They walked up the hill past the heliostats and down the other side a little. The sound of the motor faded.

They sat together in silence for a few minutes.

"The desert is so beautiful," whispered Tony,."The sky is so clear. The stars are so…. beyond description."

"Yes," said Clara. "We have been concentrating so much on our work that we haven't spent the time to appreciate it."

Tony didn't know why he was whispering but Clara was too.

"There is so much beauty here," he breathed as he looked into Clara's eyes. As they looked at each other they came together and their lips touched. The kiss was long, warm and tender.

Chapter 33

The puzzle of Rossborough Electronics had ticked over in Mike's subconscious for weeks. One morning in December he started looking online again for more information. Eventually he found a financial article about the management team. The MD had changed recently, since the last annual report to Company House. Mike didn't feel he understood the commercial side well enough so he called an old services friend to ask if he could do a bit of digging about Rossborough Electronics. His friend Chris worked in the city. Mike was sure that if anyone could cast some light on what was going on, Chris could.

Chris asked why he was interested so Mike gave him the background of his brother's project and the problem with the equipment from a reputable manufacturer.

"Something does sound a bit off there," said Chris. "I'll have a look into it and get back to you. How's things generally?"

They chatted for a while about 'things generally' and about old friends and Chris said again that he would call back when he had found something.

They had talked about Brian, who was now running his own security company; Mike hadn't talked to him for ages so he dialled his mobile to have a chat.

"Hello B. E. Security, how can we help?" answered a very pleasant female voice.

"Hello, I'd like to speak to Brian if he's available please," answered Mike.

"Hold the line please."

Mike could hear tapping of keys then a voice said,"Hello Mike, how the hell are you?"

"Brian, how come a girl answers your mobile and how did you know it was me?"

"That's my old mobile number and it routes to our switchboard. Sarah just checked your number on her system and put you through."

"Very slick," said Mike. "It sounds like you are doing OK."

"Thanks, that's the impression we want to give and actually we are doing OK although we are still a small company. What are you doing with yourself?"

"Not much at the moment," answered Mike,."I'm flat sitting for my brother in Edinburgh and thinking a lot about what I want to do next."

"Well, I could use your skills when I get any big contract. This business is pretty erratic but it would be good to know I could call you if I need help."

"Thanks Brian, I'll think seriously about that, and I have a sneaking suspicion that I might need your help with something now."

"Whatever I can do," said Brian. "But if it starts to take a lot of time I'd have to start charging," he paused. "Or you could pay me with your time."

"I get the message Brian, everyone has to make a living."

"What is your security issue?" Brian asked.

"It's just something that doesn't sit quite right with me," Mike said and went on to explain about the solar project and the problem with Rossborough Electronics.

"I'll get Sarah to do a bit of digging, she's very good at that, and I'll get back to you when she's done."

"Thanks, I appreciate it and I will seriously consider your offer. Cheers."

Mike wasn't sure whether he wanted to be in private security but it was definitely worth considering.

Two days later Mike's mobile rang.

"Hello, Mike Collins," he said.

"Hi Mike it's Chris. I've found a few odd things, do you fancy a pint and we can chew them over."

Mike hadn't told him he wasn't in London, he hesitated for only a moment and made a decision.

"I'm in Edinburgh just now but I'd love a pint and I can be in London tomorrow. Which pub and what time?"

They made the arrangement and Mike started looking up train times on his laptop.

He decided on the 07:30 from the Waverley which would get him in London before lunch. He'd have time for a wander and maybe have a look at Brian's office. His phone rang,

"Hello, Mike Collins."

"That sounds very professional," said Brian.

"Talk of the devil," said Mike. "I was actually just thinking about you."

"Good thoughts I hope," said Brian. "I have some things to tell you."

"That's great," said Mike, "and I'm going to be in London tomorrow, can I visit your palatial offices?"

"If that's your expectation you might be disappointed but you will be very welcome."

"Is 14:00 OK, and what's the address?"

They made the arrangements and Mike started to pack a few things.

The train into Kings Cross was on time, within five minutes anyway. Mike took the circle line to Farringdon and changed to Thameslink for Blackfriars. He was there at 12:15.

He'd gone there because he wanted to walk by the river. He walked onto the Victoria Embankment briefly then onto Blackfriars Bridge where he paused in the middle for a few minutes to watch the river. He thought of the last time he had been on that Bridge. He looked at the water and remembered the comrades who were with him then on a brief leave before a fateful deployment. It was in the third year of his service and he remembered mostly those comrades who hadn't returned.

Having paid his simple respects he walked back across the bridge. The other reason to visit this area was because he wanted to be sure he knew exactly how to find the pub where he was meeting Chris later.

He walked up New Bridge Street and Farringdon Street to the pub where he had a swift half and a snack.

Feeling ready, he walked to St Paul's and took the Central Line to Shepherd's Bush. It was only a few minutes walk to Brian's address which faced onto Shepherd's Bush Common. The front door was between two shops but when he went up the stairs to the second floor he found the office door with a B. E. Security sign on it. He was still ten minutes early.

"Hello," said Sarah, standing up from her desk and holding out her hand. "You must be Mike."

"That's right," he replied taking her hand,."And you must be Sarah."

"Also correct," she said. "Brian will be back any minute, please take a seat."

The office was modest but tidy and clean and the computer that Sarah was using looked new. Mikes also noticed that Sarah was very tidy.

He was sipping his coffee when Brian came bustling in with an armful of flowers and a big box of chocolates. Brian gave Sarah a kiss which she returned with more enthusiasm than just a receptionist and took the proffered gifts. He turned to Mike, "It's Sarah's birthday today and welcome to our humble office." They shook hands with the feeling of real remembered comradeship.

"Let's go in the back and have a talk," said Brian.

Sarah dropped the latch on the front door and they all went to the back room and sat in soft armchairs chairs around a coffee table.

"As you may have guessed," said Brian."Sarah is much more than a receptionist, she is key to the business," then added, "and to me."

She smiled at Brian, then turned to Tony, "The company Rossborough Electronics, I dug around to find some of their customers and talked to them. Several of them are going elsewhere, just recently. They didn't say it in so many words but the message was the same from them all, the quality of service has changed for the worse. This is strange for what was a very successful and respected company and may have something to do with changes of top management. Brian has done a bit of snooping outside the headquarters building in London and took a few pictures."

Brian brought up some pictures on his laptop and flicked through them.

"These first ones I was able to identify from previous company reports and some journal articles, but this one hasn't appeared anywhere before."

He handed an A4 print of the man to Tony.

"I'm not one hundred percent sure of this, but from his bearing his bodyguards and my gut, I think he's Russian. There is a lot of Russian money coming into London and not all of it clean."

"So if we can identify him I think we might discover more," added Sarah.

"If it's a money trail that is going to give us answers," said Mike. "I hope Chris can help, I'm having a drink with him tonight."

"Our Chris Downey?" asked Brian.

"The very same," answered Mike. "He's a money man now and works in the city."

"Pity it's not tomorrow night. I'm busy tonight, I'd love to meet up."

"Maybe that's possible too," said Mike with a grin.

"Are you in touch with any more of the old team?" asked Mike. He had just decided that he would like to spend another day in London meeting some old comrades.

"I think I have one or two numbers, I'll ring around."

They talked about the work that Brian and Sarah did and it became clear to Mike that this was an even partnership with Sarah contributing just as much as Brian, albeit in different fields.

As Mike was preparing to leave he asked, "Can I keep this photo?"

"Yes, that's for you," answered Sarah. "And take this printout too, it covers all the important things that we discovered. If you need more detail just call."

"That's great," said Mike as he slipped them into his rucksack next to his laptop. "I'd better be off now, thanks for everything. It's been lovely to meet you Sarah, maybe I'll see you both again tomorrow evening."

Back on the Central Line to St Paul's Mike looked at the photo again and the list of bullet points from Sarah.

From St Paul's he walked to the pub and arrived at about 17:30. Chris had said he'd be there between 17:30 and 18:00 depending on how quickly he could get out of the office.

Mike had found a table and had his first pint in his hand when Chris walked in. He was wearing a very smart city suit complete with white shirt and tie and carrying a briefcase. He came straight over to Mike and they shook hands warmly.

"What would you like?" Mike asked.

"Getting the priorities right as usual," replied Chris. "Pint of Spitfire please," as he sat down next to Mike's rucksack.

Mike came back with the beer.

"Lets talk about what I learned regarding Rossborough Electronics before we have too many of these," smiled Chris as though he had every intention to have quite a few more.

"Great, what did you dig up?" Mike asked.

"Well," said Chris. "I think someone is making a lot of money on Rossborough Electronics, selling short."

"Wait a second, I've heard of selling short but what is it and is it legal?" injected Mike.

"It's legal with a caveat," answered Chris. "Let's say it's Mr Smith doing it. What happens is Smith borrows shares from his broker when they are at a high price thinking that the price will go down. He sells the shares to someone else at that high price. But, he still has to give shares back to his broker at some point. If the price goes down then Smith buys shares at the low price and gives them back to the lender, his broker."

"Let me get this right, I borrow a million pounds of shares and sell them straight away for a million pounds. The price goes down and I buy the same number of shares for half a million and give them back to the guy I borrowed them from and I have the extra half a million."

"That's about right," said Chris.

160

"But what if I knew the price would go down or I caused it?" Mike queried.

"That's the caveat about the legality," answered Chris. "If someone inside a company has private knowledge about the company which will cause the stock value to change and makes money out of it, he's committing the offence of insider trading, illegal in the UK since 1980."

"OK, I've heard of that too," said Mike. "Is there any logical reason why the stock of this company, Rossborough Electronics, should go down?"

"That's the odd thing," said Chris. "This is a long standing well respected solid company in a sector that is needed and going well. There are always threats but I've seen nothing to suggest any weakness."

"Until recently," added Mike.

"Precisely," finished Chris as he also finished his pint. "another one?"

"Definitely," Mike handed over his empty glass.

When they were replenished, Mike asked, "Is there any way to see who is doing this short selling?"

"Difficult," Chris grimaced. "Most of what goes on in the city is pretty confidential. My guess would be the Russians but I have no evidence for that. It's just a bugbear I have."

"That's the second time Russians have been mentioned today," said Mike as he brought the photograph out of his backpack. "This is someone that Brian saw frequenting Rossborough Electronics. We haven't identified him yet but Brian thought he might be Russian."

Chris looked at it, "I don't recognise this guy but he looks a bit familiar." He continued to study it as he sipped his beer. "It's just that he looks like someone I know of." Chris put his glass down and smiled, "I still don't know who he is but he seriously resembles Vladimir Solovyov."

"Who is this Vladimir?" Mike asked quickly.

"Steady on Mike, it's not him, he just looks similar. Anyway, Vladimir Solovyov is a Russian multimillionaire. He lives in London and he's not someone I'd like to tangle with."

"Why do you say that?" Mike asked.

"It's just things I hear, little snippets of information, companies he's been involved with. Lots of little things."

They had more beer and continued chatting about Tony's project and of course they also talked about old times.

Mike asked, "Are you free tomorrow night? Brian can come and he's going to see if he can find any more of the old crew."

"More beer and old mates, let me think. Of course I can! Where and when?"

At the end of the evening they made a plan and left the pub, Chris to his flat and Mike to his hotel on Old Street in Shoreditch.

Mike had a late leisurely breakfast and lingered over his coffee mulling over the discussions from the previous day. He decided to call Laura in Edinburgh to see if she had any more information.

"Hello, Laura McLeish"

"Hi, this is Mike Collins, Tony's brother."

"Oh hi," said Laura warmly. "You gave Tony the SatPhones, that was brilliant."

"Well, I have to look after my little brother," he said light heartedly, then, "do you have any more updates on the problem he's had with the electronics?"

"He told you about that did he," she replied, "well basically the supplier let us down badly and aren't doing much to help. I have to write a report for our Prof. by the end of the month and he'll send a summary to Renshaw & Collier."

"Who's Renshaw & Collier?" he asked.

"They're sponsoring the project, it came out of the blue and it's been great to have the finance to do it all properly. But basically I'm just working on what Tony told me on the call on Monday. What's your interest?"

"Just looking out for my little brother. I guess you have my number on your mobile, can you let me know if there's any more information, if anything important happens?"

"No problem," she answered as she put the number in her Contacts.

Laura sounds nice thought Mike after he hung up.

Mike sounds a bit worried about Tony, Laura thought after she hung up.

In the afternoon Mike called B. E. Security and talked to Sarah. She told him that Brian had found one other buddy who could come to the pub with them. "He's called Jerry but I haven't met him yet, he's coming here about five o'clock. Have you decided a time and place?"

Mike gave her the details and asked, "Aren't you coming?"

"I'll be giving it a miss thanks. Actually it's a friend's birthday and she's taking me and some other girls to a spa. Not that I wouldn't enjoy listening to you guys chewing over old times and drinking vast quantities of beer."

"Actually," said Mike. "I think you might enjoy the spa more."

He sat in his room thinking, 'Jerry the quartermaster, *Mr Find and fix anything*, I wonder what he's doing now.'

They had arranged to meet in the same pub as the previous night.

Mike was there at 17:45. Chris came in a few minutes later while Mike was still at the bar.

"Better order four pints I guess," said Mike.

163

"OK Give, who else is coming?" Chris asked.

"Look behind you," answered Mike. Jerry and Brian had just walked in.

"Jerry, Brian," Chris beamed. "How the hell are you?"

"Spitfire OK for you two?" Mike asked.

They both just nodded as they were already talking with Chris.

"Make that four Spitfire please," said Mike to the barman.

They found a table and all had a good swig of their beer.

"So what are you doing now Jerry?" Mike asked.

"People need stuff, I find it for them. I use my superior purchasing acumen, marketing skills and contacts well enough to make a living."

"Sounds a bit dodgy to me," said Chris who was himself so well burdened with regulations.

"Oh no, all above board," said Jerry. "Well, mostly," he added more quietly. They all knew Jerry of old. He was a good guy who could always be relied on, but he tended to bend the rules a little to get the job done.

"What's the occasion that brings us all together?" asked Jerry.

"Isn't this enough?" Brian answered holding up his pint.

"It's good beer for sure, but what was the trigger?"

"Mike had some questions," said Brian, "and he thought we might be able to help."

"What questions?" Jerry asked. He was always tenacious and wanted all the information straight away.

They told him about Mike's brother and his project in Namibia and what they knew about the company Rossborough Electronics.

"Russians are usually bad news," said Jerry,."Where's this photo?"

"Sorry, my copy is in my rucksack back in my hotel room," said Mike.

Brian looked at his watch, "Sarah might not have left the office yet."

He dialled her mobile and took his phone outside so he could hear better. As he came back to the table his phone pinged. He opened the email and downloaded the photo.

"That's the guy," said Brian passing his phone over to Jerry. He looked at it for only a second and said, "That's Igor Solovyov."

They were stunned that he knew the face so well. "I've only seen him in person once but I don't particularly want to repeat the experience. He's pleasant enough on the surface but underneath, not nice. He has some very nasty connections."

"I think I can guess one," said Chris. "Vladimir Solovyov, too much of a coincidence that they both have the same surname, look so similar, and come up in the same context."

"Then as far as I'm concerned," said Jerry,."That puts this Vladimir guy in the same bad category as Igor."

Chris nodded.

"I phoned one of Tony's colleagues in Edinburgh today," said Mike. "I wanted to get an update and she mentioned that the project sponsorship came out of the blue. She also told me the sponsoring company is called Renshaw & Collier."

Chris turned sharply to Mike, "I looked up some of Vladimir's interests this morning and Renshaw & Collier was one of them. He owns it lock stock and barrel."

"So Vladimir's company is sponsoring your brother's project," said Brian. "And Igor is involved in a company that is screwing it up. That is very interesting."

Chapter 34

Mike was back in Tony's flat in Edinburgh. It was Monday morning and he had really enjoyed being with his old friends but he was still very concerned about his brother and the Russian angle. He decided he needed to talk to Laura so he picked up the phone.

"Hello Laura, It's Mike Collins. I've been doing some digging into your Rossborough Electronics and I'd like to discuss it with you. Face to face if possible."

"OK Mike, when?"

"How about I buy you lunch?"

"Sorry Mike, I'm busy but I'm free after about five o'clock, I'll need something to eat by then."

"Is there somewhere handy for you?"

"I'll be walking back towards town, there's the Old Bell Inn on Causewayside, do you know it?"

"I'll find it," said Mike. "About five thirty good for you?"

"Fine, I'll see you there."

The bar was fine for Mike's tastes: real ale, fairly traditional and a buzz of talk. He was there at 17:15, he ordered a pint of Pentland IPA and studied the menu. He stood at the bar where he could watch the front door. He guessed she'd come in that way even if there was another entrance. He was right, a good looking girl about the right age and with a confidant bearing walked in.

Mike stepped away from the bar and said with a question in his voice, "Laura?"

Laura answered, "Mike?"

"That's right," he answered. "Drink?"

"Yes please, I'm parched. If that's Pentland I'll have a pint of that and how did you know it was me?" she continued.

"I was just looking for the best looking woman to come through the door," he answered and ordered her drink. Laura gave him a wry smile.

They sat and Laura started right away with no small talk, "Something is worrying you and it must be important for you to want to discuss it only in person."

'This girl is very astute,' he thought. Mike didn't think that he had sounded worried on the phone but he knew that he was concerned. "OK," he said. "This is what I know so far."

After he had told his story Laura was looking concerned too.

"What can we do?" she asked, trying to think of something herself.

"Well, the long and the short seems to be that these Russians don't want the project to succeed, although they pretend the opposite," said Mike. "I think that the safest thing, for now, is to let them think they are succeeding with their devious plan."

"Then they won't think they need to do anything else to rubbish the project," she commented.

"Exactly my thinking," said Mike.

"Did Tony tell you about Plan B?" Laura asked.

"No," he replied. "So he has some contingency plan then?"

"Well, during our planning the technicians in the department thought that a lower tech solution would be better in a hostile desert environment. They suggested using Raspberry Pi micro computers and making a cheap relatively low tech backup solution, Plan B."

"It sounds as though your techs were right but maybe for a different hostile reason. Did you tell the sponsor about Plan B?"

"I haven't done yet."

"Well, I think telling them now is a definite no-no," said Mike with feeling.

"I agree one hundred percent after what you've told me," she replied. "I'm glad we talked now. I have to do the report to the Prof. at the end of the month and he sends a summary to the sponsor."

Chapter 35

The two metre parabola was sanded with electric rotary sanders while it was still mounted on the rotating baking tin. When the sanders had progressed to their finest paper, three thousand grit, the polishing started. Soft cloths and polishing compounds were used while the parabola was rotated. To reach the centre easily, sticks were used to hold the cloths. The polishing and sanding were both done by a pair of people opposite each other so as not to put stress on the rotation bearings. The polishing was a happy community activity with as many as five pairs of polishers at a time chatting cheerfully together over the bowl.

After the mirror was polished it was covered with soft cloth and the whole baking tin and bearing was lifted from underneath with timbers. One edge was lowered to the ground and it was tipped upright and rolled carefully away from the millstone to a pile of soft fine sand with more soft cloths on top.

The mirror was eased away from the cement and as it parted from its mould the edge dug deep into the sand and many hands grasped the edges to keep it stable. The baking tin was rolled away and then lowered onto the sand with the bearing pointing up to the sky. The two metre parabolic mirror was called Big Dish by the villagers and the name stuck. The Big Dish was gently laid, mirror side down, onto the cloths and soft sand. The larger protrusions on the back were filed and drilled ready to fix it to its frame.

On Christmas Eve, the Big Dish was in its frame and ready for testing. Almost all the villagers decided to stay on site for the Christmas celebrations and the population of the village was swelled by an influx of family members.

169

Truck loads of provisions had been brought for the celebrations. The management team turned its attention from work to organising the festivities and helping the Minister prepare for the Christmas Day service.

Progress had been excellent in the preceding months. All one hundred glass mirrors were on the hill in frames and the Big Dish was ready for trials. The villagers were proficient at all the processes, from steering the heliostats right through to polishing.

On Christmas Eve a good lunch was prepared. Towards the end of the meal the Chief spoke quietly to one of his men who went to pass on instructions to others.

The management team members were sitting together and thinking of getting some jobs done when Chief Daniel said, "Please sit with me for a time, my people have something to show you."

Clara, Tony and the Minister looked at each other quizzically. "What do you have up your sleeve father?"

"Have patience daughter," he replied.

Smoke and Spark were uncovering something on the stone where the Big Dish was mounted but from where they were sitting they couldn't see what it was. The villagers and visitors sat or stood around in anticipation.

After a few minutes Chief Daniel stood and boomed to the assembly. "My people, we have done many things in our history and these last months may crown all those past achievements, but we will nor forget our past. Once we were a proud nation of warriors and today we fight as warriors still for our whole country to create energy and employment for everyone." He paused and then continued with even more volume. "We will not forget that we were and still are warriors!"

170

At those last words there was movement on the skyline of the hill, flashes of light could be seen, then the flashes disappeared and the whole skyline became alive with a hundred men in traditional costume carrying shields and marching together into view. They came closer and stopped in a line divided by the heliostats on the hill. At a gesture from their chief, each man held his shield high and removed the covering and then planted one tip on the ground in front of him.

At another gesture, starting at one end of the line, one by one the shields were tilted forwards to reflect the sun's energy onto the Big Dish. The crucible in front of it heated rapidly and after a few minutes Smoke raised his hand and the shields angled skywards again. He and Spark skimmed the dross and then lifted and poured the melt.

"This is an awesome power which we wield," bellowed the Chief. "And we must use it wisely."

There were cheers and chants from the people for several minutes then Chief Daniel spoke again.

"Now we will continue our Christmas celebrations with more singing and beer."

True to his command this happened to everyone's pleasure. The casting itself was forgotten by the majority in the revelry but later in the afternoon Clara asked her father what it was.

"Patience my girl," he said.

What she didn't know was that when the casting had cooled a team of villagers would take it to sand and polish it.

In the morning the whole company was busy setting up for the Christmas Service. At nine everything was ready, Chief Daniel had asked the Minister if he could say something before they started.

171

The Minister announced, "Chief Daniel will now say a few words."

The Chief came to the front of the congregation and said as he turned to the Minister, "This congregation is a family and you have ministered to us both spiritually and, in some cases, medically." There were widespread murmurs of approval. "As is the custom in many cultures, we would like to present you with a small gift."

He signalled to two of the ladies in the front of the congregation who were wearing flowing brightly coloured dresses, they stepped forward and the first produced from behind her voluminous skirts a bundle of cloth which she placed on one end of the table, which was their altar. The second lady produced another smaller round bundle and placed it in the centre of the table.

The Minister looked bemused.

"Well, unwrap them," said the Chief.

The Minister carefully took the cloth from the round object and revealed a shining dome with a hole in the centre. He was still looking bemused, a significant number of the congregation smiled broadly.

"The other one," prompted the Chief.

As he unwrapped the second gift its shape became clear to him and he grasped it and raised the gleaming mirrored cross in front of him. The whole congregation erupted in applause and cheers.

"This is a wonderful, beautiful thing," he beamed. "It will be a glorious centrepiece for our worship."

It was eighty centimetres high and weighed well over ten kilograms. He looked around for a place to put it.

"It fits here," whispered the Chief indicating the base in the centre of his altar. The Minister set it in the base and stood back with a smile from ear to ear.

172

The service started with hymns and gospel songs and an old testament reading by Clara. Tony had been cajoled into reading from the New Testament, he had been nervous about doing it but afterwards was pleased to have done it.

After the service the congregation set their minds to their dinner and some drinks. The Christmas festivities went on until late in the evening so the following morning was not an early start for anyone.

The extended families who had come for Christmas gradually left the village and thoughts turned to the future.

The management team were sitting together drinking coffee.

"Do you think it is fair to say that we have proved the project concept?" Tony asked them.

"We still have a lot of work to do," answered Clara. "But we have definitely proved the concept. We wanted to set up a Solar Furnace which could melt aluminium scrap: success. Use the aluminium to make more mirrors: success. Make some other items with the aluminium: success.

"We are confident we can make another solar furnace and that we can produce other items."

"I agree," said Tony. "Our vision was to provide more benefits to the country, is that what you mean by a lot more work?"

She nodded and the Chief joined the discussion. "Many industries use heat for their processes, the trick will be to tailor the solar furnace to those applications. For example, if they don't need such high temperatures."

"The solar ovens we've been using here don't get to such high temperatures," added the Minister. "But with an abundance of mirrors we could make better and cheaper ovens."

173

As they drank more coffee they added more ideas to their list of uses for the mirrors. The Chief was keen to do something to generate cash flow and suggested making souvenirs. The Minister took this up and told them that he had contacts in churches and religious shops around the country and proposed making small crosses to be sold there.

"And maybe if that's successful they can be exported," said Clara.

"Now that would be very popular with the politicians" added the Chief. "But the big prize would be electricity generation at a low cost."

"In Namibia we have a limited power grid and that makes big power plants an issue. A good solution would be if we can make smaller low cost power plants," added Clara and so the discussion continued.

Chapter 36

Laura was in her lab on 27 December, she didn't take a long break at Christmas, just the statutory holidays. Her mobile rang, and she knew the number.

"Hi Tony, did you have a good Christmas?"

"It was great thanks Laura, very different but great. I called because of the monthly report, are you OK to write some stuff down?"

"Sure, just give me a second to get sat down with a pen and paper. OK, what's been happening?"

He told her about Plan C, using manual steering for everything so far. He explained setting up the glass mirrors and using the small parabola to make one metre square mirrors, about making the two metre parabola and then making the shields and the cross.

He gave her a quick rundown of what they had planned for the first quarter of the new year but said not to include that.

"That's great progress Tony, I'll get the report ready for the Prof. before the end of the month but I don't think the timing is critical; he'll be away till at least the second of January. Look, I have a meeting can I call you tomorrow?"

"Make it after six in the evening my time and I'll make sure the phone is on," he answered.

"Great," she said, "got to dash."

She didn't have to dash, she didn't know what to do. If all this information got back to the Russian sponsor she didn't know what would happen. While she was sitting worrying about it she suddenly realised that Mike was the only person she could really talk to about it.

She called him, no preamble, "Mike, I have to write the monthly report and I can't do it. Can we meet?"

"Sure," he answered, he could tell she was worried. They arranged to meet that evening at the same pub as before.

Mike had the drinks at a table before she arrived.

Laura sat down took a big swig of her pint and launched. "They have done so much stuff it's unbelievable and I don't know what I can write up and I don't want to lie in the report and I don't want to lie to Tony."

She stopped and took breath to try and calm herself.

Mike took her hands which were shaking a little and looked steadily into her eyes, he could tell that she had grasped the severity of the situation. "We will figure it out," he said calmly. "There is always a solution and we will find it."

She felt as though she was drawing his strength through his hands and those steady eyes. "We don't have very long," she said, growing gradually calmer.

"We have all evening," he said. "That should be plenty of time."

"I hope so," she smiled at him. "Do you have a plan?"

"First we will write a list of all the key facts. Second we get food and eat it. Third we look at the list and think hard. OK?"

"OK," she said. "I had no idea I was so up tight about this until I let it all out just now. Thank you."

They wrote their list and ate the food and felt a bit stronger when they started to tackle the hard part, the thinking.

It was late when they sat back a little from their scribblings and considered their conclusions.

"Some things I think we've agreed," said Mike. "We have to tell Tony what is going on, at least as much as we know.

We can't report on the real progress that they have made. We have to warn him that Russians are involved and they can get rough."

"I think we need to make sure that Chief Daniel knows about it too," she added,. "Because if there is a threat it could be a threat to the whole village."

"Agreed," said Mike. They discussed more details and made a few more notes.

"It looks pretty obvious now," she concluded. "Thanks Mike, you have been great."

"You have done nearly all of this," he said. She wanted to give him a big hug but it made her think of Tony again and she said, "You do want to look after your little brother don't you?"

"When we were kids I used to look out for Tony. Like at school. But I haven't been around much for the last ten years and he's done all right."

"Tell me about school," said Laura. She wanted something to think about other than their present predicament.

"You sure?" Mike asked. She nodded.

"Well, there was a bully in the upper sixth called Mason. He liked to push the smaller kids about. I was two years below him and Tony was two more below me.

"One day this big guy started on Tony. I wasn't about to see my little brother roughed up by a big hulk like Mason so I told him to leave him alone.

"He'd lifted Tony up by his blazer lapels so he just dropped him and rounded on me. He swung a big punch but I grabbed his hand and judo threw him over onto his back. All the wind was knocked out of him."

"Go on," she said.

"There isn't much more. He didn't know I was in the judo club so he wasn't excepting someone smaller and younger to throw him. Then a teacher arrived and we all went to our classes."

"Was the big guy cured of bullying?"

"No, he tossed a first year onto the playground and broke his arm and was excluded, permanently. That was before A Levels so I don't know what happened to him after that."

They walked back to her flat and agreed to talk to Tony together the next evening and parted, without any hugging.

At six the following evening, Mike and Laura were in a seminar room in her department. Laura called Tony's satellite phone.

"Hi Laura, Clara is here with me," said Tony,."How's things?"

"Hello Tony, I have Mike with me and we have a lot to talk about."

"This sounds a bit ominous," answered Tony,

"I believe it is," said Mike. "We have been doing some digging into the backgrounds of your sponsor and Rossborough Electronics and they aren't as you might think."

"Well, I thought there was something up at Rossborough Electronics but Renshaw & Collier, that's a bit more difficult to get."

"Let's talk about Rossborough Electronics first," said Laura. "Mike you tell him what you have found out."

"Here we go," said Mike. "Rossborough Electronics has been a reliable reputable company with a good stock market performance for years. Recently they have been having big problems. A new boss, many customers not happy and leaving them, and the stock price going down like a lead balloon."

"And we are one of the customers suffering," commented Tony. "Why are they turning bad?"

"The new boss," said Mike. "He's just a money man and knows nothing about running the business and he has disturbed the whole staff and many have left. I think that someone has made a fortune from insider trading and selling short on the stock."

Tony asked what that meant and Mike explained.

"And that's not the worst," continued Mike,."This new boss is a Russian and his brother is the money behind Renshaw & Collier, your sponsor. I'm pretty sure he is the one who has made the stock market killing."

"How did you find out all this?" asked Tony.

"I have some ex-service friends in London, they helped a lot. There is more," said Mike. "The vast majority of the money that Renshaw & Collier makes is from the oil and gas industry so they have vested interest in the failure of renewable projects like yours."

"So why did they sponsor us?" asked Tony.

"To have control," said Mike. "They have done the same with other projects. They finance a promising idea, make a good public relations story and then quietly the project fades away. The money they spend on that is a drop in the ocean to them."

"This explains a lot doesn't it Tony," said Laura.

"It does indeed and you are telling me all this now because you are concerned about telling Renshaw & Collier about all the positive work," said Tony.

"Exactly," said Mike. "And I'm more than concerned. When I said that some other projects were made to fade away, actually some of the people in the projects were made to fade away."

Laura looked sharply at Mike,"You didn't tell me that!"

"You already had enough to worry about yesterday without that angle," answered Mike.

"What do you mean, fade away?" Tony asked.

"Bribery, blackmail, accidents, these people are ruthless," said Mike.

Clara had been scowling at the phone, "Tony, we need to bring my father in on this."

"Definitely," said Mike.

"I think you are right," said Tony. "We'll go and talk to him now and call you back."

Laura and Mike talked and drank coffee for at least an hour and he told her more details from the investigations. Her phone rang.

"Hello Laura, I have Chief Daniel with me, Clara and also the Minister but I don't know if they will be able to hear easily."

"Hi Tony," said Laura. "I have Mike with me and he can hear you OK."

"The four of us are a sort of management team here on site, the roles evolved and we work together," explained Tony.

"Have you briefed them on the situation?" Mike asked.

"Yes," said Tony. "And I think I should introduce them. Chief Daniel is obviously the chief of the people, but he's a lot more than that. Clara is a post Doc at NUST who has been involved in everything technical here. And our Minister who is also our medic. He came to conduct a Sunday service, and he's been here ever since."

Mike and Laura were a bit concerned about a larger group knowing about this situation when the Chief came on the line.

"This is Chief Daniel. First I would like to thank you both for the work you have done, and thank you Mike specifically for the SatPhones, we would be in the dark about this issue without them. I gather that these phones use encryption so we should be fairly secure in our conversation about this situation. Can I name it the Russian Connection for want of a better description?"

Mike recognised the authority in the voice and replied, "That Sir, is a good name for this situation, I believe that Moscow is driving all this."

"I believe the same," said the Chief. "Our first concern is the safety of all the people here and secondly I do not want these Russians to succeed in destroying this project. If they are successful here they will use it as a platform to disrupt other projects in order to maintain my country's dependance on imported energy. Everyone may not be aware of this but since the split up of the USSR, Russia's influence in Africa has waned, that is until recent years. Russia is now pushing to increase its influence again and has a foothold in most of the less democratic states."

After this mini dissertation the Chief asked Mike. "What do you think we should do?"

"We need to prevent these Russian brothers from knowing that you have made so much progress," said Mike. "And somehow we have to protect your people and the project if possible."

"Keeping the Russians in the dark may be difficult," said the Chief. "But I do have some ideas about how to protect my people here in the desert."

"I think," said the Minister. "That it will never be one hundred percent possible to protect the project here, however it should be possible to protect the technology and the essence of it."

"What do you mean Minister?" Tony asked.

181

"Well," he answered. "An attack on this site could do a great deal of harm and if it was severe enough, maybe stop the project."

"We could just start again," said Carla forcefully.

"Yes," said the Minister. "If all the key people are safe, if funding continues and if there is a political will in the country to continue in the face of adversity." Everyone was quiet and realised that he was talking about real scenarios.

"However," went on the Minister. "If the project is spread out, dispersed in relatively small units, then even if one was completely destroyed, others could continue."

"I think this wise Minister is a great asset," whispered Mike to Laura. She nodded.

"This is indeed a good proposal," said the Chief. "We are grateful, as always, for your wise council."

This was reiterated by all and Tony was already thinking how to implement it.

"The key things we must protect are the parabolas," said Tony.

"And some mirrors," added Clara.

"The key things to protect," interrupted Mike,."Are people and particularly Clara and Tony, and not just because he's my brother. If someone wants to destroy this project, and yes they will try to destroy the equipment, but their priority will be to remove the key people driving it."

"I think that you may be right Mike," said Chief Daniel. "I will implement some security here immediately. Tony and Clara, you will need to be especially vigilant while you plan the dispersal of the project."

"What about the monthly report?" asked Clara.

Laura had been remarkably quiet but spoke up now, "Mike and I will contrive something convincing and call you tomorrow evening so we all have the same public story."

"Thanks Laura," said Tony. "Does anyone want to add anything?"

There were a few moments of silence, then the Chief said, "This has been most informative and useful, I think we are done for now and we need to get on with our work, so thank you all and goodnight."

Tony hung up.

"That's a good team out there," said Mike.

"Not a bad team here," said Laura smiling at Mike.

That night Chief Daniel chose twenty-four of his men as lookouts. He divided them into day and night shifts. Each shift with six teams of two. One shift was to go out the following morning and find six positions on high points around the village as far away as possible but still in sight of the village. Each team also had to be able to see the team either side of them. They would take their mirror shields and practice signalling to each other and to the village. The other team would join them mid morning and also practice signalling.

Both teams would return to the village at midday and then repeat the process at dusk to try signalling at night.

When the teams returned during the evening Chief Daniel sat with them and checked how successful they had been and discussed what equipment and supplies each team would need. Daytime signalling was fairly easy and nighttime was OK as long as there was some moon which there was almost every day of the month.The Chief didn't plan to deploy them yet as the risk was low but he wanted them ready when the time came.

The next morning the Chief himself set out in one of the trucks with some more of his men to locate a new site to set up a furnace. He had studied maps of the area and had a good idea where he was going. He planned to keep the location secret.

In the afternoon he returned with only one of his men, the others had stayed at the new site to mark it out.

The route that the trucks had been using to bring supplies to the Village had become a well worn and compacted track, they all thought that was the most likely way any undesirables would approach so they set about devising an early warning system for that route.

In Edinburgh Laura and Mike had collated all the difficulties that the project had encountered into a fairly bland report. They called Tony's satellite phone the following evening as planned to run it by Tony and Clara.

"That sounds good," said Tony after Laura had read it. "Well, it's bad really but it's all we want to say. The Prof. won't be impressed but it will be interesting to see the reaction from Renshaw & Collier."

Chapter 37

The management team sat together with beers in hand after eating in the evening. The Chief began the discussion.

"I don't think we have to worry about outside interference for some time, it will come when some products or project results become obvious outside this village or when the Russian brothers get suspicious about the monthly reports."

There was general agreement, they planned a number of products. They made aluminium crosses to hang around the neck on a leather thong; the prototypes had been chunky, twelve millimetres in section ten centimetres long, but everyone agreed they looked and felt good.

Various shapes and sizes of ingots and slugs had been made for specific manufacturers who would use them for their processes.

"We have a lot of ideas for further work," said Tony.

"We've sketched out a new design for a solar oven," added Clara.

"There are also discussions to be had about electricity generation," said Tony, "but that's for the future. There has been some good practical progress here. Smoke and Spark have found locations where the desert sand is really fine. Smoke says it's ideal for casting."

"With a few magical additions of his own I think," added Clara.

"What we really need to do next," said Tony, "is get started working on the Plan B. The Heliostat control system." Given all the information that they now had about their sponsor and Rossborough Electronics they had more or less given up on Plan A although Laura kept the university pestering them.

Tony, Clara and Liode worked together on one heliostat with a Raspberry Pi microcomputer, an interface and small model motors. For a power supply at the heliostat, Liode rigged a car battery with a solar panel to keep it charged. They now had all the parts and they began getting it all together.

Mike and Laura phoned towards the end of January to discuss progress and the monthly report.

"I've just experienced my first desert rain," said Tony. "A massive thunderstorm but it didn't last long."

"Is all your electrical equipment OK?" Laura asked.

"It's fine," answered Tony. "But I had to do a bit of scrabbling about to get everything covered."

"How about your laptops Tony, are they all backed up in at least in a couple of places?" Mike asked.

"They are OK," answered Tony. "But I admit we do need to be a lot more rigorous with the backups."

Laura chipped in, "I'll set up a laptop the same as your's Tony, and send it to you."

"I suggest you copy all of your files onto that laptop," added Mike. "And make sure that only what you need gets transferred. No viruses or anything else, and make some hard drive backups and ship them back to Windhoek."

The backups were agreed and so was the January report.

Two weeks later Tony received the new laptop and a number of solid state hard drives. They were in a small Peli Case which was inside a larger one plus a couple of padlocks. There was a note inside;

'These should keep things safe, Laura'.

It was from Laura but Tony could sense Mike's influence. He got to work immediately making backups of everything while another thunderstorm was hammering on the outside of his tent.

He decided to put the laptop in the small Peli Case and send it to the new secret site which they had agreed to call Site 2. He also shipped a complete backup of his laptop drive back to NUST.

They sent the small parabolic mirror and a hundred one metre square aluminium mirrors to Site 2.

Liode was making fairly regular trips back to the university for supplies and to take the monthly reports. He made a point of being in and out as quickly as possible and only exchanged smalltalk with his fellow technicians. He didn't want to meet the Professor or any of the lecturers who were sure to ask difficult questions.

One evening while they were relaxing, Tony said to the Chief, "I think we should make another Big Dish, but I really want to get on with the control systems."

"Good plan," said the Chief with a smile.

"What plan?" Tony said surprised.

The Chief laughed, "You get on with the electronics and I organise the Big Dish."

Tony looked a bit doubtful.

"This is what the project is all about Tony," said the Chief. "You have brought the technology, seeded the ideas and the enthusiasm and now the people will continue. They will make some mistakes but I would only worry about someone getting hurt. However I have the Minister to make sure that sort of mistake doesn't happen."

"You are right of course," said Tony. "I have to start letting go. It's always hard for technical people to let their babies go."

"It's not only technical people," said the Chief.

Chapter 38

JJ was in his stylish fortieth floor office at Renshaw & Collier high up over London. The view over the city was calm and relaxing, as was the February report he was reading, at least at first sight that was how it appeared. However as he thought more about it he became just a little concerned. The Solar project reports for December and January had all shown little progress and this one for February showed much the same. Things were going according to his plan but he didn't sense the dejection that he expected from the scientists. He called Sellick & Arrowsmith to see if they knew any more.

"Good morning Mr Sellick," opened JJ. "Have you any recent information from the Solar Project?"

"Not since the project leader was in Windhoek, I believe that their desert site has no internet connection."

"That's quite likely I suppose," said JJ. "I am sending you the monthly progress reports. At first glance they look OK but I am becoming uneasy with the lack of progress. Please look at them and then find out what is happening on the ground."

"Understood," said Mr Sellick and the call ended.

Mr Sellick called Phil Arrowsmith.

"Phil," he said. "We need Miss M again, I hope she isn't involved in anything critical."

"Nothing we can't rearrange George," he answered. "When do you need her?"

"Monday morning 09:00 my office for her briefing, thanks Phil."

Maria called her Mum as usual on the Friday evening but as usual she couldn't tell her anything about her work, and she didn't have any idea yet what Monday would bring.

"Hello Mum, how's things?"

"Oh, hello darling, we are getting along just fine. Dad is in the bar serving a few locals as usual. I'll be going in when I hear it get a bit busier. How are things with you, job going OK?"

"Yes thanks Mum, everything here is fine."

"Will you be home for Easter this year darling?" her Mum asked in the way that mums do.

"Sorry I don't know yet, my work is interesting but I would enjoy a holiday."

"Well, your room is here whenever you want to come."

"Thanks Mum, I'll call you next Friday unless I'm really tied up. Love you."

"And you darling, bye."

Chapter 39

A party of wildlife and landscape photographers arrived at Cape Town International Airport. They hired two Toyota Pick Up trucks at the airport and drove north. A local agent met them en route and provided some more equipment. All the new gear was checked over carefully before stacking it in the trucks with their original camera cases. They set off north again and joined the N7. It took them seven hours to reach the Namibian border, which they crossed without incident.

During that same week Maria flew from Frankfurt into the international airport near Windhoek.

The immigration officer asked, "What is the purpose of your visit to Namibia Miss Bassett?"

"I am here to visit a project which my company is sponsoring. I work in the new projects department and have come to see first hand if there is any more assistance my company can give."

He stamped her passport, "Have a good visit Miss Bassett."

"Thank you," she said with a smile and went to get a taxi.

From her room at the Hilton she called Mr Sellick at S&A headquarters.

"Hello Miss M, I hope your journey was comfortable. We have contacted Professor Hamutenya at NUST and he has sent a message to the site that you will be visiting. The message has gone with the supply vehicle so they should be expecting you. You need to liaise with the University to travel on the next supply vehicle to the site. Then it's up to you. Any questions?"

"No Mr S, everything is clear. Thank you."

Liode arrived back at the village on a Wednesday evening with supplies and news.

"I am to bring a visitor from Renshaw & Collier on my next trip," he announced to the management team.

Chief Daniel was the first to break the silence. "I believe that it was only a matter of time before the company would become suspicious. We must be as polite as possible and give away as little as possible."

"I am worried," said the Tony. "That we won't be able to conceal our progress."

"I am also concerned," added the Minister. "It will be obvious that we have not been idle. And with so many people here there may be some loose talk. It is good that your colleague Laura has continued to pester Rossborough Electronics to produce a good control board, which we are eagerly anticipating, but we need to remove all trace of your Raspberry Pi Plan B."

"We can blame the rains for some of our lack of positive reporting in the last couple of months," said Clara. "Not enough sun."

"I suggest that we ensure everything we need to for the future is at Site 2," said the Chief. "Including Plan B, and there can be no mention of Plan B or Site 2. These are key."

"We will need to keep our visitor occupied somehow," said Tony.

"I think that it is now time for us to demonstrate some progress," said Chief Daniel. "We should demonstrate melting aluminium with the manual glass mirrors, we will be demonstrating what we have achieved during the last few weeks, since the last report, which of course had no mention of this. Since we are so new to this," he smiled. "It will not be a very convincing demonstration but we will prove it is at least possible."

"We need to get the small parabola back here and take the two metre one to Site 2," said Tony.

"A very good point," said the Chief. "Also I will speak to my people about maintaining their traditions."

They all looked blankly at the Chief so he continued. "They will revert to their traditional dress and the vast majority will forget that they ever spoke English. We will arrange demonstrations of traditional dancing and singing for our visitor and also considerable quantities of our traditional beer."

The Minister grinned. "Of course. To refuse to participate would offend the locals. I'll ensure that our visitor is made aware of that as I'm one of the few with some English."

"When is he coming?" Tony asked.

"The techs told me that it's a she," said Liode. "And I'm to pick her up on Friday. She is supposed to fly in today."

"So we have tomorrow, Thursday and most of Friday to prepare," said Clara. "Two and a half days, it should be enough."

It was hard work but they made it happen. All the technical equipment they had discussed was moved to Site 2 together with all their spare provisions. They had to transfer a lot of provisions as they didn't know how long the team at Site 2 would be on their own. Liode and Tony each took a truck to NUST on Friday morning. They left early in order to make it back in good time and took two trucks to be able to re-provision thoroughly.

At the university Liode organised the loading while Tony went to find the visitor. He had been told she was with Professor Hamutenya.

192

When Tony was ushered into the Professor's office he stared in amazement at Maria.

The professor spoke immediately, "Let me introduce you, this is Miss Maxine Bassett, Dr Tony Collins,"

"Hello Tony," she said putting her hand forward to shake his. "It's so nice to see you again."

"You know each other!" said the professor in surprise.

"We met in Edinburgh last year," she said pleasantly. "Purely by chance, I had to leave again on business before we really got to know each other well."

"Yes, that's right," said Tony. "It was a lot cooler then." He couldn't think of anything else to say, he was somewhat taken aback.

"I know you will be eager to get back on the road Tony," said the Professor. "So I've taken the liberty of getting some sandwiches and coffee sent up here."

"That's very thoughtful," said Maria. "I gather it's a long drive."

"It'll take us all afternoon," said Tony, "but luckily, there won't be much traffic." He was regaining his composure.

They talked generally about Africa and specifically Namibia over lunch but not much about the project.

Maxine sat in the second truck, with Tony, of course. They chatted about their work but Tony was much more inquisitive at this meeting than he had been in Edinburgh. She explained that she had moved role from HR into New Projects, this was her first on site visit and she was delighted to have been sent to Africa. She wasn't sure if this was just chance or if someone in the office had heard her mention that she had met him. Anyway she was very happy to be there.

"I didn't know you worked for our sponsor," he said

"I guess it just never came up that I worked for Renshaw & Collier. It's one of those big companies that nobody's ever heard of. They invest in all sorts of things, from pharmaceuticals to Eco. projects."

He noticed that she didn't mention petrochemicals. He explained that they had a village on site providing the manpower and some skills for the project.

They arrived before dusk and Tony introduced Maria to the management team. He started with the Chief.

"Maxine, this is Chief Daniel, these are his people around us."

"Welcome to our humble village," he said holding out his big hand. The Chief was surprised how firm and strong her handshake was. He normally liked that in people but this person was a potential threat so he was reserving his judgement about her.

"Maxine," continued the Chief. "Let me introduce you to some other key people here. Dr Collins you have already met, this is Dr Bella from NUST, which I believe you visited in Windhoek."

"Please call me Clara," she said as she shook hands.

"It's a pleasure to meet you Clara," said Maria.

"And this," continued the Chief, "is our Minister."

"Bless you for coming all this way to see us," he said. "You can call me anything you like but most people just say Minister."

"Thank you for your welcome Minister," she answered. "And thank you all, it is a wonderful opportunity to come here and see your spectacular country."

"We have prepared a tent for you to rest and get a little privacy when you wish," said the Chief. "We usually all share the same meal together, it will be ready in about half an hour. Do you require any special food?"

194

"You are very kind," she answered. "I will eat whatever is provided."

Two ten year old children picked up her bags and carried them to her tent. They had strict instructions to not speak or understand English. Being inquisitive ten year olds, the soft bag received considerable prodding on the way but the more interesting things were in the aluminium flight case which was locked.

Maria was happy to get into her small tent so she could check her luggage, particularly the contents of her flight case. The contents included a camera, a laptop, a satellite phone and a small GPS unit. She tested out the satellite phone by calling her Mum as she normally did on a Friday evening.

While she was in her tent, Tony told the others in the management team, with some embarrassment, that he had met Maxine before, briefly, the previous year in Edinburgh.

They were all surprised by this, not least Clara!

"When I met her in Edinburgh she was working in HR but she only mentioned that it was a big corporation. I now find it was Renshaw & Collier and that she has transferred to the New Projects department."

"How did you meet her?" asked Clara, who was interested on more than one level.

"It was a chance meeting while I was photographing an early morning scene in the Meadows. It's a public open space with grass and trees. She was running for exercise, but now I'm doubting that it was just chance."

"I am very sceptical about that," said the Minister. "And I don't believe in coincidences, unless they are the result of divine intervention and I don't think that's the case here."

"I agree completely," said the Chief. "In short, she is spying on us for Renshaw & Collier."

Reluctantly Tony had to agree with him.

Despite their private discussions they entertained their visitor politely and with enthusiasm that evening.

The following day her head ached and she didn't feel on top form, 'that local beer must be stronger than it seemed' she thought, but she had work to do.

She spent the day taking photographs and asking questions about the project.

Tony reiterated what had been in the February report, mainly that they were waiting eagerly for Rossborough Electronics to send new control boards. He went on to describe that around the time of that last report, they had started trying to do some work manually with the mirrors they had brought with them.

"I would love to see that," said Maxine.

"It is too late today to organise another test," he said, and explained that safety was an issue because of the high powers involved, so they would organise it for the beginning of the week. In fact they had contrived to tell her late in the day about the manual trials and as the next day was Sunday, there would be no demonstration then either.

On Saturday evening she wrote a short report, copied her photographs onto her laptop, selecting the ones which showed the functions and layout of the site. With all the files encrypted and zipped she sent them to her HQ using her satellite phone data.

She knew she wouldn't get much more information until Monday so she resigned herself to enjoy the hospitality on Saturday night and Sunday.

The villagers entertained Maxine, and themselves, in their traditional way with food, beer and singing and dancing.

The Minister insisted that she attend the Sunday service and preached on Isaiah Chapter 35. He held up his Bible,

196

"This is the Good News," he declared.

He opened it and read powerfully,

"The desert will rejoice!"

'Very appropriate,' thought the Chief.

"*The desert will sing and shout for joy,*" the Minister read and then continued with the rest of the chapter.

"I want us to think about verse eight," he added.

"There will be a highway there called 'The Road of Holiness.'

"No sinner will ever travel that road;

"no fools will mislead those who follow it."

When he preached about them all being on a road and that they would not succumb to being mislead, Maria had a feeling which she had never experienced before. She felt that he was looking directly at her and right into her heart. She concentrated on breathing steadily and put the thought out of her mind.

She had to admit though, that he was a powerful orator. He seemed to be surrounded by a sort of peace and strength.

She had realised some other things too: Chief Daniel was a force to be reckoned with and Tony and Clara seemed to have a bond which made them much stronger together.

On Monday a demonstration of melting aluminium was staged for Maria. Tony explained what would happen, although with all her previous investigations she already had a pretty good idea.

"The principle is very simple," said Tony. "The square glass mirrors, the heliostats, on the slope up there are in frames which were designed to be easily made with basic materials and a bit of welding skill. They can swivel in any direction to reflect the sun's rays. We point them all at the parabolic mirror, which we made in Edinburgh, and it focuses all the energy onto the black crucible."

"Is the parabola fixed in position?" she asked.

"Yes, after its initial adjustment it should remain in the same orientation." Tony answered. "We have put weights under each heliostat so it points up when not in use and can't accidentally reflect energy where we don't want it."

Chief Daniel bellowed something in his own language to his people and a group of forty men walked up to the heliostats and stood in pairs beside twenty of them.

"Why not use all the mirrors?" Maria asked.

"It's hard enough to get them to all work together manually and we think it would be too dangerous to use more people, that's why we so desperately need the electronic solution."

Chief Daniel bellowed more commands and the process started.

One at a time the mirrors came down to point the sun's rays on the parabola. The accuracy of the steerers was nothing like as good as it had been previously and Tony was worried that something or someone would get burned. Eventually all twenty mirrors were more or less in the right positions and the crucible of crushed aluminium cans started to heat. Some of the mirrors drifted off course and the process took much longer than it needed to. Eventually the Chief ordered the mirrors up and Smoke went to pour the melt.

They deliberately made it look very amateurish and haphazard but eventually the result was a flat slab of aluminium which was then left to cool.

"Our objective is to prove that we can make mirrors or other aluminium parts to start up a sustainable industry here," Tony explained to Maria.

"That looks as though it will need a lot of work to make it into a mirror,"

"I think you are right Maxine," he answered looking a little despondent.

While she was in her tent that evening writing up her notes and sending her report to HQ, the management team were sitting together.

"We all know she is here to inform Renshaw & Collier about us," said Clara. "But she seems quite nice really."

Tony was surprised to hear that from Clara who had been eyeing Maria suspiciously, particularly when she was with him.

"She appears quite thorough and professional," said the Chief. "It is unfortunate that she is on the wrong side, as it were."

"Nobody is all good or all bad," said the Minister. "And it is not for us to judge others only to try to do the right thing ourselves."

The following morning Maxine approached the management team who were discussing the plans for the day.

"I'm sorry to say I will be leaving tomorrow," she announced. "I have enjoyed being in the desert and you have been generous with your hospitality and your company." She smiled warmly at them.

"That is a great shame," said the Chief, half believing it. "It has been a pleasure to host such a charming lady."

He's laying it on a bit thick thought Clara.

"Do you need us to take you back to Windhoek?" Tony asked.

"Thank you but no, my plans have been changed. I am to go to our office in Cape Town, then later back to the UK. Someone is coming to pick me up," she explained.

The expressions of the management team were all quizzical.

When she saw that she added, "I received the message on my satellite phone, I suppose I didn't mention that I had one."

I wonder what else she hasn't mentioned thought the Minister.

That night Tony and Clara had gone to their favourite spot over the brow of the hill to sit together and look at the stars.

"I still don't know what to make of her," said Clara. "But I'm relieved that she's going."

"I feel the same," said Tony as they snuggled together.

Chapter 40

On that same evening the group of photographers were sitting around their camp relaxing. Two of their number had just returned from near the top of a high dune observing Chief Daniel's lookouts through night vision scopes.

"It's all quiet as usual up there Mr K."

"Good, get settled down and pay attention," said Ken Heaton their leader.

They had moved to that location on the same night that Maria had arrived in the village and had been observing since then. They were well trained and cautious and had seen the Chief's lookouts with their high powered binoculars well before they were seen themselves.

"Our insider is leaving tomorrow," said Mr K,."HQ have processed all the intel and we now have a good map of the site. We know the two people that are to be extracted are a couple, and they like to visit a certain hill in the evening for a bit of fun. That location is just out of sight of the village for obvious reasons. They do not know that we are coming so we will approach them quietly with minimum fuss but without them seeing our faces. We are then to deliver them to another team who will transport them safely to their destination, which incidentally, I don't know.

"Also, I do not know the other team, only that they have been tasked by the same client as ours."

"So they aren't one of our S&A teams then? " asked his second in command, Mr F.

"Not as far as I know, and as we are in Africa with no backup we will treat them with caution. Understood?"

"Yes Mr K," the three replied.

"Why are we extracting these two?" Mr F asked.

"I've been informed that they are in danger but they do not know it or do not accept it, hence the covert rescue."

"What if they don't want to come Mr K?" Mr F asked.

"We must take them anyway for their own safety; silently and with minimum force," their leader answered. "Now, this is a simple radio transmitter," he said, showing them a device much like a small VHF radio. "The leader of the second team has been issued with a compatible receiver.

"Before we make the final approach to the couple I will send a signal on this device and the other team will provide a distraction. The plan is that our couple will turn to see what is happening and we will approach them without being seen. Any questions?"

"What if they don't turn away Mr K?"

"We will be wearing these bandanas over our faces," he produced them from his pack. "They are light but not see through, we will be well enough disguised."

"Not as scary as black balaclavas," said Mr F.

Chapter 41

The village said a goodbye to Maxine with traditional dancing which included a war dance from the men using spears and shields, not the aluminium ones which were well concealed in individual huts and tents.

The Chief spoke to Maxine after the entertainment, "I hope you have seen enough of the project, if you have more questions we will be happy to give more information and if we make some progress I would like to be able to tell you about it, I would be very grateful if you would give me your satellite phone number so we can contact you,"

He now knew she had a satellite phone and not giving him the number would have seemed suspicious so she answered, "Of course Chief Daniel."

A Land Rover with South African registration plates arrived just after eleven in the morning and Maria left.

"That was an interesting display of African culture," said Tony to the Chief with question in his voice.

"We have borrowed a few things from other peoples to broaden the appeal of our demonstrations. The spears and shields are Zulu, they are the main addition. In the past we have done displays for groups of tourists. It has helped to supplement the income of my people. It also has the effect of making us seem rather primitive and unsophisticated which, I believe, in this instance is beneficial."

"Also, I wonder why you wanted her SatPhone number?" asked Tony.

"That was the Minister's request and I have found that his wishes are to be ignored at one's peril, whether they come from divine inspiration or not."

As they sat together in the evening the Minister was uncharacteristically introspective.

"What is on your mind Minister?" asked Chief Daniel.

He snapped out of his reverie, "I am concerned that the next few days might be hazardous for this village."

"Why do you think that?" asked the Chief.

"The girl Maxine's job is to report our status to Renshaw & Collier. It matters not whether she is doing it maliciously. It is just a feeling inside me that we are vulnerable. That big corporation, that she works for, wants us to fail."

"I have learned to trust your feelings my friend," said the Chief. "We will discuss this tonight and tomorrow we will take action."

Maria arrived in Cape Town on Wednesday evening, dusty and tired. She just wanted to get to her hotel room, shower and go to bed.

She went to reception to check in.

"Hello, you should have a reservation for me, Maxine Bassett."

The receptionist checked his screen.

"Yes Miss Bassett, for three nights but we have space if you decide to stay longer," he smiled. "Here is your key, room 307 and there is a letter for you." He handed her the sealed envelope and added, "Have a pleasant stay."

"Thank you," she replied as she went to the lift.

She opened the envelope in her room, the note was printed on Sellick & Arrowsmith paper with the Cape Town office address at the bottom. It simply said: *'Wait in Cape Town for instructions.'*

'Excellent,' she thought as she undressed and entered the bathroom.

Chapter 42

A man in shorts and a shirt staggered from behind a dune and made wobbly progress slightly away from the lookouts then veered a little towards them. Another man appeared from the same direction, only made it a few metres and collapsed face down in the sand. His buddy turned and staggered back and knelt beside him. He sat him up against his knee and poured a few drops of water into his mouth from a clear plastic bottle. He shook the bottle, looked at it and cast it aside. He swayed a little then collapsed in a heap with his buddy.

The lookouts left their post with their water bottles in their hands and ran and slid down towards the collapsed men. Each helped one to a sitting position and gave them a little water. They seemed to revive a little when a click was heard and a voice said quietly, "Be silent. Make no sound." Two armed men were standing over them pointing rifles at the lookouts. One had a finger to his lips in an obvious sign. The lookouts were relieved of their belt knives and the two casualties got up and bound and gagged them and leaned them back to back.

The leader, Ken, said quietly, "Don't move or make any noise and you will not be harmed. Nod if you understand."

They both nodded enthusiastically. Their zip-tie bindings were then tied together so the two were attached to each other and Ken tied a chord to each man which was attached to something which he buried in the sand about a metre away from them. They couldn't see what.

Ken pointed to the chords and the places he'd buried things and said, "Remember, don't move. We will release you when we leave."

They both nodded very slowly.

The two casualties collected their gear and they all moved cautiously towards the village.

Unfortunately night vision goggles and scopes gave little advantage that night as the sky was clear and the moon full, so deception had been needed instead. They had been observing the Chief's lookouts since they arrived and knew the routines. They had also observed the couple from afar with their powerful scopes. They crept as close as they could without being seen and removed their heavy gear. They would have to run up a sandy slope, not easy even under the best of conditions.

Tony and Clara were in their favourite spot looking at the night desert, they embraced and leaned together for a long kiss when they heard revving engines and gunfire from the direction of the village. They both turned in that direction and started to crawl up the hill to see what was happening. Before they reached the top, strong arms grasped their arms and legs and they were turned over to face Ken.

"Don't be frightened," he said firmly. "We are here to rescue you and take you to safety."

Tony and Clara were too alarmed to take that in, or to believe it if they had, and they both started to struggle.

It was to no avail. The team quickly bound them hand and foot and carried them bodily away.

Ken said to one of his men, "Deal with those two lookouts."

Mr B veered off at an angle towards the lookouts. He had clear instructions.

When he arrived the two men hadn't moved at all. Their eyes went wide as he grasped the chords and yanked them out of the sand. There was a small rock on the end of each not an explosive device as they had thought. Mr B pulled their knives out of a pocket and indicated for them to look at the knives. He then walked away about twenty metres to the top of a dune and very obviously dropped the knives before disappearing over the top.

Trucks came roaring towards the village spreading automatic fire in every direction with no noticeable effect due to their distance. About fifty metres from the first hut the front of the lead vehicle dropped about half a metre and its front end slammed into the side of the pit, the passengers were projected forward as the rear end lifted and flipped over the bonnet. It settled upside down. The next truck stopped just before the pit but the one behind ran into it and pushed its front wheels over the edge.

The remaining trucks tried to drive around the obstacle but the pit had been placed carefully. To one side was a rocky outcrop, the other appeared drivable but was very soft sand and the first vehicle started to sink.

"Leave the trucks. Attack on foot," shouted the commander from the sinking truck. His men all leaped out and ran towards the village, the front ones firing the odd burst towards the huts.

As soon as Chief Daniel had heard the revving trucks he shouted orders to his men. They grabbed all their shields and weapons, mostly spears, and sprinted into the desert. The Chief followed them.

At those first sounds the Minister also ran, but towards Tony and Clara's tents to warn them. He called to them to run. There was no reply and he realised that they weren't there he hesitated and then rummaged in Tony's tent. He came out with the satellite phones but he was too late to catch the Chief and his men. He dived behind a discarded millstone and peered cautiously towards the attackers. The satellite phones slipped from his hand and slid under the stone. He plunged his hand underneath to retrieve it and was surprised when he started to slide underneath it. He slithered round and pushed in his legs and was able to slide his whole body under the stone. Sand trickled on top of him but with his face close to the stone he could still breathe. He had concealed himself well but barely in time, the attackers were busy riddling the huts and tents with their automatic weapons and some were firing after the Chief and his men. The Minister heard rounds ricochet off the millstone. Then annoyed shouts and some orders. After a short pause he heard the sound of smashing glass which went on for minutes.

A little later he heard trucks revving and eventually moving away, then he smelled burning. As he lay there his hand had touched one of the dropped satellite phones. He realised what it was and felt around for the other one. That was when he remembered the children playing around the millstone, they must have been making a den. "God bless the little children," he sighed.

The attackers tried to chase the Chief and his people but they had deliberately run over soft desert sand where they knew the vehicles couldn't follow. After the marauders had stolen or broken everything that looked worth anything, they recovered their trucks and went back the way they had come.

Chapter 43

Tony and Clara bounced along in the back of a pick up truck. They were stuffed in amongst a lot of kit so they didn't roll about much.

"Are you OK?" Tony whispered.

"No," she answered hotly. "I've been kidnapped, my hands are cable tied behind me and I'm bouncing around being taken who knows where or why. So no, I'm not OK!"

"Sorry, stupid question. Are you hurt?" Tony asked.

"No." was the curt reply. She was not happy.

Tony could just see the sky. He knew the moon took roughly the same path across the sky as the sun and he could see the moon was generally behind them. He was thinking hard. 'Southern hemisphere, sun and moon in the north, so they were going roughly south.'

He wasn't thinking at his best so he wasn't sure about anything right then.

"Clara, I think we are going south."

They hadn't been searched so he still had his watch and he whispered to Clara, "Can you see anything?"

"No, the sides of the truck are too high and I can't get up," she replied. They were both in the foetal position so they didn't roll about too much, and back to back.

"Can you feel my watch to take it off?" Tony whispered.

They wriggled till their hands were together and she managed to undo the watch strap and get the watch in her hand.

"Got it," she whispered.

Tony wriggled round so he could see her hands and she held the watch face where she thought he would see it. He could, just.

"It's nine thirty, sunset was just after seven, we walked up to the hill about eight after eating, so I guess the attack was about eight thirty."

"So you think we have been driving for less than an hour." she whispered

"Yes, and I think we are doubling back."

He could on longer see the moon and as the truck was turning and weaving so he guessed that they were heading towards the moon now; doubling back. Eventually, after another half an hour, the truck slowed.

"See if you can push the watch into my boot," he whispered. "If we are searched they may take it."

As they were being helped out Tony demanded. "What the hell is going on, who are you people and where the hell are you taking us?"

Ken faced them and said very quietly, "Sit on the ground and be very quiet and I'll tell you, and do not move."

They were facing away from the trucks but could hear equipment being shifted about, like loading or unloading. The engines of two trucks were ticking over quietly. The ground beneath them was sand not a road but the trucks could obviously handle driving cross country.

Ken gave some orders to the other men, then kneeled in front of Tony and Clara and spoke to them very quietly.

"We have intelligence that your lives are in danger and we have been sent to extract you from that danger. We are taking you to meet another team which will take you to safety. Who we are is not important and that's all I can tell you. Please remain quiet, we do not know how far away the threat is."

Tony and Clara were a dumbstruck with this information.

"Not far to go now," said a voice quietly and they were lifted into the back of the pickup again.

The trucks rolled down a hill and carried on for about ten minutes when voices and laughter could be heard. Then a welcoming voice with a distinct accent boomed out in English, "Here are the clever men with our gifts."

The trucks stopped, doors opened and closed and rough hands dragged the couple out of the truck and made them stand.

"Are you prepared for these people?" Ken asked a bit doubtfully as he surveyed the camp.

"Course we're prepared," came back a voice filled with offence and aggression. "Throw them in that truck." He pointed to a dirty Land Rover.

"This is a rescue," said Ken sharply. "Be careful with these people."

"Keep your mouth shut Englishman," he shouted back. "This is my camp, my orders." The atmosphere stiffened and the men in the camp gripped or lifted their AK-47s. He was their boss and that was what he was called, Boss.

"OK, then we'll leave now," said Ken; 'Englishman,' he thought and with so much aggression, this was not what he had expected.

"Why the bandanna?" Boss asked. "You can see my face, I want to see your's"

"It stops us breathing sand," said Ken but he slipped his bandanna down below his chin, Tony moved to turn and look.

"Don't turn," Ken ordered, Tony and Clara froze.

"You are not frightened are you," said Boss in a soft and menacing voice. "With all your skills and fancy equipment and vehicles." He looked enviously at the two nearly new Toyotas.

Ken ignored the taunt and nodded back to the trucks; his three men understood and walked backwards towards

211

them. His men were carrying assault rifles but Ken had only a holstered pistol.

"Stop!" shouted Boss as he stepped behind one of his men.

In that moment many things happened very quickly. Boss's men raised their rifles towards Ken and his men. Ken's team dropped to one knee and raised their rifles in response. Boss's men responded by opening fire, this was returned but there was only one outcome. Ken's team was outnumbered ten to one and they were gunned down.

Ken stood amongst the carnage, he had not moved and nor had Clara and Tony, miraculously the three were unharmed.

"Remove that holster," said Boss as he let the man he was holding in front of him slid lifelessly to the ground.

"Now you will not be needing both of these nice vehicles," said Boss maliciously. Then he scratched his head theatrically then he added. "Actually old chap, I don't think you will need either of them." His men all laughed despite the carnage around them.

Ken thought he was about to be shot too but instead he was told to stand still and his hands and legs were bound.

"You may stay here and enjoy the beauties of the African desert when we are gone," laughed Boss sadistically and pushed him over onto his back.

They stripped his men of their equipment and boots and also took Ken's boots. He didn't think he'd need them anyway.

Eleven of their own men were dead and their weapons were collected but their personal belongings were put with the bodies. Two of the Land Rovers were parked side by side facing a patch of sand. The winch lines from the front of each were run out across the sand and a tailgate from one of the trucks was connected to the cables. Two men leaned heavily on the tailgate and as the winches pulled it, it dug into the sand like a plough.

Tony and Clara watched what looked like a well practiced process; several passes were made over the sand until a trench was created; the eleven dead were laid in it and then covered. Tony thought this was so practiced, almost routine, that they must loose men regularly. He doubted that Boss cared as he spent the burial time examining his two new vehicles. The three dead S&A Security operatives were just left to rot.

The captives were loaded into a Land Rover, Boss switched to one of his new vehicles and they drove away leaving Ken to die in the desert.

"Say some prayers for your dead men as you watch them rot," laughed Boss as he drove away.

Chapter 44

"How many people are injured?" asked the Minister when he met with the Chief.

"There are two men and one women," replied the Chief. "They are awaiting your attention."

"My medical attention I pray," said the Minister and added, "I thank God that you sent everyone else to Site 2."

He went immediately to attend to the casualties.

An hour later he returned to the Chief's side.

"They will recover well," said the Minister. "They just need rest now."

"Thank you," said the Chief. "Now tell me why didn't you run with us. And how did you escape the bullets?"

"I went to Tony and Clara's tents to warn them but they weren't there."

"I know," said the Chief seriously. "We have searched and we find signs that they were taken by other men from the hill where they like to sit. The lookouts were overpowered and bound but the men who did that were very different to those who attacked the village."

"I pray they do not fall into the hands of those animals," said the Minister, then added as an afterthought. "I have the SatPhones."

"That is good," said Chief Daniel. "Those animals stole the small parabola and burned or smashed everything else including all the glass mirrors." He then added, "Please give me one of the SatPhones, I will call Tony's brother and explain what has happened. And I think I must also tell the professor at NUST."

All the phone numbers that Tony thought they might need had been programmed into both satellite phones. The

Minister sat alone in the cool evening where he would not be overheard and looked through the list, he selected one and called it.

At about ten that evening Mike was channel-hopping to find something interesting to watch on the television. He wasn't having much success but perked up when his mobile phone rang showing Tony was calling. 'It's a bit late for Tony to call,' he thought.

"Hi Tony," he said, "whats up?"

"A lot, but it's not Tony,"

"Chief Daniel," said Mike with surprise,."Something is up isn't it."

"I'm afraid so, the village has been attacked and Tony and Clara have been kidnapped."

"Bloody Hell!" exclaimed Mike, then. "Sorry Chief Daniel."

"Don't be Mike. I feel the same and have said much worse."

"Please tell me every detail. Starting with when did this happen?"

The Chief explained all he knew and Mike asked what they planned to do next.

"We have just come back to the village to salvage what we can," he answered. "We will let you know when we have assessed the situation."

"Please do. If you can't reach this mobile number call me on this satellite phone number." Mike gave him the number, pausing to allow the Chief to program it into the satellite phone.

"I will be with you as soon as possible," said Mike, "probably tomorrow."

"How is that possible?" Chief Daniel asked in surprise.

"I am in South Africa," answered Mike.

"Oh, having a small vacation?" Chief Daniel queried but not really believing it.

"Something like that," said Mike. "Please keep me informed and I'll be in touch. Charge the SatPhones if you can."

Mike was staying at the Hilton Sandton, Johannesburg, about half an hour from Jan Smuts Airport (JNB). So he called a car hire company and reserved a pickup truck for later that evening.

Mike hung up and then called Jerry the quartermaster.

"Where are you Jerry?"

"In a pub of course," he replied.

"Have those parts I ordered been shipped as planned?" Mike asked.

"They are at the docks, do you want me to forward them to the factory?" Jerry asked.

"Yes please, can you get them on the road by 08:30 tomorrow?" Mike replied.

"Will do," answered Jerry. "Anything else I can help you with?"

"Not at the moment thanks. The project issues that I was concerned about have materialised so I'll call if I need something else. Thanks,"

They ended the call.

There was a small crate in a warehouse near the dock in Luderitz on the coast of Namibia. It would take three and a half hours to have it driven to the *factory* and a regular pickup truck would handle it.

He knew it would take him about twelve and a half hours to drive to the *factory* from JNB.

An airport was a good place to get some provisions and a vehicle late at night. He had a long drive ahead, right through the night, so he needed sustenance and caffeine.

216

It was 23:30 as he drove south from the airport then west on the N12 Southern Bypass and kept going west. He had SatNav and a GPS unit for backup. He didn't intend to get lost.

At 09:45 the following morning he approached the South Africa to Namibia border. He was glad of a short stop and poured coffee from his vacuum flask. He could hardly believe he had made such excellent time. He estimated he would reach his destination in the required two and a quarter hours to make the rendezvous at midday.

Chapter 45

Maria had a restful Thursday relaxing at the hotel. Her concession to Sellick & Arrowsmith being that she kept her mobile and the satellite phone charged and with her constantly. It was evening and after a good meal in the hotel restaurant she was having coffee in the lounge when the satellite phone rang.

"Not HQ already," she sighed, but it wasn't.

"Hello Maxine," said a voice she recognised.

She was surprised to hear it though. "Hello Minister, what can I do for you?"

"I'm not sure," he replied and went on to relate the story of the attack and the kidnap but without any mention of Site 2.

When he stopped she asked, half to herself, "Who were these people?".

"All we know is that they were Africans and had what looked like AK-47 assault rifles and Land Rovers."

"Thank you Minister, I will call my HQ and see what we can do."

They hung up and she Looked at her watch, it was ten thirty in the evening, eight thirty in the UK; she called her headquarters.

"Hello, Sellick & Arrowsmith, how can I help you."

"This is Miss M, we have a *situation* and I need to speak to Mr S immediately."

"Hold on, I'll try to get him."

She waited as they tried to locate Mr S and eventually Mrs Smith from Special Ops came on the line, "Hello Miss M, we are still trying to locate Mr S but in the mean time please relate this *situation*."

"As you know from my communications I have completed my project and I am now in the hotel which was reserved for me. I have just received a call from the people that I was assessing and they have the *situation*. Do you wish me to describe their *situation*?"

"Yes, if it is possible without revealing company confidential information," instructed Mrs S.

Maria went on, "It appears that the people running the project which our client is sponsoring have been attacked by a militia type group of African men. Three local people were injured by gunfire from this militia and two of the project leaders were kidnapped. Much equipment was destroyed or stolen. The militia has withdrawn."

"Do you know the identities of those kidnapped?" Mrs S asked.

"Dr Tony Collins the Edinburgh University project leader, and Dr Clara Bella the Namibian University project leader."

"Thank you Miss M, I will relate this to Mr S as soon as possible someone will get back to you. Please stand by."

Maria had no intention of standing by. She wanted to know what was going on. First she called Car Hire at the Airport and reserved a 4x4 for that evening, airports were always the easiest place to get a vehicle late at night. She packed, ordered a taxi and went down to reception to check out. She was still in the lobby when her mobile phone rang.

"Hello Miss M, this is Mrs S again, please return to the site and gather as much information as possible. There is one other thing; we have another team of operatives in that area which has failed to report in on schedule. Please make contact with them and inform us of their status. I will text you the IDs of our personnel and the SatPhone numbers, which are not being answered."

219

Maria got her taxi to the airport.

There were some shops still open and she bought provisions, far more than she would need for herself but if there was a team in trouble she would need much more. Although she had a first aid kit she bought more first aid items just in case.

"Hello Miss Bassett," smiled the man at the car hire desk. "I'm afraid the only 4x4 we have available is a Range Rover Sport, 5 litre V8."

"That will be just fine," she smiled as she passed over her credit card.

"Would you like the full insurance package?" he asked.

"Yes please," she answered, thinking, 'I may well need that.'

By midnight she had just cleared the northern outskirts of Cape Town and she was on the open road. She should be at the site around ten in the morning.

Chapter 46

"Are you hurt Tony?" Clara whispered as she struggled to get her head closer to his.

"Just a bit bruised I think, what about you?"

"The same but I need to pee," she replied.

"Hey you two, no talking!" shouted one of their captors who had been assigned to watch them. When Boss had ordered a stop for the night to make camp, they had been taken off the Land Rover. Their hands were still cable tied behind them and they had been searched again, with Clara getting far more attention than necessary.

"Langa," hissed Boss. "What you making so much noise for? Wakin' everybody up."

"They was talking Boss."

"And what were they saying?"

"Don't know Boss."

"You are useless, sunshine," said Boss walking up to them. "What were you two talking about?"

"We need the toilet," said Tony.

"No toilets here," said Langa. "Do it where you are."

"And the stink," said Boss. "You gonna clean them up?"

Langa remained silent.

"Get more ties and put their hands in front," said Boss loosening the pistol in its holster.

Langa cut the cable ties and zipped up a new one with their hands in front of them while Boss watched.

"Now you can go and shit in the desert," said Boss. "And you watch them, don't let them out of your sight," he added to Langa.

Their leg bindings were removed so they could walk.

They walked away together as far as they could until Langa hissed, "Stop!"

Clara undid her shorts but with her hands in front of her she couldn't get them over her bottom.

"Tony, stand behind me so that animal can't see and slip my shorts and pants down." He stood as requested and put is fingers over the waistbands and slid them down. His fingers touched her bare skin and he felt himself tingle. "Stay there till I've finished peeing," she added.

She squatted down and squirted into the sand.

"What do these people want?" she said quietly. "Are we to be ransomed?"

"That seems most likely," said Tony."Otherwise I think that would have killed us already."

"Why did they kill their accomplices?" asked Clara. She was frightened now and, for the first time in their relationship was really relying on Tony to support her. Tony was trying to figure it all out and suppress his own fear at the same time.

"I don't know for sure, but I think the first group was genuinely trying to rescue us and maybe they met up with the wrong people. I don't know."

When she stood again she nodded to Tony to pull up her pants and shorts.

When she was zipped up again Tony stepped to one side, undid his fly, without assistance, and started to pee.

"Do you think we can make a run for it?" Clara whispered.

"That guy would catch us or shoot us, so not now."

"We wouldn't run very well with our hands tied anyway," she conceded. "We need to get these ties off somehow."

"If we get to keep our hands in front then we have a chance, quiet, he's coming."

"You two finished?" he demanded as he came up to them. Tony was just zipping up his fly and they turned and started walking back to the camp.

Langa told them to lie down and keep quiet.

"We should try to get some sleep then," whispered Clara and to their surprise they dropped into a deep sleep together.

"Wake up you two. Get up and get in the back of that truck," said Boss loudly, pointing to one of the Land Rovers.

They climbed in without assistance but at least now they could sit with their backs against the sides. They could see where they were going now but even that was a bit worrying. They didn't know what the Boss had in store for them and they were sure that whatever it was, it wasn't good.

The ride was rough and seemed to last for many hours but was really only an hour and a half. They stopped near a high voltage electricity transmission line. A concrete hut stood nearby and they were hustled out of the Land Rover towards it. Tony was pushed towards the door and put his hands on it to stop himself falling, the door opened and he and Clara were pushed inside and made to sit on the floor. One of the men brought in an aluminium case, opened it, handed the contents to his comrades and then passed the empty case to Clara who automatically grasped the handle.

"Put it in the corner," the man ordered Clara. She did as she was told.

"What was all that about?" Clara whispered to Tony.

"Crazy," he replied. "Could you see what was in the case?"

"It looked like white chocolate," she answered. "What are they doing now?"

"No talking, get back in the truck," instructed Langa and they were taken outside to the Land Rover again.

As they watched, one of the men was taping a block of the white material onto one leg of the nearest pylon.

"It's plastic explosive," whispered Tony as he realised the significance.

The man went to tape another charge to the next of the four legs.

"What are you doing?" shouted Boss, "I want four pylons down. I want to see a whole row crashing over. One charge per pylon will do it."

"But Boss if I do that...."

"Don't argue! Do as I say!" Boss cut him off aggressively.

"OK Boss," he answered, with little conviction, and went back to push a wireless detonator into the C4 then jumped into a Land Rover and was driven along the power line to the next pylon.

Twenty minutes later he came back and Boss demanded to have the transmitter so he could push the fire button.

The convoy drove away from the pylons and stopped. Boss climbed into the back of his truck and stood up in readiness to bring them down. He grinned like a naughty child and pressed the fire button. The charges exploded on the four pylons and they all lurched dangerously. The top earth cable took the strain and the insulators swung wildly but then gradually stopped swaying and the pylons leaned but still stood.

Boss's face dropped and he thought about going back but he had been given only four charges and the instruction had been to take down one pylon. In an effort to

224

save face and maybe try to convince himself, he shouted, "They will fall when the wind blows. Now let's go."

But they didn't fall.

Chapter 47

At the same time that Maria was leaving Cape town, Ken sat in the sand and considered his predicament. The negatives: he was on his own in the desert, his hands and feet were bound and he had no weapon or blade. The positives: he was still alive, he wasn't injured, it was night, there was a full moon, his hands were bound in front of him and the equipment that he had offloaded earlier had not been discovered. The downside of the last thing was that it was five kilometres away and mostly uphill.

He swayed from side to side until he could roll over onto his front, he pushed himself up onto his hands and knees and could make out the tracks they had made coming to this unfortunate meeting.

Ken started crawling towards his stashed equipment, his lifeline. He tried crawling like a caterpillar, arching his back, he tried making bunny hops, he rolled over, any way to make progress over the sand. All the different methods had two things in common: they were slow and they hurt. The ties rubbed and cut his skin but he was moving. He used all the different methods in the hope he could just keep going. He rested regularly, actually he collapsed exhausted every twenty minutes or so. The only idea of time he had, was the moon tracking across the sky. By the time he had covered one kilometre his wrists were raw from abrasion by the sand and the plastic ties. He couldn't find any sharp stones to cut his bonds so he just kept going, trying to ignore the pain and exhaustion. Eventually his hand came across a sharp edged stone and he managed to sit and saw his way through the zip-tie binding his feet. He tried to cut the tie on his wrists but the stone kept slipping when he gripped between his feet. The process was painful so eventually he gave up. At least now he could walk and that gave him a little hope.

He walked and staggered through the night until dawn and rested for half an hour, then set off again. He kept a track of the Sun's position in the sky, it had travelled about a quarter of its route along the ecliptic. It had been gradually getting hotter and he was dehydrated when he stumbled up to his cases and collapsed in the sand. He was semi conscious and gradually drifting into real unconsciousness. It was 09:00 and the heat of the sun was increasing rapidly, he knew if he just lay there he would never get up again, so close but he didn't have the energy to move. "I'll just rest for a couple of minutes then get up," he told himself as his eyes closed.

Maria had been driving for about seven hours and was in Namibia already. She decided to try to call the S&A Security team so she pulled over, opened her flask of black coffee, poured some and picked up the satellite phone. It gave her a few minutes rest from driving but she got no reply. She looked at her watch, it was 07:00, "Maybe they are asleep and have the phone off," she thought, "I'll try again about 09:00."

She had a quick nap for half an hour and then carried on her journey to the Village that she had left only two days ago.

The road passed through sandy scrub with a few small trees and she could now see rocky outcrops on both sides of the road. Glancing at the time she pulled over and took out the satellite phone again. She found the number of the Team's phone and called it, it appeared to be ringing, it rang and rang and eventually she gave up and hung up the call and drove on towards the Village.

227

Ken was in a deep sleep, dreaming about sitting on a stool in a pool bar drinking a cool beer but there was an annoying noise. He tried to ignore it and enjoy the beer but it just kept going. "Somebody answer that phone!" he shouted in his dream, and then he realised he was actually shouting but there was no-one to answer a phone. He snapped out of the sleep and stared at his surroundings. There was a noise coming from one of the boxes, he shook his head, it hurt. He crawled to each box until he found the one making a noise and it stopped.

"That shouldn't happen," he muttered. "Some idiot has left a SatPhone switched on, the battery will go flat." He thought for a moment and realised that he should get the phone out of the box. He kneeled in front of the box and flipped the catches one at a time and opened the lid. Yes, one of the phones was on and the battery was almost gone, he couldn't remember when it was charged last. As he pushed a button the display faded completely, the battery was flat.

Maria was only five minutes along the road when she stopped again thinking, 'Had there been two numbers for the Team?' She checked the satellite phone, there was a second number and she called it.

"Thank God," rasped a voice.

"Who is that?" Asked Maria.

"K," came the short reply.

"I'm from S&A, you don't sound good, what's your status?" she asked.

"Alone, others dead, hands bound, need transport."

"Can you give me your location?" said Maria, "I'll come to you."

"Need to find GPS, battery flat, hanging up, call me in five," and the line went dead.

She checked her watch and watched the minutes tick off. She had a notepad and pencil ready and after a long five minutes she called again. He answered straight away, and rattled off the coordinates.

"How long?" he asked.

"Two or three hours, I'll be as quick as I can. Switch the phone on every hour, on the hour, for one minute. I'll call then if I need to." He clicked off.

He sounded as if he was in a real state and she didn't think she could rely on him to get her number and call her, even if the phone remembered it and she didn't want him calling her when she was driving anyway, that would just waste time.

She swigged coffee, unwrapped sandwiches and set off, eating while driving. The village would have to wait until she had found Mr K.

Chapter 48

Mike was making good time across Namibia. The border with South Africa had been no problem but there was no reason it should have been. He shuddered to think about crossing a border with the crate he was about to collect.

At about ten minutes before midday, Mike was driving into an industrial area in Keetmanshoop, one of the bigger towns in southern Namibia. He parked beside a specific *factory* sign as agreed with Jerry and poured himself coffee from his flask. He had waited twenty minutes when a pick up came and reversed up behind him. The driver got out and Mike was presented with a delivery note for tools. He signed it, printed his name and received the top copy. Both tailgates were dropped, the delivery truck reversed right up to Mike's and they dragged the crate across and the transfer was done. The delivery truck set off to pick up another cargo and Mike drove away to find somewhere quiet to unpack the crate on the road towards the village.

Mike had general directions to the village from his conversation with the Chief and he was driving in that direction. On a quiet track he stopped and opened the wooden crate with the tyre lever from the truck's tool kit. Inside were a number of top of the range Peli Cases. He opened them in turn, quickly checking their contents and their functions. He repacked some of the cases but put the Glock 17 in his belt, and the MK 13 Mod 5 Sniper Rifle on the front seat. One case contained a range of combination padlocks which he used to secure the cases. He set the combination to a number he wouldn't forget and he knew that Tony would guess it too if need be.

He called the Chief's satellite phone, "Hello Chief Daniel, any news?"

"Hello Mike, I'm sorry there's no sign of Tony and Clara,"

"Are you still at the village?" Mike asked

"We have moved to the other side of the hill where the mirrors were. We have a good view of the village and we have tidied and repaired as much of it as possible so it looks lived in."

"If these militia come to attack the village again will you keep hidden?" Mike asked.

"That is our plan but if they find us we will fight," replied the Chief with steel in his voice.

"Can you give me your exact location, GPS coordinates?"

"Sorry no," answered the Chief

"Was there anything left in Tony's tent?"

"Everything was collected from each tent or hut, his and Clara's were bagged," replied the Chief, "I'll send someone to get it."

Mike waited while the Chief gave instructions and in a very short time he was unzipping a bag.

"His rucksack is still intact," said the Chief. "And there are few things in it. Anything in particular you are looking for?"

Despite the years apart, Mike still knew Tony well. "Is there a very small Swiss army knife. It's red and only about four centimetres long."

The Chief tipped everything out onto a blanket and spread it out with the help of some children. "No," he replied, "definitely not here."

"I'm not sure if that's good or bad but I think it's good," said Mike. "Is there a small GPS unit? Fits easily in the palm of your hand, brown with a small screen."

"This looks like it," said the Chief. "It says Garmin at the bottom."

231

"That'll be it," said Mike getting excited, "can you turn it on? It's a press button on the side."

"Got it," said the Chief. "It shows a little man, now it says, 'searching for satellites'."

"Great, when it says, 'ready to navigate,' push the 'Page' button, three times I think, until it gives your location."

After about half a minute the Chief answered. "Yes, I have the location."

He read the coordinates to Mike who promised to be there as soon as possible.

Mike had given Tony the GPS to use when he was in the mountains a lot skiing. At the time Mike had one the same and he had kept it as a backup so he, like Tony, knew its functions well.

Now that he knew exactly where to find the village he set off directly towards it. The Chief had told him exactly how to approach their current location because of the pit and other potential obstacles. The Chief had also asked for his truck's registration so they would know it was him and not a bandit.

As suggested by the Chief, Mike arrived at the new encampment from the open desert, coming from the side directly opposite the Village

"Welcome," said the Chief. "It is excellent that you are here Mike and I see that you have come prepared. Tony did mention that you had military experience."

Mike was carrying a soft brown bag with the Sniper Rifle in it. The bag was mainly to keep the sand out not to disguise the rifle. In fact it was quite obvious what he was carrying and it elicited considerable interest.

The Chief took Mike to the ridge of the hill and they peered over at the village. It was a good vantage point, they would see vehicles approaching miles away especially with the dust clouds vehicles created during the day.

"We have lookouts all round this camp so we can hide if these bandits return," said the Chief. "We had lookouts before the attack but two of them were tricked by a group of men who we believe took Clara and Tony."

"Were they some of the bandits who attacked the village?" Mike asked.

"I think not," replied the Chief. "I have questioned my lookouts carefully and they were a different type of soldier, much more disciplined and organised and much less violent. In fact my lookouts were bound and told to stay still but were not harmed and were given a means to release themselves, with a little time. Also the bandits were Africans, the other group was European.

"The bandits just came in shooting and shouting with no regard for human life or property. It is a miracle that no-one was killed or seriously injured."

"That miracle," injected the Minister. "Assisted by your good planning."

"Thank you Minister but we still lost Clara and Tony."

"For now," said Mike. "We'll get them back. One positive thing is that they weren't taken by the barbarians."

"Thats true," said the Chief while looking carefully at Mike. "Where did you drive from after we talked last night?"

"Jo'burg."

The Chief looked at him with surprise. "You must be exhausted, you must eat and sleep, we will keep watch tonight and plan what to do in the morning."

233

Chapter 49

On Friday night Tony and Clara's captors had made camp and told them. "Shut up and go to sleep." The former they did, the latter was not in Tony's plan.

Later Tony moved close to Clara so he could whisper into her ear. "When they searched us they missed the little Swiss Army knife in this little jeans pocket." He pointed with his right elbow. "Can you get it out?"

She wriggled around so she could get her hand there. "Move a bit your belt is almost covering it," she whispered.

"That's why they didn't find it."

"Got it," she whispered and passed it into Tony's hand. He opened out the small blade.

"That tiny blade will take ages to cut through these ties," she said.

"We aren't going to cut through them," he said. "If we push the blade under the locking tag in the tie we can slide it apart." He did just that and freed Clara's hands.

"Now mine," he whispered presenting his wrists. She worked the blade in until he could slip the tie apart.

"What now?" Clara asked.

"We put them back on the other way round," he turned the tie round and wrapped her wrists and then slipped the pointed end into the locking part; the ratchet tag had nothing to lock into on that side and it could slide apart again easily.

"Just pull it tight if someone comes nosing around, they won't notice in the dark," he added.

Clara put his back on the same way.

"Did you notice that Boss was very protective of his new vehicle," Tony whispered. "The keys on all the others were taken by his men but he didn't let them have his, even the spare one. He put it in the glove compartment when he thought nobody was looking. If it is still there we can take that truck."

"It would be good if we could disable the other trucks," she whispered. "Then they couldn't follow us."

"Yes, but if we made any noise we'd be caught."

They continued planning while keeping an eye out for Langa who was still allotted the job of watching them. He came looking in the early hours and they quickly pulled the ties tight with their teeth and pretended to be asleep. He noticed nothing unusual.

Just before dawn they made their move. They crept towards the vehicles giving the sleeping men a wide berth and pausing every few metres to look for any night guards. The one guarding the vehicles was fast asleep in the front seat of the second new Toyota. It had more comfortable seats than the Land Rovers and ,of course, he was forbidden to go in Boss's truck.

They reached the passenger door and tried to open it very gently. Even so it clicked. The guard stirred and gripped his Kalashnikov but relaxed and went back to sleep.

Tony reached in and looked in the glove compartment, he realised that he wasn't breathing, nor was Clara. He allowed himself a small grin when he felt the key. He took it out as quietly as he could and examined it; just a single key and a car rental fob. He slid across to the driver seat and Clara slipped in behind him. She grasped the door handle and Tony hissed, "No!"

Clara stopped abruptly and realised that she had been about to shut the door just from habit.

"Leave it till we are going," he added. "They will hear the engine start but no sense giving any advanced warning. Can you reach both seatbelt buckles?"

She nodded.

"OK, when I start the engine, you click them in."

"Do you know which way to go?" Clara asked.

He could see a glimmer of light from the eastern horizon and knew their orientation roughly.

"I think we go straight ahead to get back to the village," he answered. "It seems roughly the right direction from where we have travelled so far. I also think that they are intending to go back there to finish their work, whatever that is exactly. Ready?"

She nodded again.

Just before he turned the key Clara handed him a hat she'd found on the floor and whispered, "It's the Boss's, I saw him wearing it. You put it on and I'll bend right down."

He put it on then turned the key and drove away steadily accelerating.

The guard woke with a start and sat bolt upright and saw what looked like Boss going for a drive. "What the hell is he doing?" he said to himself, thinking more about the beating he would get for not being awake. There was stirring from the camp and he heard the Boss bellowing, "What the hell is going on?"

The whole camp was waking now and the men ran to where Boss was striding towards the vehicles.

He dragged the guard out of the truck and shouted in his face, "Who is driving my truck?"

The guard was terrified and shaking. He blurted out, "You are Boss."

Boss pulled out his pistol in a rage but he'd lost enough men recently so with all the self control he had he knocked the guard to the ground with his gun. Then he turned and fired two rounds at the truck but it was two hundred metres away already and his shots were nowhere near it. One of his men raised his AK-47 towards the fleeing truck.

"No! Don't shoot!" Boss shouted. "You might hit it. I don't want my truck damaged." Then the truth dawned on him and he bellowed, " Langa! Where are the hostages?" There was no reply and he knew who had taken his truck. He pointed to two of his men, "You two, go and look for the hostages and fetch Langa."

The hostages were gone and Langa was dragged before Boss and beaten viciously then thrown into the back of a Land Rover, meanwhile they broke camp as quickly as they could and set off in pursuit.

Chapter 50

When Maria was on the open road she put her foot down, which was very effective with five litres under the bonnet. By 11:30 when she was driving over soft desert dunes. She was coming down over a ridge into a dip between dunes when she had to brake hard and turn to avoid the body on the ground. He was lying motionless next to some equipment cases.

She jumped out with a bottle of water in her hand and gently tilted the man so his head was upright enough to take some water. She dripped a little onto his lips and moistened her scarf and covered his head. The nearest case was within reach so she dragged it over behind him to support his back. She thought about providing some shade but the sun was almost directly overhead and she didn't have the equipment. He took a little water into his mouth and swallowed. She splashed a little water on his shirt and started to examine him properly. His wrists were raw and still bound by the cable tie, blood had dried on the tie and looked as though it would be painful to remove. She poured water over his wrists and got a knife from her bag and cut the tie and peeled it away. It started bleeding again so she washed it and put on antiseptic and dressings.

He moaned quietly, possibly the pain was bringing him round. She gave him some more water and his eyes opened. "Have I died?" He muttered, "Are you an angel?"

"That's corny," she said. "You must be recovering."

"My God am I glad to see you," he said. "I didn't think I was going to wake up, it's so hot."

"As soon as you can move we'll get you into the truck out of the sun," she told him. The truck had air conditioning but she was aware to be careful not to shock his body with a rapid temperature change.

After about twenty minutes, having drunk some water and cooled down a bit from the water on his shirt and Maria's scarf, she was able to move him into the back of the Range Rover. The air con temperature kept the temperature below that of the desert and he gradually started to recover enough to lift the water bottle himself and then take some food. After that he fell into a deep sleep. Maria was concerned and monitored him carefully but he seemed to be breathing normally and his pulse was steady.

The sun was going down and Maria was dozing in the driving seat.

"You did a good job with my wrists," a voice said. "And thanks for saving my life." He climbed into the passenger seat, "I'm K," he said holding out his hand.

She gripped it and shook, "Miss M, it's good to meet you." They both felt the other's firm and confident grip.

"Can you to tell me what this is all about?" she asked.

"Then you can tell me how you come to be here," he answered

"I think my story is a lot simpler," said Maria, "so maybe I should go first."

"Fine by me," he said.

"I was sent to gather information on a solar project which is being run between Edinburgh and Windhoek Universities and the trial site is not far from here. I flew in to Windhoek a week ago Wednesday, went to the University on the Thursday and arranged for travel to the site and was taken there on the Friday. I stayed a few days observing their

239

progress or lack of it, not their fault actually, problems with a supplier which are out of their control. I reported by SatPhone to HQ and was picked up on Wednesday of this week and taken to Cape Town. The message I received there was to wait for further instructions.

"On Thursday night I had a call from the site which they call the Village. They had been attacked and two people kidnapped. I reported the situation to HQ and got instructions to return to the site and gather as much information as possible.

"I was also told that there was another team in the area which had failed to report in on schedule. They asked me to make contact and I have."

"And I'm very glad you did," said Ken, and then related his story. "We arrived in Cape Town, there were four of us, we drove to this area collecting equipment on the way. Our operation was to rescue two people who were apparently in danger but didn't know, or didn't want to know. Therefore we had to collect them at night with or without their consent."

"So you were to kidnap them," she said, in a very flat tone.

"We thought we were rescuing them, the kidnap came later."

"So what happened?" Maria asked.

"Our instruction was to hand them over to a second team at a designated location, down this hill in fact," he said pointing. "And when we arrived things weren't as expected. This other team was a group of about thirty militia led by a man they called Boss. They were armed with AK-47s and were happy to use them. Boss was aggressive from the start. He demanded I lower my bandanna from my face."

"You were masked!" Maria exclaimed, "I bet they didn't think they were being rescued."

"No, I guess not," he replied sheepishly. "But we had specific instructions not to be recognised. Anyway we tried to retreat to our trucks, my men had assault rifles too. Boss shouted 'No' and his men pointed their guns at us. My guys went to one knee and his men just opened fire."

Ken stopped for a moment, clearly shaken by the experience, and then continued, "My men were cut down but they took eleven of his with them, including one that the Boss had held in front of himself as a shield. I think there might have been more injured."

"What about the hostages and how come you weren't injured?"

"The three of us were just standing still, I was only armed with a pistol which was buttoned down in its holster. Boss now has that. They buried their dead which looked like a frequently practiced operation. They took anything worth having from my men and my boots and tied my hands and feet and left me to die. They took the trucks of course and my guess is that they will try to ransom the hostages but who the hell they are and why we were instructed to contact them I don't know."

"And the hostages?" asked Maria.

"Yea, they were put in the back of one of the Land Rovers."

"How come this equipment is still here?" she was afraid that she was beginning to sound like an inquisitor but she wanted to know.

"I was wary of this second team even before we met them because I didn't know who they were, so we dumped a few boxes here before we drove down to meet them. And we are in Africa."

"With no backup," she added.

"Well, it turns out there was some," he said looking at her. "And I guess all the information we got about the village came from you, via HQ?"

"I suppose so," she answered, now feeling pangs of guilt about her part in this disaster,."And your men are still down there?"

"They must be," he answered. "I should go and bury them. At least until we can arrange repartition." He was staring at the floor trying to control his emotions.

Maria put her hand on his shoulder. "We will go down and bury them," she said quietly emphasising the *we*.

They put all the equipment boxes in the Range Rover and drove down to the site of the carnage. Before they started Maria picked up her satellite phone.

"Are you calling in?" asked Ken.

"No, I'm going to call my Mum, I call her every Friday. If I didn't she would just worry and worry. I never tell her anything about my work," she added reassuringly.

"Hello Mum. How are you and Dad?"

"Oh, hello darling, we are fine, busy as usual. There are some locals in the bar, Dad is looking after them. How are things with you, job going OK?"

"I'm fine too, busy, busy, busy, out travelling again for the company. It's hard work but the situation is interesting."

"Do you know when you'll be home to visit us?" Mum asked as she usually did.

"I'll come and see you as soon as I get back," she answered. "I'm dying to see you and have all my old friends round me."

After some more friendly chat they finished their call.

Following that call to her Mum, a technician in GCHQ downloaded the recording, encrypted it and sent it to Rob Riddle, section head in Thames House.

The moon was near its zenith now and the whole desert was flooded with its pale light. Maria and Ken sat side by side on the sand a little above the graves. The three graves were side by side and a small pile of stones marked the head of each.

Both of them had shed tears during the evening and they were tired from the exertion.

"I need a pee," said Maria and walked away across the sand. Her mind was busy, Ken had been badly affected by the deaths of his team, Maria had never met them in life so it wasn't quite so bad for her. She needed to get him thinking about something else, to snap out of his mood, to get him back on track and start thinking to help her figure out what to do next.

She stopped and didn't walk as far as she had initially intended. She undid her belt and slipped her shorts and pants down, squatted and relieved herself. Still facing away from Ken she stood and pulled up her pants and shorts, as she buckled her belt. She could feel Ken's eyes on her.

Ken had been sitting idly watching the figure walk across the desert, when the figure stopped and reached for her belt he automatically focused and felt his heart beat a bit faster and stronger as her shapely buttocks became visible. He'd said she was an angel when he was delirious but he had since noticed how good looking she was. As she walked back towards him he shook his head quickly and became much more aware of his surroundings. Maybe it was due to that little pump of adrenalin he thought.

"I've been thinking about this situation," said Maria. "And there is something fishy about the whole thing."

Ken thought for a moment. "Yes I agree," he said. "And I don't think I want to report in until I know what the hell is going on."

"That is exactly my feeling," she was happy he was thinking. "We don't know who has been involved in this or where it is leading."

"One thing is for sure," said Ken vehemently, "Boss and his crew are not going to get away with murdering three of my men."

"Also," said Maria. "I know the hostages, they are academics and not guilty of anything except trying to complete an environmentally friendly project."

"We need to start from the beginning," he said. "And put together all we know."

"I agree," Maria replied. "But I am dog tired, lets sleep first and thrash it out in the morning."

"You're right," Ken conceded. "Let's get some shut-eye."

On Saturday morning there was no planning; neither had slept properly since Wednesday night and they didn't wake until the heat of midday disturbed them. Both felt much more human and after some breakfast they were ready to plan.

"Our operation," started Ken. "was to observe the village without being seen and take the two academics safely to another team who would evacuate them. We were to insist they came using the minimum force but without alarming the other villagers. When we got close to the village we found that they had set a perimeter of lookouts which we couldn't get past without engaging them in some way, so we planned to do that on the night of the evacuation. We didn't have any information about S&A's client."

244

"How did you identify the targets?" Maria asked although she had her suspicions.

"We were fed intel from HQ," he answered. "We guessed that there must be someone in the camp telling HQ"

Now she knew. "That was me," she said. "My task was simply to report in detail on the progress, or lack of it, of the project and my client was the project sponsor."

"Well, if you provided all the intel for our operation then we were both tasked by the same client," he said.

"I agree, and it is weird that the sponsor sabotages their own project, but," she went on. "The project has been dogged by other setbacks which aren't easily explained."

"There's a more worrying angle," he added. "Boss and his crew must have been hired by the same client too, and they are a bad lot."

"Are you up for going after them?" Maria asked.

"Bloody right I am," he answered.

"Good, then we had better take stock of our supplies."

Chapter 51

After some hours of exhausted but solid sleep Mike woke early on the Saturday morning. He found the Chief and the Minister at breakfast and joined them. After he had eaten and drunk coffee his brain was getting back in gear.

"Trucks from the north!" shouted the lookout from the brow of the hill overlooking the village.

Mike collected his rifle and went to the ridge with the Chief and the Minister. The Chief gave instructions for everyone to stay behind the hill. Mike peered at the dust cloud with the telescopic sight of the rifle.

"I can make out a white truck followed by a group of dark ones," he said. "Perhaps it's the leader at the front."

As the white truck came closer it was clear that it was in a hurry.

"I could probably take the driver very soon," said Mike.

"No," said the Minister.

Mike wasn't sure whether it was the Minister's fundamental aversion to taking a human life or something else but he held his fire.

"The bandits' trucks were all dirty Land Rovers," said the Minister. "They didn't have a white truck, maybe they are chasing someone."

"Maybe they are," conceded Mike. "The Land Rovers are following," he could see them better now, perhaps the Minister was right.

The white truck was well ahead of the others and Mike was getting a better view with every passing moment.

"It's a man driving," said Mike. "and a girl in the passenger seat."

"It's them," said the Chief excitedly, he had a pair of powerful binoculars and was sure, "Clara and Tony."

Mike thanked God for the Minister, he had been a hair's breadth from shooting his own brother.

The white truck came racing into the village and skidded to a halt in a cloud of dust. Two of the Chief's men emerged from a tent in the village and ran to the truck, waving their arms and pointing. Tony and Clara got out and the four of them raced up the hill. The Land Rovers were three kilometre away and bouncing around so the bandits couldn't possibly have seen them scrambling up the hill.

When Clara reached her father they hugged with relief. Tony was amazed to see his brother and they hugged briefly but they both knew there was trouble coming across the desert.

"Those guys are crazy," said Tony. "Their leader won't stop unless he's dead or wounded." He looked at Mikes rifle. "That would do it but he won't be near the front." He borrowed the Chief's binoculars while Mike looked through his telescopic sight again.

"That white truck at the back, that's where Boss will be," said Tony.

"Boss is what his men call him," explained Clara.

"There are only about twenty of his men left now, he lost about ten in a firefight with the people who originally took us," said Tony.

"What about the guys who took you?" asked Mike.

"All dead I think," he answered. "Three were shot and one was tied up and left to die in the desert."

'Less potential enemies to worry about,' thought Mike although he also thought that those four soldiers must have acquitted themselves well to take ten of the Boss's men with them, pity they didn't get the Boss.

"Tony, in my truck there's an assault rifle in a case, it's locked but you'll know the combination," said Mike.

Tony raced off down the hill to get it. Mike's truck was at the bottom of the hill on the opposite side from the village.

"They look to be about one and a half clicks out," muttered Mike keeping his eye to the scope.

"That gap in that line of rocks they are approaching is one kilometre out from the Village," said the Chief. Mike didn't ask how he knew that but the information was very useful.

There were six Land Rovers and the white truck, probably two or three bandits in each.

"Any objections to slowing them down a bit," asked Mike. There were none.

One of the Land Rovers was approaching the rocks that the Chief had mentioned. Before it reached the rocks, Mike steadied himself, took careful aim and gently squeezed the trigger. 'Now's the time to pray Minister, that he doesn't swerve,' thought Mike, the round would take over a second to reach the target and he had aimed to hit the driver's windscreen centre so had a little leeway. The delay after the report of the rifle seemed like many seconds and nobody was breathing, then the Land Rover veered to one side hit a half metre high rock and turned over spilling its passengers.

There was a general sigh of relief not least from Mike, it had been a bit of a speculative shot especially as he was so out of practice.

The other vehicles all stopped to look at the damage.

Mike took some easier shots and put holes in three vehicles before they realised what was happening and beat a hasty retreat.

Boss, in his white truck, was way ahead of the rest and already at the limit of sniper range.

248

Mike took a shot anyway and managed to put a hole in the tailgate which greatly annoyed Boss.

"I'm guessing we'll need this later," said Tony holding the assault rifle.

"I am sure that they will be back," agreed the Chief.

"What is to be done about the men they left down there?" asked the Minister.

"We need to go and see what happened to them," answered Mike. "Tony and I can go. Better bring that weapon."

"I will come with you," said the Minister, "First-aid or last rights, I can do both. I'll get my kit."

"Take as many of my men as you can," said the Chief. "I will provide them with shovels."

Three of them sat in the cab with six of the Chief's men in the back of the white truck that Tony had taken from Boss. Tony drove and Mike held the assault rifle by the window.

Two men were on the ground, one had a bullet wound in his shoulder but also a crushed skull from the crash, the Minister checked him and he was dead. The other appeared to be alive, he was lying on his back, was just conscious but unable to move. The Minister examined him and offered words of comfort and a little water.

He spoke to the others as a group. "A grave for this one," he said pointing. "The other one is in a bad way, I think he probably has a spinal injury, if he is moved it must be very carefully."

"They are returning," interrupted one of the Chief's men. They all turned but there was only one vehicle with a makeshift white flag being waved by the passenger. Mike gave quick instructions, Tony turned the truck to face back towards the village and kept the engine running, they all boarded with Mike in the back pointing the assault rifle over the tailgate towards the oncoming Land Rover. When they were close enough the passenger with the flag shouted, "Boss wants to bury his dead."

"OK," shouted Mike, "but one is alive."

They drove back to the Village and stopped the truck by the tents and huts.

From their vantage point on the hill they watched as Boss approached the crash site in his white Toyota. Some of his men jumped out and continued the grave that the Chief's men had started. Boss went and looked at the dead man, then went to the wounded one. He kneeled down beside him and put his hand compassionately on his chest, he waved the other men away who were approaching. When they were well away digging the grave, he slid his hand over the casualties face clasping his mouth and nose tight. His eyes came wide open as he struggled to breathe but he couldn't move to save himself. Boss spent a few minutes in that position apparently speaking words of comfort until there was no life left, he stood and walked away with his head down and told his men to make the grave wider.

Mike and the Chief watched his every action until the burials were finished and the trucks had retreated.

When Mike told Tony later he was sickened but not surprised.

"There are still too many of them for us to chase down and attack with the weapons that we have," said Mike as he sat with the management team in the mid morning.

"I agree," said the Chief. "However we now have these which my men recovered," two AK-47s and some ammunition were placed in front of them.

250

"That's excellent," said Mike smiling as he checked the weapons. "A bit dirty but functional," he added. "Do any of your men know how to use them?"

"We have a few who were in the Namibian Defence Force," answered the Chief. "They all get basic training at the Military School north of Windhoek. I'll pick some men to report to you, I think they will need to refresh their skills."

"That's a good idea," said Mike. "The more the merrier, we may pick up more weapons."

"Good," said the Chief. "We have a lot to do but I think we are in a better position here than chasing across the desert and I suspect that they will be back."

He was right. At around three in the afternoon they could see a distant dust cloud.

The vehicles stopped one and a half kilometres from the village, it was another hundred metres to their hill position. Sixteen hundred metres was beyond the range of Mike's rifle and Boss, or one of his men, had guessed it right.

"I can't hit them there," said Mike. "My maximum range is about thirteen hundred metres."

"They are setting up something," said Tony lowering the binoculars.

Mike looked carefully through his gun sight,."They have a mortar."

"Can they reach us from there?" asked the Minister.

"They definitely have the range," answered Mike. "Whether they can hit us is another question but I don't plan to wait to find out, I'm going down to those rocks and see what mischief I can cause. That's only five hundred metres to the mortar. Fancy a run Tony?"

"Sure thing. It could take us ten minutes in this terrain. I'll bring this." He grabbed the assault rifle. "I hope they can't see us."

"I think we can help there," said the Chief and called for shields.

Tony and Mike started running down the hill, "I don't know how shields will help us," said Mike as he ran.

"Mirror shields," said Tony. "They will dazzle them with the sun even if they don't burn them."

"Mirrors down!" commanded the Chief, and his one hundred Zulu style mirror shields focused on the mortar site. It caused consternation among the militia, at first they couldn't understand this dazzling light from the village direction. By the time they realised what it was they were mostly temporarily blinded from staring at it.

As a consequence they didn't notice Mike and Tony running towards the rocks and it also took them more than ten minutes to set up the mortar.

When the Chief saw that Mike and Tony were in position, he ordered, "Mirrors up."

He watched carefully through the binoculars. As the first shell was being taken to the mortar he judged when Mike would fire and he ordered, "Mirrors down."

Mike saw the light, steadied and shot the man carrying the shell through his shoulder. He could easily have put the round through his heart but saw no point. He dropped the shell and fell clutching the entry wound. All the men scattered but the shell didn't explode. The casualty was helped to the truck, they made no attempt to dismantle the mortar, they just picked it up base and all, put it in a Land Rover and hastily drove away. Mike could have done more damage but he was wary of giving away his position. The militia had no idea where the shot had come from because of the mirrors dazzling them.

When the Land Rovers had gone, Clara drove down to pick them up in the white Toyota. Before they went back they had a look at the wrecked Land Rover to see if anything could be salvaged. In one of the compartments, under the seats in the back, Mike found a canvas bag full of hand grenades. He took one out and examined it. It was old but looked serviceable, 'Probably the dry climate' he thought. Three of the wheels were OK and the fuel tank was also intact and at least half full.

They drove back, left their truck in the village and walked up the hill.

Chapter 52

Phil Arrowsmith was in George Sellick's office at the farm.

"I'm sorry to drag you in on a Saturday morning Phil but we have a situation. Shall I get us some coffee?"

"That would be good," he replied. They had worked together for eight years, most of it at Sellick & Arrowsmith Security, and were good friends. They used first names when they were alone. George called the canteen and asked them to bring coffee and biscuits.

"A call came to me on Thursday evening from Africa but unfortunately I was not available. Mrs S dealt with it adequately but time has moved on and I want to get your take on it."

"OK," said Phil. "What has happened?"

"Five months ago Renshaw & Collier, our biggest client, gave us a contract us to get first hand information about an environmental project which they are sponsoring. We initially sent Miss M to Edinburgh and she covertly acquired all the information needed in two weeks."

"That's fairly quick," said Phil, "I thought she was good."

"Recently they came back with a similar request relating to the same project. Apparently there had been very little progress and they wanted to know what was happening on site in Namibia. So we sent Miss M to audit the project again, this time as an employee of Renshaw & Collier."

"How did she do this time?" Phil asked.

"Very well again," answered George. "She had a SatPhone and gave very precise reports each night. After a few days we called her to Cape Town in readiness to re-deploy or come home. Then the real situation arose."

"And what happened?" Phil questioned.

"First I have to tell you about another contract from Renshaw & Collier." George added. "This was more sensitive. They told me that they feared for the lives of the two project leaders, one from Edinburgh, the other from Windhoek. They told me that some persons unknown were sabotaging the project, which was why it was going so slowly, and that they needed to extract these two project leaders urgently for their own safety. They also said that they might be unwilling to leave the site because of their personalities. They cited an African militia which has been causing trouble in the country and intended more, and that if the project leaders stayed there, they could be assassinated."

"I presume this militia is from outside Namibia."

"I believe that might be the case but I don't have any direct evidence. Anyway we sent a team led by Mr K. His instructions were to extract the two people and if necessary use minimal force and take them to a safe rendezvous with another team contracted by Renshaw & Collier. We received all the intel from Miss M, who was at the site, and we fed it back to Mr K's team. She was not aware of their task."

"What went wrong?" Phil asked, puzzled.

"Listen to this recording," answered George and replayed a recording of Maria's explanation to Mrs S describing the militia attack and the kidnap.

They discussed some of the details and Phil asked, "What was she told to do next?"

"We instructed Miss M to go back to the site and investigate. We also informed her about K's team being out of contact. We have heard nothing from her or K's team since."

"I know this sounds like biting the hand that feeds us," said Phil. "But it looks as if our client is being duplicitous. The distraction which this other team was supposed to provide, to let the project leaders be removed easily, appears to have been a full on attack by a militia. And, the description 'militia' and their behaviour appears more like the group that the client told us to protect the project leaders from."

"I cannot disagree and that leaves us with a problem," said George. "We have a very important client who is using our services in an unacceptable way. What we don't know is how high up in our client's organisation this is coming from."

"I think we could use some outside help on this, George. I wonder about asking the government intelligence services, they might be interested in this."

"Do you have contacts there?" asked George.

"I know a few SIS names in Vauxhall Cross but I wouldn't call them contacts. I do, however, have a good relationship with an MI5 section head in Thames House. I've a good idea that my MI5 contact talks to SIS regularly, he would be my first port of call."

Mr Sellick thought for a moment then said, "Go ahead and contact him or her and see if they can be of any help. At this stage I think we will have to be as open as necessary with our information."

"Understood George, I'll get onto it right away."

Chapter 53

"That was very well done gentlemen." Chief Daniel was addressing Mike and Tony. "Do you think they will attack again today?"

"I think they will attack tonight," answered Mike. "They probably think that we have an incredibly long range rifle and they have no idea how close they can come. But at night shooting at distance with any accuracy is not so easy."

"The moon is still almost full," said Tony. "That should help."

"We are lucky," added the Chief. "That moonrise is about the same time as sunset."

"We had better spend the remaining daylight hours preparing as best as we can," concluded Mike. They all agreed.

The sun had set and it was well into the evening when the lookout called down the hill, "Headlights Chief Daniel!"

Mike got into position on the hill and viewed them through his telescopic sight. All he could see clearly was the headlights. When the vehicles were about a hundred metres from the rocks he sighted on the vehicle at the rear of the column. He judged where the driver would be and fired. He didn't know whether the shot wounded or killed, but the vehicle swerved violently, teetered and landed on its side.

The column stopped and Mike called to the others, "Watch the front vehicle and see if it tilts one way, I'll try to hit a tyre."

He took careful aim where he judged that the tyre would be and gently squeezed the trigger. Nothing happened at first, then, "It's down a little on the right," said the Chief. "Good shooting!"

All the headlights went out. "They have realised how they are being targeted," said Mike. "I can't hit much now but we can see where they are in the moonlight, if only it was brighter I might slow them up more."

"Almost time for our little surprise," said Tony. They had been busy in the afternoon.

"Yes," said Mike. "There's enough light for that," and he sighted on the Land Rover which had been wrecked earlier.

He was actually sighting on a door which they had removed and draped a high-vis jacket over. It was precariously balanced on the side of the truck.

As the column entered the pass between the rocks, Mike fired several times in quick succession at the top of the door.

Nothing happened for a few seconds, then the door fell to the ground pulling on a strong line which ran over the Land Rover body and was then attached to the pins of the grenades that they had recovered.

Most of these were buried in the sand across the path of the vehicles except one which was taped to the wrecked Land Rover's fuel tank. The centre of the column was over the grenades when they detonated and the fuel from the wrecked landcover was projected towards the column.

The damage was considerable, several men were injured, one vehicle was disabled and two others damaged.

Mike was scanning the vehicles for the Boss with the intention of putting him out of action but he was nowhere to be seen. The white vehicle, where he was most likely to be, wasn't there, it must have been the first one he'd fired on and had turned over, so Boss could be anywhere.

258

In fact Boss had stayed with his Toyota, and with his remaining men, rocked it onto its wheels again ready to make his escape.

The other vehicles which could move, set off again towards the village, in the remaining light of the fuel fire Mike picked off two more of the men but they were quickly in the dark again.

"We're a bit buggered now," said Mike. "If only I had a bit more light. "But he kept trying to sight on the vehicles.

Mike heard Tony talking urgently to the Chief behind him, then a lot of scurrying about and some words from the Chief to his people which Mike didn't understand. 'Perhaps they are making plans to retreat,' thought Mike still looking through his scope. As he watched, the image became clearer, a mysterious glimmer of light appeared on the trucks, not enough at first but gradually the ethereal glow intensified around the lead Land Rover. Mike didn't question where this eerie glow had come from he just took aim and got back to work. He aimed at the driver of the first truck and hit him in the shoulder, the truck veered sharply to the left, the right front wheel dug into the sand, increasing and increasing the turn until it rolled over. He fired through the tyre of the next truck and it too swerved to one side but the driver managed to control it and it just ploughed to a stop in the sand. He fired a shot which hit the roof and ricocheted away but was enough to encourage the occupants to abandon the truck and run for another. Realising that they were in plain sight of a sniper, they turned their trucks around and headed away out of range. The men from disabled vehicles, those that were able anyway, climbed in before they left. Mike fired a few more shots to encourage them to leave and perhaps do some damage.

259

The Chief selected some men to remain on the hill and everyone else prepared to go down to see what had been left by the attackers. Mike carried his rifle and some of his other kit that he had collected into a rucksack.

Mike and the management team got in the white Toyota and drove down from the village to the wreckage of the column. Tony and Mike were in the back of the pickup leaning on the cab roof with their rifles at the ready for any hidden trouble. The rest of the villagers walked or jogged down after them.

When they arrived they could hear groans from survivors. Mike left his rifle and jumped down with his revolver in his hand, he called back, "Stay in the truck Tony and keep alert." He was worried that some of the injured would still be armed and aggressive. He went round all the injured and apparently dead and removed their weapons and told them to lay still and he'd get help. When he'd checked them all he went to the truck, "OK, Minister, they're all yours, but watch them, they might still be dangerous."

Clara and the Minister started examining the casualties and doing what they could to help them. While the Minister was making each medical assessment Clara made a careful examination too but she was looking for weapons not injuries. She relieved several of the casualties of knives and handguns, not only from their belts but also from boots and shoes.

Mike was surveying the site more carefully now, scanning the ground with a powerful torch. Suddenly he shouted urgently,

"Move away from the truck!"

People started to obey but hesitated when they saw Mike running towards it. The Chief reacted quickly, he trusted

Mike's orders and bellowed, "Get moving!" Everyone ran. Mike jumped into the back, grabbed his rifle and ruck sack.

The moment before when he had scanned the scene with the torch his mind had raced, he had seen the row of craters that the grenades had made. When the Chief had stopped the truck he'd thought that they had parked beyond the last crater in the line but with the torch he had seen another one on the far side of the truck and from the spacing there should have been another right where the truck was. There was no crater, which meant there was still a grenade under the truck, probably with no pin in it. The sand must have prevented the safety striker lever from flying off. It had taken him only a fraction of a second to realise the potential danger.

He was on the truck just behind the cab when he heard the faint telltale noise from the grenade, again his mind was in overdrive and a thousand thoughts seemed to race through in a millisecond, the striker lever had eventually pushed it's way through the sand, probably with being disturbed by the tires of the truck, the striker had hit the percussion cap and started the fuse. The fuse should be four seconds but he knew that in practice that it could be as little as two. 'Not again,' he thought, 'another IED under a truck.' The last one had been in the desert too but set by insurgents. This one he had set himself, 'such irony,' he almost laughed as he turned to jump from the truck.

Chapter 54

Maria and Ken were opening all the cases and checking the contents.

"This should be our best help in finding them," said Ken as he produced a tablet and switched it on. "The password is pelicase," he added as he typed it in. "One word all lowercase."

The screen came on showing an image the earth, "Looks like Google Earth," she said.

"The user interface is like that but it does a bit more." He zoomed in to Namibia using the touch screen.

He tapped the icon to go to my location and it zoomed in on the desert where they were, although there wasn't much to identify it by.

"This is the good bit," he said and tapped a blue icon that looked like a target. The image zoomed out and then in on another area of desert where there was a blue pulsing spot.

"What's that?" Maria asked.

"That's one of my Toyotas, that the Boss took. I fitted a tracker to each one when I picked up our kit."

He tapped a red target and again the image zoomed out, moved a little and zoomed in again to a pulsing red dot. He zoomed out again so all three positions were on the screen.

"So we can find them with this when we are ready to go," Maria said with a smile. "That was a great piece of advanced planning."

"The odd thing is that they are not together," said Ken.

They repacked all the kit carefully in the cases and arranged them in the truck so they knew where everything was.

"These are interesting," said Maria in the afternoon as she studied a tranquilliser rifle a case of darts and some surveillance equipment. "And you have an assault rifle and a Baby Browning."

Just then the tracking App on the tablet started to bleep. "What's that?" Maria asked.

"One or both of the trucks are moving," said Ken.

They studied the screen and watched the red dot move towards the blue one.

"Can it show the coordinates of the blue dot?" Maria asked.

Ken moved the curser over the blue dot and the coordinated appeared at the bottom of the screen. She looked at the numbers and said, "That's in the village."

The red dot stopped about a kilometre from the village and then moved away.

"What do you think are they doing?" Ken asked

"No idea," she answered.

They watched the dots moving backwards and forwards during the afternoon still bewildered by the activity. When the dots stopped moving they finished their preparations and had some food.

It was dark and they were still trying to work out a plan. They picked up the tablet to assess the distance to the trucks. While they were looking at then screen the blue dot unexpectedly blinked out.

"That's weird," said Ken. "It shouldn't do that."

He rebooted the tablet but the blue dot had definitely gone, they couldn't know that the tracker had been destroyed by a grenade along with the truck.

"Could they have found the tracker?" Maria asked.

"I don't think so, it was very, very well concealed. I think it is much more likely that the whole vehicle has been destroyed," answered Ken.

"I guess that makes our planning easier, we've only one truck to follow now," said Maria.

Chapter 55

Mike leapt from the back of the truck and pumped his legs as hard as he could shouting "Get down!" at the top of his voice. When he judged he was three seconds away he threw himself down. He didn't think he had made even ten metres and he knew he was still within the grenade's kill radius, he hoped everyone else was clear and down.

He threw the bag down and the rifle as gently as possible under the circumstances and put his hands over his ears as he hit the ground and pushed his head forward into the sand. He had dulled the sound of the explosion but shrapnel fired in every direction. He felt a shock and pain in his left leg. A few seconds later he rolled over and sat up to examine his leg.

"Damn," he said through a mouthful of sand, "I should have checked all the grenades first."

"You can't do everything," said the Chief as he walked up to him. "We should all have checked. Are you injured?"

"Don't know yet," he answered. "This leg hurts."

The Chief looked and there was a twenty centimetre length of exhaust pipe sticking out of the sole of Mike's left Boot.

"Let's get the boot off," said the Minister and went to work unlacing it all the way down. As he eased it off the prosthesis came away with it.

The Minister looked curiously at it.

"It a prosthesis," said Mike. "It replaces a chunk of my foot that was blown off by an IED."

"Well, it appears to have taken the impact," said the Minister, "I hope it's not damaged. We can repair a boot but this is bespoke."

265

They prised the pipe out of the sole and examined it. The Chief called one of his men and sent him to their camp with the boot to get it fixed.

The Minister looked at the prosthesis. "There isn't much wrong with this as far as I can see."

"It's made of strong stuff," said Mike. "Army issue."

The Minister bandaged the prosthesis into position on Mikes foot as a temporary fix until the boot was ready. Tony had been examining the truck.

"How's the truck?" Mike asked.

"It's not going anywhere," answered Tony. "Way too much damage."

"We'd better look at these Land Rovers then," said Mike. "And see what we can salvage."

They started taking stock of what was available which wasn't so easy with only the moonlight and torches.

There were six Land Rovers but no sign of Boss's favourite white truck.

Three of the Land Rovers were complete write-offs but might be good for some spares. One of those had severe damage, another had turned over and the third one, they had fixed a grenade to the fuel tank.

Of the three that were relatively serviceable, two just needed tyres replacing and the other one had only shrapnel holes in the doors and panels.

There were two corpses in the badly grenade damaged Land Rover, the Chief's men set about burying them.

That left four casualties, two with bullet wounds inflicted by Mike and two with shrapnel wounds from the grenades.

The Minister and Clara had completed their first aid and arranged all the casualties together ready for transportation. It was also good to have them all together so that one of the Chief's men with an AK-47 could guard them.

The villagers had also collected another six AK-47s, with some ammunition, but only three were serviceable. The Chief allocated two to Defence Force veterans who had worked with Mike during the afternoon and the other to himself.

One veteran he sent to the village as security in case there was more trouble.

Mike was looking at a Land Rover when he saw one of the villagers rolling a wheel towards him. "Where did he get that?" Mike asked the Chief.

"I believe it was removed from the first damaged vehicle before you blew it up," answered the Chief. "My people don't like waste so it was put amongst the rocks in case it might be useful."

"Your people are a very resourceful," said Mike.

"Here is another of my resourceful people coming," said the Chief. "I believe he has your boot."

It was well repaired and when Mike put it on it still fitted perfectly. "Thank you," he said to the repairer. "You have done a great job."

The Chief smiled at his man but nothing like as broadly as the cobbler.

Three of the Land Rovers were repaired, two were loaded with the casualties to take them to hospital. The other one they planned to use to find Boss and his militia.

Mike was determined to find out what had really been going on. He and Tony were planning their trip and what they should take. Mike put his bag and rifle in, they would need extra fuel and a lot of water.

In a quiet moment Mike at last had time to think about the eerie light that had appeared earlier. It was much too bright for the moon, and they didn't have spotlights, then it clicked.

"I just realised what you did Tony, you clever bugger, you got them all to reflect the moonlight onto our attackers."

The Chief joined them. "We have collected some jerry cans of fuel," he said. "And we are bringing bottles of water and one SatPhone from our camp."

"That's great," said Tony.

"We need to decide who is going with us," said Mike seriously. "It could be very dangerous and some of us may not return."

"I will go and some of my people wish to go also. I presume that you two are going?"

"Yes, we'll be going. I want to take only one Land Rover because we might be able to fool them into to thinking we are stragglers from their own force. That might help us get closer to them. Anyway the other two are being used for the casualties."

"Clara and the Minister have agreed to take the casualties," said the Chief. "And I'm sending two veterans armed with the first two AK-47s we recovered. One in each truck."

"That's good," said Tony. "I was afraid Clara would want to come with us."

"She did," said the Chief. "It was the Minister who eventually persuaded her, a girl doesn't always listen to her father, even if he is chief."

"I think that the three of us had better set off," said the Chief. "We will collect some of my men on the way."

Tony and Mike looked at him with puzzled expressions.

"Oh, did I not tell you, a group of our best trackers set off some time ago after the escaping vehicles."

Mike drove and the Chief was in the front passenger seat, Tony went in the back with his assault rifle so he could see, or shoot, in any direction.

They drove as fast as the terrain would allow for about ten miles and Mike thought they must have missed the trackers when the Chief held up his arm and said, "Stop here."

Mike pulled up gently, he didn't want to plough the wheels into the sand and get stuck.

Ten figures appeared from the surroundings, some were carrying Zulu style shields and spears, the short stabbing spear developed many years before by the great Zulu king Shaka.

Geoffrey, who carried only a knife in his belt, came and spoke to the Chief who then gave instructions. Geoffrey and two spearmen climbed in the back with Tony.

The Chief nodded and said, "They definitely went this way."

Mike accelerated away but soon had to ease off as the edge of the plateau gave way to a steep slope. A track zigzagged through a series hairpin bends. It was dirt and gravel so the truck slewed alarmingly at every turn.

Mike was scanning for a shortcut as he drove but the road wound amongst short trees. The only tracks which cut off the wide bends were too narrow and steep for a vehicle.

Even with the help of the moon the Land Rover lights didn't show up much of the road ahead. Mike's expression was constantly concerned, he was looking in front for an ambush at any turn but they reached the bottom of the zigzag track unscathed.

The track came out into open country scattered with a few piles of massive rocks, some scrub trees but very little other cover. There was no dust cloud to be seen from

269

escaping trucks. 'Too far ahead,' thought Mike. But they were on what resembled a road so it was highly likely they had gone this way.

They sped across the flat plain in uncomfortable pursuit.

"I can't think that anyone is hiding out here," said Mike but he was still looking around warily for any small sign that the trucks they were pursuing had left from the road.

Suddenly on instinct, or perhaps a subconscious assimilation of tiny signs, Mike slammed on the brakes. At the same moment a volley of fire hit the ground in front of the truck and a couple of shots ricocheted off the bonnet.

"Hell! That was us if you hadn't hit the brakes." Tony was shaken but he pointed the AK and sent a short burst in the direction of a rock pile less than hundred metres to the right.

Mike's mind raced to assessing the situation, 'There's no cover, we're completely exposed for hundreds of metres, in a moment the gunmen will have us in their sights and it will all be over.'

He hauled the steering wheel round and floored the throttle. The Land Rover went round in a tight circle temporarily putting the attackers off their bead. But he continued doing it raising a dust cloud around them. They weren't visible at least for a moment but what next. Some random shots came towards them and he realised that sooner or later the shooters would get lucky. He tried to judge where the fire was coming from.

"Tony," he shouted, "I'll give you a mark and you let some short bursts go out of the side of the truck."

"What?"

"At right angles, just do it"

"OK"

"On my mark."

"Fire! Fire! Fire!" Mike shouted at short regular intervals.

Some of the short bursts from the automatic could be heard hitting rock.

The incoming fire stopped momentarily.

"Good," muttered Mike. "Chief, get ready to pass me my rifle as soon as I stop."

Mike slowed the rate of his marks to Tony as he slowed the rotation of the truck. They stopped and he lined up his rifle over the windshield.

As the dust cleared he glimpsed one of the attackers just above the line of the rock.

His rifle fired once and he immediately swung it one eighty degrees to the rocks at the other side of the track in case there were more attackers there.

In an instant all the attackers were out of sight.

As the dust cleared further the Chief saw a dried up river bed, more like a big ditch, down one side of the track and pointed to it.

Careless of damage Mike put his boot down and drove the vehicle into the trench leaving only the top of the windshield sticking up and vulnerable.

They all jumped out as a round shattered the windshield. More shots were fired but without more damage to the vehicle.

Mike was pumped up with adrenalin and thinking hard.

"We are safe for a moment but we're stuck here," he told Tony and the others. "Get everything out of the truck and run that way, keep low in the ditch and don't stop. I'll catch you up."

They grabbed the kit and ran as best they could, keeping well below the site line of the shooters. There were still occasional rounds coming in and bouncing off the windshield.

271

Mike had taken his bag and rifle the other way and the Chief had followed him.

Mike and Tony were both about a hundred metres away from the Land Rover in opposite directions when they heard the first thump.

"Bloody hell the mortar, hit the deck!" Mike shouted.

The first mortar shell went right over their heads and landed just in front of the rocks on the opposite side of the road where Mike suspected there were more militia. His suspicions were confirmed as there was an angry shout from behind those rocks. The second mortar landed a couple of metres short. The third landed smack on the Land Rover. It exploded throwing sharp shrapnel in every direction. The petrol tank went up in a fireball and everyone kept their heads down as they were showered with hot metal.

"They've got the hang of it," muttered Mike without much enthusiasm.

He chanced to cautious glance over the edge of the bank.

'They aren't that good,' he thought. 'They think we're done.' He slid his rifle over the edge and sighted on the man, who appeared to be their leader, walking forward towards the wreck of the truck. The round hit him between his eyes. Mike's second shot didn't find a target as the other men scurried so quickly behind the rocks again.

"Back towards the Land Rover," he hissed to the Chief.

They were scurrying along when they heard the three thumps.

"Down! Cover your head!"

This time the first one landed right where Mike had fired from. The next mortar landed a few metres further away from them and in the river bed and next landed a few metres further again, also in the river bed.

272

"Good guess," muttered Chief.

"We can't keep this up for long," whispered Mike. "But we'll have just to keep low and keep quiet." They moved in as close as they could to the burning remains of the Land Rover.

Their attackers were being very cautious now.

"It looks like maybe they don't have too many mortar rounds left, maybe they're saving them up for a sure target."

All they had, was Mike's bag and rifle and the cans of fuel, that the Chief had grabbed. They had no water, that was with Tony and they couldn't get past the smouldering Land Rover to join him. What they really needed was a miracle.

The attackers didn't know if they were all dead now or if they were trying to escape down the dried up river bed. If they were trying to do that the attackers reasoned that they would all die of thirst in the desert anyway so they just kept their position and kept their eyes open for any movement.

There were less of the militia left now but they had the positional advantage and more weapons so they weren't worried and were prepared to sit it out. A few clouds drifted across the moon and the night darkened. The Land Rover engines started and two spot lights swept over the dry river bed. They shone the lights from random points above the rocks to prevent them being shot and occasionally aimed a burst of fire in the direction of the ditch.

Mike felt like he was in a WWI Trench and was preparing with the Chief to go over the top. He was expecting the same result that many of his ancestors had experienced in the mud of Flanders.

He whispered with the Chief. They had to break this stalemate. Immediately after a burst of fire and when the

273

spotlight has swung away, Mike and the Chief scrambled out of the river bed and ran low towards the nearest attackers. They heard movement ahead and threw themselves down between a small scattering of rocks not enough cover really but maybe they wouldn't be seen. Laying there, completely vulnerable they expected the light and the bullets to come at any moment. Their hearts beating so loudly they felt that they could be heard from anywhere

It seemed like an eternity but the lights didn't come on again and they couldn't understand what was happening. Maybe this was another trick or perhaps the mortars were coming again. They could still hear activity behind the rocks.

Tony and the other three kept running as Mike had instructed. They heard a shot and then three more explosions. Then all was quiet. Maybe that was it, maybe his brother and the Chief were dead.

They were well away from the action already but what could they do? They had water but only one rifle so they just kept going quietly and keeping their heads down.

The terrain they were entering had some small scrubby plants between the road and the ditch. Tony was getting tired although his companions looked as though they could go on all night.

"Can we stop for a while?" Tony said.

"Yes," said Geoffrey. "This is a good place to stop, we can watch the road through the bushes." They all rested and listened.

Tony got the binoculars out and scanned the horizon in the direction they had come from.

He saw soft faint lights flickering intermittently and after a while the occasional bursts of fire. That was encouraging it meant that there was somebody alive, unless they were just being executed. However the firing continued and it appeared that there must still be some sort of fight going on.

Then the firing stopped. Tony looked at the other guys they all had the same thought, 'It was over.' Now they'd just have to find the best cover they could and rest up.

Half an hour after the firing had stopped, they heard the sound of an engine on the road. As it approached they could see a lot of lights and actually could make out two engine sounds and eventually they saw two vehicles approaching them. This must be the militia. If that was true, then the last shots they had heard were the murder of Mike and the Chief.

They crouched low in the ditch and Tony readied the AK-47. Geoffrey had the sharpest eyes so he agreed to watch through the scrub. As the first vehicle approached they could all see the glow of lights then Geoffrey suddenly jumped up and ran out. Tony tried to stop him but it was too late, he was in full view. In that instant Tony had flashes of what Geoffrey might be doing. Was he going to avenge his chief by killing the Boss, it was a heroic idea but he had nothing in his hand except a knife. The truck roared to a halt. In the trench they waited for the sound of gunfire but it didn't come, only shouts, flashing lights and then Mike's voice.

What sort of a miracle was this? Tony dragged his weary body out of the trench with the AK-47 at the ready, if it was a trick it was all over now anyway. But it wasn't a trick! Mike sat on the bonnet of the first truck with a spotlight light shining up on him so he was easily visible. Geoffrey had recognised him immediately and so leapt out of the trench. There were hugs, slaps and incredulous looks; everybody was OK.

"Mike you're a genius." shouted Tony

"Nothing to do with me, it was these guys," he said pointing back down the road.

In the distance they could see a group of the Chief's men jogging along the road at a good pace.

"Where did they come from?" Tony exclaimed.

Mike filled in the details, "It seems like they can take shortcuts when trucks have to zigzag down a hill.

"When the ambushers put the lights on they knew exactly where they were. The Land Rover engines covered all sounds of approach.

"They just crept up behind them on both sides of the road at the same time and bashed their heads in with rocks."

They had commandeered the vehicles and had all the spare petrol and water plus the weapons from their attackers and Mike's rifle and bag.

"We are in a better position now to do something about this Boss and his men," said Mike.

Tony thought about Boss, "He seems to be totally careless of life, even his own men's. I wonder why they stay with him?"

"He cares only about himself," said Mike. "And I would guess he controls them with brutality and fear."

"Well, he doesn't have so many men behind him now," said Tony. "When we first saw him he had thirty. He lost eleven in that first encounter. Two more in his first attack and in the night attack he left two dead and four injured that we sent to hospital."

"That means he only had a force of eleven when he left some to ambush us," summarised Mike.

"How many did he loose in the ambush?" Tony asked.

"He had three on each side of the track," answered the Chief.

"That means he only has five men left, six with himself," said Tony.

"Unless he has a camp somewhere with more," said Mike. "But my guess is that he is not so well organised." Mike was drawing on his experience of warlords and terror groups from all over the world and comparing them with this man.

"What weapons did we get from the ambushers," said Tony and then thinking he had been callous for not asking before. "Did any of his men survive."

"No," said the Chief bluntly.

Chapter 56

"Where are we going now Boss?" Kabo asked.

"Shut up, I'm thinking," said Boss fiercely. There was quiet after that in the Toyota cab as they drove along a good tarmac road. Kabo, sitting in the passenger seat, knew better than to speak again.

Boss was actually thinking about what to do next. Since Thursday he had lost most of his current gang of men. He'd had thirty men when he first attacked the village and now he had only five and one of them was injured. There were another six but he didn't know where they were, whether the ambush had been successful or another disaster, and they had the mortar. He wasn't going to get his second payment for this job, that was for sure but at least he could keep most of what he had been paid. There weren't so many men to pay. What did the English say? 'Every cloud has a silver lining.' His best option would be to offer his services, and those of his remaining men, to another mercenary group and he knew exactly who that would be, his brother Seth. It would be a bit of a climb down but maybe if his brother had an accident or was killed in action there would be a good chance to take over the group. But first he needed a place to rest and get communications.

He started watching the road more carefully, he needed to find somewhere quiet and out of the way. After driving for another five minutes he braked hard. The Land Rovers nearly hit him but just managed to stop leaving rubber on the road.

"Tell them to reverse," he commanded.

Kabo walked back to the other vehicles and told them and just managed to get back in before Boss followed them. He stopped again and pulled off the road. He drove onto a dirt track with a small sign advertising holiday accommodation in a lodge.

"Rip up that sign and throw it behind a bush." Kabo dutifully went to pull the signpost up and discard it.

Boss drove till he was well away from the road and stopped again. He called all his men together.

"We are going to find some nice comfortable accommodation for a few days," he said. "I will go in first with my truck. Can Kabelo sit up." Kabelo had a bullet hole in his shoulder.

"Yes Boss, but he won't be happy," answered Kabo.

"I don't care if he is happy, just make sure he doesn't bleed on my seats," said Boss, "Thabo, you and Thabang lay down in the back of my Toyota."

They started to climb in, "Get your guns idiots, you're not going on holiday. Kabo, get the canvas and cover them."

The canvas was the dirty remains of a Land Rover's canvas roof.

"Kabo and Langa, wait here with the Land Rovers," Boss ordered. "And come when I signal or you hear gunfire."

Boss drove the Toyota with Kabelo in the passenger seat wincing at every bump in the road. He had put his holster and belt in the back of the truck but kept the pistol with him. It was on the seat beside him, ready to put in the back of his waist band. There were no weapons visible.

Dawn had still not yet come as the truck pulled up at the front of the house. Boss got out, ran round and opened the passenger door and tenderly helped Kabelo out.

The residents had heard the truck and seen them arrive, a man and a woman came out and ran to help when they saw the injured man.

"Let's get him inside," said the woman. "What happened to him?"

"It's a bullet wound. We were attacked last night but we escaped."

"Berni," she called as they went in. "Get my first aid box. Nadi get some sheets for the spare bed, and a plastic one."

By the time they had guided Kabelo into the spare room, the teenagers had the sheets on the bed, the bedside table cleared and the first aid box was open on top of it.

The casualty was laid on the bed and Selma sent her children for some more supplies. She cut away his shirt with scissors and Kabelo cried out as she pulled it away at the front and some fragments came out of the wound.

After more examination and cleaning she said, "The bullet went right through, which is good, but it dragged material into the wound and I'm afraid that might fester. Jo he'll need hospital or a doctor at least."

"I'll call the doctor," her husband Johannes answered. "And if you've been attacked I'd better let the police know too."

"No," said Boss, rather too quickly, then. "No need to bother them, he's very strong he'll recover with some rest." He actually didn't care if Kabelo recovered or not but calling the authorities was definitely out.

Jo was already half way to the door. "It won't be any bother for the doctor, he's only lives half an hour away."

"I said No!" shouted Boss as he quickly grabbed his pistol from behind him and shot Jo in the leg.

Jo fell, Nadi screamed, Selma gasped and went to him and Berni glared at Boss with the sudden fiery hatred of a teenager seeing his father hurt. His eyes flashed round the room looking for a weapon.

"Don't even think about it boy," said Boss coldly as he pointed his gun straight at Berni's face.

After a tense moment Selma said urgently to Berni, "The box, here," he complied immediately.

The bullet had just caught the bottom of Jo's shorts. She pulled the cloth away gently bringing some fragments of fibres out of the entry wound. She saw that the bullet had passed right through, she washed it and checked again for foreign material in the entry wound then dressed both holes and bandaged his leg.

"Stay there on the floor for a few minutes to rest," she instructed in a tone that did not brook dissent.

While she was dressing the wound, Thabo and Thabang burst into the house with their guns at the ready.

"All under control here," said Boss. "But keep an eye on that boy."

The Land Rovers arrived and Boss issued instructions to his men to secure the dwelling.

"Langa and Kabo put the Land Rovers round the back out of sight of the drive, Langa, you stay there and watch them. Kabo, come back and sit in that chair on the front porch and keep watch on the drive, keep your gun out of sight unless you are going to use it. You other two get Kabelo into a chair and get him his gun, then put daddy onto the bed," he said pointing at Jo. "Kabelo can watch him. When you've done that sit in the front room in those two chairs with your guns out of sight. You two kids sit down and shut up and I'm going to tell you all what's going to happen."

281

Selma checked Jo's dressings again and Kabelo was moved from the bed into the chair and given his gun.

"OK, get him into his bed," Boss pointed at Jo again.

"Now this is what will happen," said Boss making himself comfortable in an easy chair. "I will stay here with my friends for a few days," then he looked at Selma. "You will look after us and nobody will get hurt. Do you understand that?"

They all reluctantly nodded, Selma thought, 'If you think I believe that you are an idiot.' But she kept quiet and looked at her children as if to say, 'Do as he says, for now.'

"Now you two get outside and wash my truck and don't complain or I'll put a bullet in his other leg," he said pointing his gun in the direction of their father. They went out the front door with looks that could kill.

"I need to tend my husband," said Selma moving towards him.

Boss grabbed her arm, "Oh no lady, I have some plans for you and don't kick up a fuss or hubby here will be bleeding even more. Now go and get us some beers and some food."

Selma fetched three beers and then went to get some food for them, but took her time getting it, all the while trying to think how she could get help.

While she was in the kitchen, Boss found the house phone and made a call, just as he hung up Selma entered with their food.

"You two," Boss told Thabo and Thabang, "while I'm busy with her you keep watch from in here, and don't even think about touching that girl out there, she's mine when I've finished with her mother, then you can have them both to play with."

They smiled and made themselves comfortable.

282

Chapter 57

Geoffrey was walking back down the road towards the front of the truck where Mike, Tony and the Chief were talking.

"What do you see Geoffrey?" Chief Daniel asked.

"Three trucks have taken this road recently," he said. "Two had worn tyres one had much newer tyres."

"That's probably two Land Rovers and the Toyota he just acquired," said Tony.

"To answer your other question Tony," said Mike. "We have another six AK-47s, two pistols and a Mortar. There isn't much ammunition for the mortar but we can take it just in case. I'll stick with my rifle and pistol which means we can arm six of your men, Chief, with AK-47s and have a couple of pistols to spare."

Mike looked to the Chief to allocate these and he picked six of his men for the assault rifles and gave Geoffrey a pistol to defend himself if needed, he strapped the other pistol around his own waist.

When Mike drove off he was feeling a lot more confident about their chances of confronting the Boss and his men. He drove the first Land Rover with the Chief beside him and Tony and Geoffrey behind. The two spear men also stayed with them in the back.

The second Land Rover had six men all armed with assault rifles.

Because of the delay, Mike knew he would have to keep going and wouldn't overtake their quarry until Boss stopped, probably to make camp.

After half an hour they approached a good tarmac road, Geoffrey made them stop before they reached it and went to look. He could see that the trucks had joined the road and not just crossed it. He examined the tracks and the dirt thrown onto the tarmac then went back.

"They went to the right on the road," he told them.

After twenty minutes Geoffrey called for another stop. He looked at the road in front and behind their truck and then walked along the side of the road behind. They backed up for fifty metres and Geoffrey showed them a track off to the left which was almost invisible in the dark.

"They went there," he told them. "They missed the turn, stopped suddenly and had to reverse, just as we did, one old Land Rover left rubber on the road."

Mike laid out his map on the bonnet and checked their location and directions with his GPS. "That track looks like a dead end," he said after studying both. "But there is a building marked near the end."

Geoffrey had been walking around the junction of the road and the track and spotted the discarded sign. He carried it back to his Chief who read it.

"This track leads to a tourist lodge," said the Chief, "which means there may be people there in danger."

"We'll have to go cautiously," said Mike.

"With luck," said the Chief, "there will be a water tower or a windmill that we'll see from a good distance."

Mike set off down the track. Tony sat down in the back as Geoffrey and the two spearmen stood and stared into the distance ahead.

It was only about ten minutes later that the three of them said, "Stop!" almost simultaneously.

Tony and Mike looked through binoculars and could only just make out the top of the wind vanes.

"Power generation or water pumping," said the Chief.

"There are some small trees it that direction," said Geoffrey. "We can approach there without being seen. Can we lower the windscreen and take those rails off?" he asked indicating the tubes which could support a long gone canvas roof.

"Good idea,"said Mike. "We can drive a bit closer if we are careful."

They managed to get within two kilometres of the house with the Land Rovers still well concealed by the trees. The six armed men from the second Land Rover stayed with the vehicles in reserve and the other six made their way carefully forward.

"I've told them to stay with the vehicles unless there is trouble or we call for them," the Chief said quietly to Mike. "Also, they will be watching that wind vane on the water tower, if you shoot that they will know to head straight to the road and prevent the bandits from escaping."

"That's good," said Mike, thinking again what a great asset the Chief was in this venture.

The land in that area was relatively flat with scrub trees and bushes but the area around the house had been cleared. When they came in sight of it first, it was still night. The Chief sent Geoffrey to scout around, certain that he could do that without being seen.

Geoffrey reappeared silently from the darkness just before the sun peeped over the horizon away to their right.

They could see the white Toyota was parked at the front of the house and Geoffrey had seen that the Land Rovers were at the back with one guard. There were lights on all over the house and Geoffrey had seen people in several of the windows.

Mike sketched a plan of the house from what they could see and from Geoffrey's information.

285

As the sun came up two teenagers, a boy about fifteen and a girl a couple of years older, came out and started washing the Toyota. They didn't look very happy about it and appeared to be whispering furtively to each other.

"Two kids," said Mike. "Likely a mother and father in the house too."

"Could we get any closer Mike?" Tony asked.

"We could try but we would risk being seen."

"There is another truck coming," said Geoffrey.

Chapter 58

Ken and Maria had some more food and watched the red dot on the screen move further away from the village and across country.

"I think we'll be working together until this is over," said Ken. "There's nobody else around so we could use our names instead of the company letter. I'm Ken Heaton."

Mary Best was her name at S&A. She didn't want to mention that her real name was Maria as she didn't want that information getting back to the Farm.

"My name is Mary Best, pleased to meet you Ken," they shook hands jokingly and continued their observation.

"They must be on a track now Mary," said Ken they are moving in much more of a straight line after that stop.

"They don't look as though they are in a great hurry," said Maria. "I think you should try and get some rest, I'll keep an eye on them and wake you when I think they are travelling straight enough for us to work out an interception point."

Ken objected at first and said he'd watch with her but conceded when he realised how much his trek across the desert on foot had taken out of him. He would need to be fresh.

The next thing he was aware of was Maria saying, "Ken, wake up."

He stirred and gradually came out of a deep sleep.

"Sorry to wake you but it's on a tarmac road and making good time. I think we need to get going."

It was the early hours of Sunday morning, Maria gave Ken a cup of hot coffee and sipped her own as she drove.

Ken watched the tablet and navigated. Just as dawn was breaking Ken said, "Mary, they've turned off this road."

"Shall I stop?" Maria asked.

"Yes, let's stop and have a look where they go, they aren't that far away," he answered.

They studied the screen and the maps.

"It looks like they are going down the drive to that tourist lodge," said Maria eventually.

"Yes," he replied. "And they are probably terrorising the occupants. We need some more information, mainly how many men Boss has."

"Let's get that drone up that you have in one of your cases," she suggested.

He agreed then went to the back of the Range Rover to get it out.

While Maria drove off the main road Ken sat in the passenger seat and checked out the drone. They stopped in the drive a few kilometres away from the lodge which they had identified on a map.

They flew the drone as high as it would go until they could no longer see it. All they had was the view on a tablet monitor. It was a very good view, they could already see the lodge so Ken guided the drone towards it.

What could be seen was remarkable when the camera zoomed in. The Toyota at the front and the two Land Rovers at the back were clearly visible.

"Mary, if they have lost the same proportion of men as they have vehicles," said Ken, "they don't have too many left."

As the drone moved toward the lodge they could see a man sitting in a rocking chair on the front veranda and another who appeared to be asleep in the back of one of the Land Rovers.

"We need to get closer," said Maria. "This is what I propose we do."

Chapter 59

Maria was driving the Range Rover and Ken was concealed in the back with the window right down. They had arranged the cases of camera equipment so it could be easily reached when the tailgate was opened.

Maria pulled up behind the Toyota, kept the engine running and called to the girl who came over to speak to her. Kabo put his hand down to locate his gun but kept it out of sight.

"Hello," said Maria, "I have come to help."

"On your own!" Nadi exclaimed in a whisper.

"Don't worry," she replied. "I have backup nearby. How many of them are there?"

"There are six," she answered. "One is wounded but he still has a gun, he's watching my Dad. They shot my Dad in the leg."

"Who else is inside?" Maria asked, "My Mum, she has been bandaging the wounds.They sent my brother and me out to wash his truck."

That didn't bode well for Mum thought Maria, she could guess why they wanted the kids out of the way.

"OK," said Maria. "Act like I'm a new guest and try to behave normally. If shooting starts get on the ground quickly, crawl away and try to find some cover. Do you understand?"

She nodded. "Go back and help your brother and explain to him."

She went back to her brother and they continued washing the truck.

"OK Ken, I'm going in."

"Be careful Mary," he answered.

Maria opened the tailgate, took out a couple of bags and walked to the front door. She smiled at Kabo and said, "Good morning, are you the owner?"

"No Ma'm, I'm only the hired help. It's open, just go in," he said knowing full well that there were two men inside waiting for her but he didn't challenge her outside because he thought she might be the first of a larger party.

Thabo and Thabang were sitting in easy chairs, each with an arm draped over the back, Maria knew what would be in those hidden hands.

She smiled politely again and asked, "Are you gentlemen in charge? I need accommodation for a few nights."

"I think we can accommodate you," said Thabo with a dirty smile to Thabang.

She took his meaning and said, "That sounds a bit naughty boys," in a slightly husky voice, and added, pointing at one of the bedroom doors. "It sounds like there's a bit of naughty going on in there already." They just smirked.

"We are always up for a bit of fun," smiled Thabang.

"Well," she said quietly moving towards them. "I haven't had a proper man for weeks, two would be a bonus." They were almost drooling, she had her hand on her crotch, they watched it as she slipped it down the front of her shorts and gave little sigh. They couldn't believe what they were seeing as their eyes followed her left hand over her breast to the buttons on he blouse.

Her hand came out of her pants holding a warm Baby Browning which she was pointing at them. Their reactions to lift their guns were automatic but fatal. She fired twice then stepped quickly through the open bedroom door that she had noted as she came in and snatched the AK-47 from Kabelo as he was drifting back from semi

290

consciousness. She handed the gun to Jo on the opposite bed. "Stay here and watch him," she said with authority.

The instant Ken heard the two shots he was out of the truck and racing towards the house. Kabo had risen with his gun in his hand and was looking at the front door and moving towards it.

"Drop the gun!" Ken ordered. He had the advantage, his rifle was aimed directly at Kabo's torso but Kabo's gun was pointing at the door.

Kabo dropped down and to his left, raising his gun towards Ken in the same quick motion. Ken's burst of fire hit Kabo on his right side and the gun dropped from his injured arm without being fired. Ken kept running straight through front the door.

He saw two men slumped in chairs not moving, then Maria emerged from a bedroom closed the door and moved quickly across to another door. Just as she got there the door burst open and she went behind it leaving Ken pointing his rifle into the room. Boss came out gripping a woman in front of him and holding a pistol to her head. Her clothes were ripped, she had bruises on her cheeks and a trickle of blood from her nose but the expression on her face was all defiance.

"You!" Boss shouted as he saw Ken. He was surprised the man was alive, "I should have shot you with the rest of your men."

"Your mistake," said Ken, his rifle was at his shoulder and he was sighting at Boss's head.

Boss quickly pulled his head behind Selma's and shouted, "Drop your gun or I'll blow her brains out!"

"No you won't because I will kill you if you hurt her, you sadistic, fat bastard."

"Watch your mouth or I'll kill you," Boss spat venomously.

"You really are stupid aren't you," said Ken calmly. "Too stupid to know that you don't have any men left to do your dirty work."

His comments had the desired effect, Boss was enraged and quickly moved the gun from Selma's head and started to aim towards Ken.

In the instant it moved away from Selma's head Maria struck. She hit his arm down, the pistol fired into the floor, she grasped it and levered it out of his hand casting it away.

At that moment Tony and Mike stepped through the door with AK-47s pointing at Boss.

Boss hesitated only a moment, he pulled a knife from his belt with his right hand and lunged at Maria. Mike raised his rifle, Maria shouted, "No!" Mike watched her sidestep, pull Boss's left hand, sweep his legs from beneath him and follow him to the floor. The combination of Maria's actions and his momentum sent him flat on his face. She held his left hand up so he instinctively opened his right hand to save himself as he hit the floor losing the knife. An instant after hitting the floor all of Maria's weight landed on his back and knocked the wind out of him. She had both his arms tight behind his back now and Ken stepped forward and zipped them together with a cable tie. Maria took another tie and zipped his feet together too and said "Watch the back door Ken, in case the other one comes in,"

"He won't be troubling us," said Mike. Tony smiled.

Maria turned to them, "Hello Tony, I'm glad to see you looking OK, is Clara all right?" she asked calmly.

"She's fine," answered Tony still a bit bewildered with what he'd seen.

"Who are you?" she asked looking at Mike.

"Mike," he answered. "I'm Tony's brother."

"Pleased to meet you Mike, I'm Maxine," she held out her hand and stepped over to him.

"Pleased to meet you too, I think," he said as he shook her hand.

Chapter 60

"Maxine?" Ken whispered the question.

"Yes," she whispered back, "S&A legend."

He nodded, understanding.

Selma stepped into her bedroom, grabbed her dressing gown, wrapped herself and started organising her home.

"Please get the wounded into this room with the other one and watch them." She led her husband out and into her own room. "And get that animal out of my house," she added pointing at Boss.

She checked that Jo was well settled in their bed and was OK, then she fetched her first aid box and administered to Boss's injured men. Mike joined her and assisted as Tony stood with his rifle in the doorway.

Ken checked Thabo and Thabang, they needed no first aid, each had a small bloody hole in his forehead, so he started with Boss. He dragged him out onto the veranda none too carefully. He did not struggle or resist but wisely tried to assist. The two spearmen appeared beside Ken startling him, his heart was racing when a confident deep voice said, "We are with Tony and Mike and we are here to help." The Chief had been squatting on the ground talking to the two teenagers.

The spearmen grasped Boss by the upper arms and lifted him to his feet.

"Please put him well away from the house," said the Chief. "Tied securely to a tree and out of sight would be best."

The spearmen took him away.

"This is all very confusing," said the Chief to Ken.

"You're not kidding," said Ken who was definitely perplexed.

"One thing I am sure of," said the Chief. "That is a very bad man and must be guarded and in time punished."

"That is something that we can definitely agree on," said Ken. "I work with Maxine, my name is Ken."

"Well Ken, I think we are on the same side. I am Chief Daniel and I hope we can all sit down together later to understand what is really going on." He held out his hand and shook Ken's.

Maria stepped out of the door and saw, with some relief, that they were shaking hands.

"Hello Chief Daniel, I am happy to see you again and I see you have met my colleague Ken."

"Yes," said the Chief. "All appears to be under control, for the moment at least."

The most seriously injured was Kabo with three bullet wounds, courtesy of Ken.

Langa appeared to be uninjured. When he was awakened by the sound of gunshots and saw the Chiefs men standing around him he did not resist. His weapons had been quietly removed during his sleep and they didn't even need to point their rifles at him. He was told to be quiet and they tied his hands in front of him.

He sat quietly awaiting his fate; he doubted that it would be any worse than he would get from Boss.

The Chief consulted with Jo about a location for graves and then had his men remove the two corpses to bury them.

Selma treated the injured as best she could but decided that she wanted the local doctor to see them so Jo phoned.

"The doctor will be here in half an hour," said Jo leaning on the doorframe and looking proudly at Selma.

"You should be lying down," she said when she saw him. "And where are the kids?"

"They are outside talking to Chief Daniel," answered Jo.

"Who the hell is Chief Daniel? In fact, who the hell are all these people?" Selma asked a bit wearily.

The doctor arrived and examined all the injured including Selma. He was more concerned with Selma than the others and, as well as treating her injuries, he took swabs and gave her a tablet to take "just in case" he had said.

After he had finished his treatments he was in deep conversation with the Chief for some time before he left.

Later, Tony, Mike and the Chief, together with Jo and Selma were talking with Maria. Ken had opted to guard the injured men, he didn't want to be talking with the others in case Tony recognised his voice. Boss was still tied to a tree and the Chief's men were watching him with instructions to listen to everything he said, threats, pleas or anything else.

Selma and Jo were itching to know what was going on.

"These bandits, mercenaries or whatever they are, attacked my village," started the Chief. "If we had not been at least a little prepared the first time, it would have been a massacre, as it was there were only a few minor injuries. They attacked us again but with Mike's help we were able to chase them off. We believe that they attacked us to derail the project that we are helping with. What we do not know is why they are trying to stop the project so we have been tracking them to get some answers."

"Are you all working together then?" Selma asked looking at Maria, "You and Ken?"

"Actually Ken and I were tracking them and we didn't know that others were here or we might have devised a different plan," explained Maria.

"I don't know that we would have come up with anything that would have worked better," said Mike who was intrigued by this woman who appeared to be endowed with skills far beyond those he would expect from an operative of a private security company.

"It was a good plan," said Selma. "It worked." Jo nodded in assent as he put his arm round Selma.

"I'm only sorry that we didn't arrive earlier," said Maria looking towards Selma and turning over all the events in her mind. "Ken and I are also very keen to find out who is behind this group of bandits."

"Oh no! You have just reminded me!" Selma exclaimed, "They aren't the only bandits! He called his brother on our phone. I got the impression that his brother is in the same business." Then she pointed out to the trees, "And that animal, out there, asked him to come here."

"Did you get any idea of how many men or when they will arrive?" Maria asked trying not to make the question sound too urgent.

"That was all I could hear," answered Selma.

"We had better make some preparations and we have a lot of questions for these bandits," said the Chief. "Lets get started."

Geoffrey went to the top of the water tower to keep a lookout. Mike went to speak nicely with the remaining bandits. Selma organised her children into making lunch for everyone. The others started preparing the vehicles in case they had to leave in a hurry.

Chapter 61

When Maria was alone in her Range Rover, she dialled a UK number on her satellite phone.

"Please can you track down Rob Riddle for me, this is Maria."

"Will you hold please?" The receptionist replied. She located Rob and said, "Agent Maria is on the line sir."

A few moments later she came back on the line to Maria, "I'm putting you through."

"Hello Maria," said Rob.

"Hello Rob, reception found you very quickly."

"I am in my office, we have been on alert since your message on Friday evening."

Her call to her mum on Friday evening was monitored, as always, and relayed to Rob. Maria knew it would be monitored and had included messages to MI5. She had said, 'busy, busy, busy,' this was a flag for important information coming. 'Travelling again,' meant that she had gone abroad, her boss knew it would be Namibia in this case. 'Situation is interesting' meant there was a developing 'situation'. 'I'm dying,' was an indication that lives were threatened and the wish to 'have all my old friends round me' was a clear call for support.

"What phone are you using?" Rob asked. She gave him the make and model number.

"Good," he said, "that has good encryption. Give me an update."

"As you know Sellick & Arrowsmith Security sent me to audit the Solar project at the village as an auditor from Renshaw & Collier. I completed that audit, reported everything live to HQ and went to Cape Town as instructed by S&A. I then had a call from the village Minister that they had been attacked and the two Doctors kidnapped."

As Maria finished the sentence, Rob broke in, "We know some of this already, I had a call from a contact in S&A, Phil Arrowsmith, you know him I'm sure. We met and I believe that he has been completely open with me and told me everything that they know and did, including Ken Heaton's operation to rescue the two Doctors. That's the part which really embarrasses them. It's right on the borderline of their covert operations but they believed it was the only way to keep those leaders safe. S&A sent you back to the village, what happened after that?"

"They also told me to make contact with the other team they had in the area. I managed to contact Ken and he was in a very bad way so I diverted to him first. Luckily I found him before it was too late. He was alone, bound and suffering from exhaustion and dehydration."

"Did he recover and where is the rest of his team?"

"The rest of his team is dead," she reported,"but he did recover and he's OK now. We found his team and buried them and then tracked the bandits who had killed them and taken the Doctors."

"Why didn't you or Ken report any of this back to S&A Headquarters?" Rob asked.

"We reasoned that the bandits, who Ken was tasked to meet, were contracted by the same client as his team. That meant that we couldn't trust the client or S&A."

"Logical," said Rob. "Where are these bandits now?"

"We have captured them. They took over a holiday lodge run by a family of four. The father was shot in the leg and the mother raped but the children, both teenagers, are physically unharmed. The surprise was that Ken and I were joined during our rescue by Chief Daniel and some of his

299

people and also that Tony and Clara, the two Doctors escaped from the bandits under their own initiative. Tony and his brother Mike were with the Chief when he joined us, it seems that Mike was a big help in fighting off the bandits"

"Ah yes, Mike, Tony's brother," said Rob thoughtfully. "It sounds as though you have the situation under control now so, to wrap up the UK end of this, we need to know who contracted these bandits."

"Not quite under control," she said. "The leader of these bandits called his brother for support and we believe that he is coming here in force. Unfortunately we don't yet have any details of this brother's whereabouts or his numbers."

"Understood," said Rob. "I have already made some contingency plans with our friends at Vauxhall Cross and some of our other friends. Try to find out what you can from the bandits and keep the satellite phone with you. I will call you with any information and if this bandit-brother arrives call me on this mobile number."

She put the number into the satellite phone and replied, "Understood."

"One other thing," added Rob. "What do you know about Mike?"

"Not much except that I think he is military and good at what he does," answered Maria.

"Not a bad summary," he replied. "He is actually ex-military, invalided out over a year ago, however extremely resourceful and experienced. After officer training there isn't much in his record that isn't redacted but he has a very high security clearance."

"He doesn't display any physical injuries," commented Maria. "Is it PTSD?"

"No," replied Rob, "he had a part of his left foot blown off by an IED. I'm glad to hear he shows no disability because I think his skills could be very useful to us. I believe that you can trust him, as much as you can trust anyone in our world.

"I think it best to explain everything to Mike, even the extraction of his brother and Dr Bella. Later he can explain to his brother. If his brother recognises Ken this could help."

Chapter 62

Chief Daniel was at the rear of the Lodge, sitting in the back of the Land Rover examining Langa. He was younger than he had appeared at first, probably only early twenties but he had a weary countenance.

"My name is Daniel," said the Chief. "I am chief of the people that your Boss attacked. What is your name young man?"

Langa thought for a moment, he had not been mistreated since his capture and there had been no threats so he made the decision to be as cooperative as he could.

"My name is Langa Chief Daniel," he replied respectfully.

"How did you come by that mark on your face?" Chief Daniel asked.

"I was hit with a pistol," he answered. The Chief guessed who had struck him since he knew that Boss carried a pistol.

"Was it Boss who struck you Langa?"

Langa nodded and as he did he winced slightly.

"Please remove your shirt," instructed the Chief.

He complied slowly, not from reluctance but from the pain of lifting his arms.

"Was this the Boss's work too?" Chief Daniel asked.

Langa nodded again.

"I will get the woman in the house to look at your injuries later Langa and see if she has something to ease the pain," said the Chief.

"Thank you Chief Daniel," said Langa.

"Now, please tell me some more about your Boss," said the Chief.

It was about midday; Selma gave the Chief's men food for themselves and Geoffrey who was still keeping watch. They took it outside to continue their watch over Boss and Langa.

The group watching Langa, gave him food and drink but the group watching Boss were happy to eat their own food and let him watch hungrily.

Most of the others sat around the big guests' dining table, there were eight of them including the teenagers. Ken was sitting in the doorway of the makeshift hospital room and Selma took food to him there.

"This is very kind of you to feed us all Selma," said the Chief.

"You are welcome after all that has happened," she replied.

"I have spoken with the man Langa who is outside with the Land Rovers," the Chief continued. "He has been quite forthcoming about Boss and his activities. It seems that this Boss character acquires his recruits as young as possible and forces them into his service governing them by fear and with brutality. Langa thinks his age is about twenty-three and he was forcibly recruited eight years ago. He has no love for Boss and I suspect that is true of most of his men."

"Why does this not surprise me," said Selma.

"Langa also told me about Boss's brother," continued the Chief. "He runs a similar gang by similar methods. The last time the two groups met, Boss had thirty men and his brother had fifty with eight vehicles and considerable weaponry. Unfortunately, he does not know their current location. Geoffrey will inform us if anyone approaches," added the Chief confidently. "And we will ensure that we

303

keep everyone safe." Given the potential threat he knew there was some work to be done to achieve that.

"I've only been to question Boss once briefly," said Mike. "But he wouldn't make a sound."

"Give me five minutes with him and he'll make a sound," said Selma pointedly.

"Is it OK if I come and talk to Boss with you Mike," asked Maria.

"No problem," he replied.

After more discussions around the table, everyone thanked Selma and the teenagers for the lunch and set about their various tasks.

Mike and Maria stood in front of Boss.

"Would you like us to make you more comfortable?" Mike asked. Boss had his hands and legs cable tied to a small tree. His hands were behind his back and he had to stand rather awkwardly.

Boss looked from one to the other, he knew nothing about them, except that the woman had attacked him, and he was now at their mercy. They were White and English though, so they wouldn't know how to hurt people properly, but he thought he might as well be more comfortable and he might get a chance to escape so he nodded.

The man went behind him and cut the wrist ties.

"Hands in front," said the woman and zip tied them tightly together.

"Bitch!" he hissed and was rewarded by a hard punch to his stomach which sent him onto his face on the ground.

"Please be more polite," she said as she placed her foot on the back of his neck and pushed his face into the ground. "I hope you are more comfortable now."

He felt the tie pulling on his feet go slack and although they were still tied together he could now move his legs.

He pushed himself onto all fours, shook his head and spat dirt out of his mouth. Then he was able to squirm round and lean against the tree. He could only see the man, the woman had gone which was a relief, and he was able to wipe the dirt from his face.

Mike was squatting in front of him, "She is quite an angry lady," he said. "It would be better for you, if you were more civil in her presence."

Boss uttered a more or less affirmative grunt and added. "What do you want?"

"What's more to the point," said Mike, "is what did you hope to gain by attacking the village?"

He was silent for a while then answered sullenly, "It was just a job."

"And who was the job for?" Mike asked.

This he would not tell, he feared the people who had hired him far more than these White English. So he refused to say any more.

"OK, have it your own way," said Mike walking away. "You may regret not talking to me."

Mike and Maria concealed themselves in the undergrowth and watched him roll about to try and find something sharp to free himself.

His wrists were getting raw when Maria walked up to him and said sharply, "You've moved from where you were put!" She dragged him roughly back to the tree he had been tied to before, made him stand and secured his feet again. He hoped she would cut his wrists loose to try and tie them behind him, then he would get her, but instead she hoisted his arms and tied them above his head to the highest branch in the small tree. Now he was even less comfortable and felt vulnerable stretched up like that.

"My colleague tells me that you refuse to tell him anything useful," she paused and smiled wickedly at him. "But I'm sure you would like to talk to me."

He was indeed more concerned about this woman than he had been about the man.

"Tell me Boss," she said quietly. "How were you contacted about this job?"

"I was telephoned," he said cautiously, "but I don't know the man's name"

"Was it this phone he called you on?" Maria asked holding up the mobile phone that had been discovered in the white Toyota. She was watching his face very carefully and saw his eyes open slightly wider in startled recognition.

"Well?" Maria asked.

He nodded reluctantly, they must know already he thought.

"How were you paid?" Maria asked quickly. He looked quickly at the phone and then away even more quickly. "Good," said Maria with satisfaction, she was now pretty sure that all the transaction details could be extracted either from the phone or the service provider when there was time.

"You have been a good boy. I have one final question, for you Boss, then I may even let you sit down."

'What now,' he thought.

She waited a moment for him to think about that, then, "When will your brother arrive?"

How did she know about that? I Didn't tell her and I can't tell her. His face showed surprise then defiance and he said nothing.

"So it's like that," she said drawing a knife with a six inch blade from her belt scabbard and a steel from another. She started to hone the blade and said as though to herself,

"We have a few options, I could cut your bonds and let you go. That's not going to happen. I could puncture your leg and let you bleed until you answer or die, or I could end this discussion now and just put this knife in your heart. Which would you prefer?"

He remained silent, he didn't believe that even this callous White English woman would kill him.

Selma came bursting through the bushes still wearing her washing up gloves from the kitchen.

"Give me that knife," she shouted in a rage, "I'll show you what to do with him."

Maria looked at her and said, "But if you kill him I won't get any more information."

Selma glared venomously at Boss, "I'm not going to kill him, I'm going to cut his dick off. Give me that knife."

Boss stared at Selma in utter terror, he was trembling and if his hands hadn't been tied above his head he would probably have collapsed.

Maria shrugged her shoulders and stepped towards Selma but Selma had already turned to Boss and pulled his shorts down to his knees. She grabbed his genitals and shouted hysterically at Maria, "The knife, give me the knife."

Boss screamed at Maria, "No! No! He'll be here at midnight. Don't give her the knife."

"Where from?" Maria asked as she took step towards Selma.

"He's coming from the north don't give her the knife, please, please," pleaded Boss.

Mike appeared. "What's all the noise?"

"Stop them! Stop them! They're going to castrate me," he pleaded to Mike.

Mike put his hands comfortingly on Selmas shoulders and whispered in her ear. She relaxed a little and then squeezed the genitals viciously before releasing them and letting Mike guide her away.

Boss screamed in pain and hung on his wrists his head down almost unconscious. When he looked up he was alone.

Some time later Mike came back and pulled his shorts up and cut the tie to the high branch. Boss collapsed on the ground and Mike checked that he was still securely bound. Two of the Chief's men appeared to watch him.

"Thank you Selma," said Mike. "You were brilliant."

"Yes, I agree," said Maria. "It was brilliant, he really thought he was about to lose his manhood."

"I'm glad you didn't give me the knife," said Selma. "If you had I think he might have lost it."

"It would be what he deserved," said Jo looking protectively and proudly at his wife. He was sitting in the circle with them with his arm round Selma.

"Well it worked as planned, and we now know when his brother will arrive," said Chief Daniel, "but what do we do next?"

"Mike and I have been discussing that," said Maria. "There are a few things we have to do, but for everyone's safety, we would like everyone inside the house tonight and nobody should go outside."

The rest of the group looked a bit shocked and stared at her and then questioningly at Mike.

"There are some things that you don't know about Maxine which she can't tell you," said Mike. "But what I can tell you all, is that you can trust her. We have a plan which is as bullet proof as it can be."

"Perhaps bullet proof isn't the best metaphor," said Maria. "But it should all work out well. When we have everything in place we'll tell you more."

"Mike," said the Chief. "I know that I can trust you and I have always had a good feeling about Maxine, so if you say that we will be OK then I am happy to fit in with your plan." This of course meant that all his men would too so that only left Selma, Jo and their children to be convinced.

"We've only known you for a very short time but I believe that I can trust you all," said Selma looking to Jo who nodded his approval. She looked towards her children.

"We're cool," they said in unison.

"There is just one thing. That animal is not coming inside my home," said Selma pointing outside to the trees where Boss was being watched.

"That's fine," said Mike. "He can stay out there."

Chapter 63

The whole current population of the lodge was much more relaxed now with the notable exception of Boss and his remaining men.

Mike and Maria went to her Range Rover.

"If you work for MI5," asked Mike, "why are you working outside the UK?"

"My initial brief was in the UK," she answered, "but because I knew about the solar project and I knew Tony, when it went abroad I started working with SIS. I still report to my section head in MI5 but he liaises, and I mean really liaises, with SIS."

Mike knew that there were rivalries between the different organisations but it was good to know that this particular relationship was working.

"I'm going to call my section head now and see what exactly he can arrange to help us, he said he could get what we needed."

"Hello Rob," she said when she was put through. "I'm still on the same SatPhone. I have more information now and I'm with Mike."

He was glad she was calling and replied, "Both those things sound good, what do you know?"

"We have the Boss's mobile phone which was used to arrange his contract and we are fairly certain that there is good information there. He has told us that his brother's ETA is midnight tonight and he is coming from the north."

"So we have less than ten hours," said Rob thoughtfully. "We should have enough time. I'll call you back in an hour."

Mike and Maria went back to her Range Rover at 14:55 to wait for the call. At 15:00 it rang.

"Hello Rob, Maria here."

"I have set some wheels in motion," said Rob. "This is the plan and I will call you in three hours to confirm that it is all in place."

He went on to explain the details.

After the call Maria outlined the plan to Mike. They sat in the front of the Range Rover and went over the details until they were convinced that everything was covered.

When they got back at the house, Maria was surprised and concerned to see Ken and Tony with their heads together talking and joking. She and Mike went to join them.

"Ken's lost his voice," said Tony. "He can only whisper but it's OK if you are close enough."

Maria leaned close to Ken, "I don't think it's infectious," he whispered. "Probably just the dry air and desert dust. It's just a bit uncomfortable."

"Well, don't talk too much," she said and she thought to herself. 'That was a good idea Ken.'

At 18:00 Rob called Maria and told her that everything was good to go, she answered, "Thanks that's great," and hung up.

"All go," she confirmed to Mike and they went to tell the others.

Geoffrey insisted that he kept watch from his high vantage point. He had made himself comfortable there and much preferred to be doing something useful. He was very pleased when Ken gave him night vision goggles to try when the sun went down.

Langa had been taken to the hospital room and Selma had treated his injuries with lotions. Ken and Tony watched their captives but they seemed quite docile now, especially as they were being fed and housed and nobody was shooting, or even shouting, at them.

The Chief and his men were on the veranda at the front of the house, they had brought all the vehicles there where they could keep an eye on them. The trucks were aligned ready to drive away in convoy. Mike had organised them with military precision, just in case.

At 20:30 Maria and Mike went to Boss and took over the watch from the two spearmen who went to join their chief. Everyone had strict instructions to stay where they were unless they were warned by Geoffrey of an imminent attack, in which case they would evacuate in the vehicles.

Mike cut Boss's wrist bonds and tied them again in front of him. He also released his legs so that he could walk.

"Sit against that tree," ordered Mike, "and don't move. Now we wait."

"What time is it?"Boss asked.

"You don't need to know," snapped Maria. He kept quiet after that.

At 20:55 Mike stood up and walked into the darkness. Boss stirred. Maria drew her knife and said, "Sit still." He did!

Mike walked about fifty metres then deviated slightly towards the sound he had heard which was now clearly recognisable as the beat of helicopter rotors. Mike held his arms high, he didn't think he needed a light as they would have IR cameras and night vision goggles.

As the rotors slowed and the sound level dropped a voice beside him said, "I thought you had retired."

He dropped his hands and turned toward the voice. A uniformed figure emerged from the darkness in a balaclava with an assault rifle at port.

"Invalided out," replied Mike, recognising the voice but not mentioning it.

"Good to see you Mike," said the soldier. "You look well. Where are the packages?"

"This way," he said. He walked back towards Maria and they heard disgruntled grumblings then a yelp and silence. Mike came across Maria ushering Boss towards him.

"No trouble?" Mike asked.

"No," she replied. Boss looked at Mike with pleading eyes and suddenly a black bag whipped over Boss's head and two more soldiers grasped his arms and led him towards the helicopter.

The first soldier stepped up and asked, "And the other package?"

Mike produced the phone from his pocket which the soldier sealed in a plastic bag and slipped inside his jacket.

"Good to see you again," he said as he disappeared into the darkness. The helicopter rotors had already started turning and then it was whirling away.

They went back to the house and sat with the others.

"Well?" Tony asked looking at Mike.

"Boss has been taken for interrogation," he answered, "and that's as much as I know and all I need to know." They all understood that they didn't need to know any more and they didn't ask.

At 23:00 Geoffrey reported lights to the north. Mike climbed up to him and looked with binoculars, night vision glasses and the telescopic sight of his rifle. He couldn't see much detail but from previous experience, he believed that the column of vehicles belonging to Boss's brother had been attacked by aircraft. Given the swift cessation of action there had not been much resistance.

313

Maria's phone rang at 23:30 and she went outside to listen to the report. When she came back she was smiling. "We can all sleep easy tonight," she reported. "Boss's brother and his column of vehicles was ambushed by Namibian Defence Forces about thirty kilometres to our north. Their resistance was subdued with a single strafing run by a Chengdu F-7 fighter from the Namibian Air Force."

The following morning two police vehicles arrived to remove the injured captives.

Chief Daniel had moved all the vehicles, except the Range Rover behind the house and well out of sight before they arrived.

When they were all safely locked in the police vans and the sergeant in charge had spoken to them all, the Chief spoke with the Sergeant and asked about their fate.

"It appears Chief Daniel," said the sergeant, "that they are not Namibian and therefore the simplest action will be to deport them. Their own countries can deal with them. It seems that the ringleader has disappeared so they probably cannot give us much useful information anyway. Someone will get in touch with you to get statements and please accept my thanks for apprehending them."

Chief Daniel graciously accepted their thanks and bade them farewell with their captives.

As well as the Toyota Pick up and the Range Rover there were four Land Rovers at the lodge when the police left. It was agreed that two would be left at the Lodge, for Jo and Selma to use. The teenagers hoped that one of them would come their way to learn to drive. The Chief would need the other two to get back to the village.

Ken drove the Toyota that he had originally rented from Cape Town, the Chief and Geoffrey joined him to help navigate back to the village. Four of the Chief's men followed in each of the two Land Rovers. Maria, still being called Maxine, brought up the rear of the convoy in her Range Rover accompanied by Mike and Tony.

On the way Mike called the airport car hire company, where he had rented his Toyota, which was still on the other side of the village. They agreed he could leave it at Cape Town Airport instead of Johannesburg, it was still in South Africa and it was about two and a half hours closer.

Maria and Ken would take their vehicles back to Cape Town Airport too.

When they arrived back at the village Clara had already returned.

She hugged Tony and her dad with tears of happiness welling in her eyes.

"I can't believe it's only two days since I saw you," she said when she had released them.

"It seems like a lot longer," agreed Tony.

"What are you doing here Maxine?" Clara asked with a hint of hostility, "I thought you had left for Cape Town and the UK."

"It's a long story. We will discuss it all over some food," interrupted the Chief with a tone that said, 'this is what will happen'.

The whole story came out over the evening meal, or at least nearly all of it. The people had moved back into the village and repaired or replaced most of the tents and huts. Clara had reported the pylon sabotage to the electricity authority and their maintenance people fixed the pylons, it would have been a disaster if Boss had followed his instructions.

Maria, Mike and Ken left the next morning and Tony and Clara settled down to pick up where they had left off.

Chapter 64

Phil Arrowsmith and George Sellick were in a conference room in the London Headquarters of S&A. There was a knock at the door.

"Come in," said George Sellick.

Maria walked in and greeted them, "Good morning gentlemen."

"Please sit down Miss Best," said George Sellick. "Or may I call you Mary?"

"Mary will be fine thank you," she answered.

The two men had doubts that it was her real name but didn't question it.

"I believe that you are leaving us," said Mr Sellick. "I am sorry to hear that."

"That's correct Mr S, I've had a very interesting time here and made some good friends but I have to move on."

She had finished her time investigating S&A and the work had led to good intelligence on their biggest client, Renshaw & Collier.

"We understand," said Mr Sellick. He and Phil Arrowsmith did understand, they knew she was not what she had seemed to be.

Also they were loosing their biggest client. They were having to restructure and lose some people so resignations were almost welcome. It was a pity though, as she was probably their top operative. "You may already know that your colleague Alison has also found another position, close protection with the Scottish Government."

Maria wondered whether John Sutherland at Scottish Parliament Security, had anything to do with that.

"She will be a good addition to their team," said Maria.

"We took the liberty of clearing your things from the Farm," said Phil Arrowsmith, "I hope you don't mind."

"Not at all," said Maria. "There wasn't much there."

He handed her a small Sellick & Arrowsmith branded ruck sack, "Please keep the bag as a memento." And that was it.

Maria walked from the Headquarters up to her flat in Shepherds Bush and deposited the bag there. She had an hour before her next meeting in the Kings Road so she decided to walk. This was a fairly relaxed day time wise, she wasn't back in the swing of things yet.

Mike was sitting at a table at the side of the café with his back to the wall as Maria walked in. She sat next to him facing the window. That sort of habit detail was ingrained in both of them.

"I've ordered a coffee for you," he said. "Black?"

"Yes that's good," she said and her mind flashed back to a café near the Meadows in Edinburgh. It was midday. "Mike, you know I said that I want you to meet someone, well, I've made an appointment for two o'clock and it's about an hour's walk if you are up for that."

"Fine by me," and looking at his watch, added, "So we have time for lunch here."

They arrived at Thames House five minutes early and were shown into a conference room.

Rob Riddle walked in just before two.

"Hello Mike, I'm glad that you were persuaded to visit us," he said holding his hand out to Mike. They shook and all sat down. Without preamble Rob began, "I gather that you haven't been doing anything specific since you were discharged. Is that fair?"

"Yes, that's fair," said Mike. "I've been involved in a couple of things, one of which I'm sure you know all about, and

317

I've been looking for an interesting opportunity. I haven't found one yet but I haven't been in a hurry."

"I understand," said Rob. "Let's cut to the chase, I have an opportunity for you here in my section. Does that sound interesting?"

"It sounds very interesting," answered Mike as he leaned forward to hear the details.

The following week, Rob called Mike and Maria to his office again. Mike had spent most of the intervening time at Thames House and had now met most members of the section.

"I think Maria has told you about some of the fallout from the recent events in which you were both involved," continued Rob. "But there are a few things I'd like to summarise.

"First Igor Solovyov has been directly linked to the militia that attacked the village. That was through the payments he made, Boss had no choice but to give up that information. Igor is also linked to the assassination attempt at Kings Cross Station in the autumn of last year. We haven't arrested him yet because we don't want his brother to know that we are closing in.

"His brother Vladimir is the slippery one and the real force behind it all. He has the contacts with Moscow and his company Renshaw & Collier is big in fossil fuels. He and Moscow don't like anything that threatens that.

"He is extremely careful with his communications of every type and has his most sensitive conversations in a very discreet and private club in Berkeley Square. No chance of getting information from the staff or bugging the place especially as there are other important people who meet there, people we would not wish to upset.

"However thanks to one of our more imaginative technicians we did get some information but we probably couldn't use it in court."

"How did you get the information, if the place is so secure?" Maria asked.

"The idea is a little crude on several levels," said Rob. "A very small microphone and transmitter are wrapped in a blob of brown and white sludge that resembles a bird dropping. When it's on the outside if a window we can hear what is being said inside."

"Surely it just gets cleaned off," said Mike.

"Eventually yes but the trick is to apply it just before the conversation starts," said Rob.

"How do you do that without being seen?" Mike questioned.

"With a catapult," said Rob. "I said it was crude."

He went on to explain that they knew, but probably couldn't prove in court, that Vladimir was involved in all of this. However, the breakthrough had come when Sellick & Arrowsmith gave up all their information. "The link was a man called Jim Jones, known as JJ, in Renshaw & Collier. He was giving the instructions to S&A. He was also instructing an engineer at Rossborough Electronics. It was this engineer who sabotaged the LSI electronics for the solar project. The engineer has disappeared but we are still looking for him.

"When we discovered JJ's links we were able to put a lot of pressure on him. He had no choice but to give up Vladimir. We are expecting warrants tomorrow, then we will move in on them all.

"Although JJ will probably have to go into protection, we still consider it a big win overall."

Chapter 65

Clara and Tony took stock of the damage at the village and visited Site 2 to see how they were progressing.

Two weeks after Mike, Maria and Ken had left, Clara and Tony had returned to the village.

"We should call Laura and find out what's going on with Rossborough Electronics, if anything," said Clara.

As soon she saw the number she answered right away, "Hello Tony, are you OK?" Laura asked.

"What have you heard?" Tony asked.

"Mike came up to Edinburgh with a woman called Maxine and told me about what happened and some other stuff, not the whole story I'm sure, but enough," she answered.

"That's good," said Tony, "saves me telling it all again. Anyway we are OK."

"That's good," said Laura. "There's some other good news too, Rossborough Electronics have done a complete U turn in attitude. It seems that an engineer there had deliberately put things in the control circuit to make it unstable with temperature. So they have removed his modules and sent trial units to Clara's University. As soon as you test them and give the go-ahead they'll replace all the faulty units."

"That's great, I wonder what changed their mind," said Tony.

"I think it may have had something to do with that woman and your brother," said Laura. "But have you anything to test them on?"

"We have," said Tony. "Site 2 has produced enough aluminium mirrors to rebuild the solar furnace here at the village. The bandits thought that smashing the glass mirrors was all they needed to do to shut us down so they hardly damaged the frames. When will we get the new control circuits?"

"They should be with you in about a week," she answered. "What will you do in the meantime?"

"The people at Site 2 are nearly ready to test the Low Tech version with the Raspberry Pi computers so we are going over there, mostly to observe I expect," said Tony.

What had happened at Site 2 was exactly what Tony had hoped for since the beginning. The local people had taken on the project and were running with it.

Over the next months Tony could feel his vision becoming a reality. This relatively poor nation was using this simple sustainable technology independently. The two initial sites produced mirrors for other sites to get started and they had already begun turning scrap aluminium into mirrors and ingots for sale. Because of the high temperatures of the solar furnaces they were also able to recycle other metals.

Tony and Clara went back to Windhoek to review the progress of the project with professor Hamutenya, and met in the professor's office in NUST.

"This simple idea of yours Tony," said professor Hamutenya, "is stimulating areas that I hadn't considered seriously beforehand. I am getting enquiries from home and abroad for all sorts of metal recycling. If this continues I believe Namibia will become the go-to country in this region of Africa for metal recycling and for the supply of metals."

"That's great news," smiled Tony.

"We shipped some mirrors to a brewery, do you know how they are doing with them professor?" Clara asked.

"It's very interesting," he replied. "Our technician, Liode, has provided them with drawings for the basic frames that you used in the desert and the brewery has had some of

321

them fabricated locally. They are heating their vats by manually directing the mirrors, as you did initially. If they are successful they plan to put in electrical control systems. It will cut their electricity bills massively. I think that this will be taken up by many other industries which use a lot of energy."

"They will still need some electricity," said Tony.

"Definitely," agreed the professor. "I have been talking to the government about Solar Power Tower technology. Until I started researching, I didn't realise there were so many installations around the world. We know the technology works, there is one in South Africa. It is only a hundred kilometres from our border so I plan to take a team and visit it. If we built one as big as the Americans have in California it would supply about a quarter of our energy shortfall. These are expensive to build but I think we can cut the costs significantly by using the technology that you have developed."

"Part of my vision," said Tony. "Is that by using the suns's energy locally and directly for heat we will be able to reduce the need for electricity generation and transmission."

"I think that's right Tony," replied the professor. "I think it's an inevitable consequence of projects like the brewery."

They discussed other aspects and when they were finished, the professor asked, "What are your plans now Tony?"

"I'm planning to travel to Edinburgh," he answered. "I have some commitments there and I need to review the project with my University department."

Clara didn't look too happy about his plans.

Later over dinner she told Tony, " I don't want to go to the airport to see you off."

"Why not?" Tony asked, surprised.

"It would be too emotional and would feel a bit final. I don't like goodbyes."

Tony was quiet for a while and eventually told her that he understood.

They said goodbye the next morning as Liode collected Tony from his hotel. "Look after yourself Clara," said Tony.

Clara hugged him tightly. "You too," she whispered.

She was too choked up to say much more but they kissed gently and long.

At the airport Liode helped him with his bags and chatted excitedly.

"I've been thinking," said Liode as they he walked towards security. "If we can make enough mirrors, we could cover the polar ice caps and stop them melting."

"That's a great vision," said Tony smiling. "Very ambitious, but a great vision."

Glossary

AK-47

Avtomat Kalashnikova, designed in 1947 in Russia after WWII. Sometimes referred to as a Kalashnikov or just an AK. It is still produced in many countries and about 75 million have been produced.

Aluminium

Aluminium is a light metal with a melting point of 660.32°C. Normally the surface is allowed to build up a coating of oxide which is very resilient to further corrosion and gives it a silver grey appearance. However it can be machined and/or polished to produce a highly reflective surface.

Baby Browning

The FN Baby Browning is a small 0.25 calibre semi automatic pistol weighing less than 300 grammes and just over 100 mm (4 inch), long. It was originally produce by FN (*Fabrique Nationale*) in Belgium in 1931 and is still being manufactured.

Bodge

A bodge is usually a repair done not very well.

Chinook Helicopter

The Chinook Helicopter is used by the RAF and the US Airforce and Army. It is a versatile support helicopter which can transport 50 troops and has a lifting capacity of 10,000 kilogram/10 tonnes.

Critical Path Network
A critical Path Network is a pictorial way to depict the activities in a project. The arrow lines represent activities and show how each activity depends on the others. The critical path is the route from start to end of the project which will take the most time.

Dinnae
Scottish slang for don't

ESF
École de Ski Francais, French Ski School, present in most alpine ski resorts in France.

GCHQ
Government Communications Headquarters. One of the three UK intelligence services.

Great Circle
The shortest distance between any two points on the earths surface, which is of course the surface of a sphere.

Heliostat

A heliostat is a flat (plane) mirror which reflects the suns rays onto a fixed point. Helios is Greek for sun, stat meaning the light goes to a static point. The mirror has to swivel as the sun moves across the sky.

IED

Improvised Explosive Device

IPA

India Pale Ale acquired its name from the popularity of beer exported to India from the 1800s. It now describes a wide range of beers.

LSI

Large Scale Integration, this is a description of complex integrated circuits also known as chips.

M10

ISO Specification of a thread with a major diameter of 10 mm (~ 0.4 inch). A 10 mm diameter bar could have an M10 thread tapped on it.

MI5

MI5 is one of the three UK intelligence services. Although sometimes described as having domestic responsibilities, MI5 works closely with the other two intelligence services to protect the UK worldwide.

NUST
Namibia University of Science and Technology in Windhoek, Namibia

Parabola & Paraboloid
If a liquid in a container is rotated at a constant speed the surface curves into a paraboloid. A section through the centre of rotation is a parabola. In geometry a parabola is one of the "conic Sections", in its simplest form the formula is $y=x^2$

Raspberry Pi
A small and inexpensive single board microcomputer developed by the British charity, The Raspberry Pi Foundation with support from Cambridge University. The charity promotes interest at school level in computer science and programming skills.

RIB
Rigid Inflatable Boat. The bottom of the hull is rigid for speed and the tubes around the sides give excellent buoyancy.

SIS
The UK's Secret Intelligence Service, which has responsibilities overseas, also sometimes known as MI6. One of the three UK intelligence services.

SNP

Scottish National Party

The Meadows

The Meadows is a public open space in Edinburgh to the south of the city centre. It is largely grass but crossed by tree lined walks.

Wildcat MK1 Helicopter

The British Army uses The Wildcat MK1 helicopter for light transport, reconnaissance and light attack.

Zero-sum

Zero-sum thinking is based on the belief that in a relationship or negotiation, the resources are   finite, so one side's gain will be the other's loss. As one gain equals the other loss the sum is zero.

Acknowledgements

Audrey: For always being there

Elizabeth: For amazing feedback and editing

Geoff: For the cover design

Friends.   For proof reading

The Author

Dr Howard Fortescue was born in London and raised in Dorset. Following the award of his Honours degree in Physics from Heriot-Watt University, Dr Fortescue stayed in Scotland before moving with work and family across the UK and the Netherlands before settling in South Wales. With a PhD in Technology, a vast experience in the fields of engineering and science and certification as a SCUBA instructor, Dr Fortescue has connections and personal experience worldwide. This experience coupled with a passion for our beautiful planet inspires and infuses his writing.

EK

Printed in Great Britain
by Amazon